Hidden Agenda

HIDDEN AGENDA

Scared and on the run, Maggie Callahan doesn't know who to trust. Something's wrong at the pharmaceutical company where she works, and patients are turning up dead. Out of options, she seeks out the one person she knows won't let her down—Gunner Everett.

Snatched from the airport, Gunner Everett has no idea why anyone would interrogate him about a woman he hasn't seen in nearly ten years. Left with more questions than answers, he realizes there's only one person who can tell him what he needs to know—the woman he'd left behind.

As each new piece of the puzzle falls into place, Maggie and Gunner race to find the answers. Can they unravel the mystery, or will they become the latest casualties to greed and corruption?

Hidden

AGENDA

By
KATHY IVAN

COPYRIGHT

NEWSLETTER SIGN UP

Thank you so much for reading my book. If you want to find out about my other books, new releases, contests, free reads, and other things that are going on, sign up for my newsletter at http://eepurl.com/baqdRX

I take your privacy seriously. I will not sell your e-mail or contact you for any other reason than to send you publication updates when a new release is available.

BOOKS BY KATHY IVAN

www.kathyivan.com/books.html

Dear Reader,

Welcome to The Big Easy! Hidden Agenda is the latest book in my New Orleans Connection series. You'll find a unique blend of suspense, romance, and intrigue set in the heart of New Orleans, filled with alpha heroes oozing Southern charm and the strong women they love. So, sit back and hold on tight for a roller coaster ride of nail-biting intrigue and sensual tension with Hidden Agenda.

And if you love contemporary romance with a comedic flair, check out my Loviin' Las Vegas series.

Laissez les bons temps rouler!

Kathy Ivan

Chapter One

*H*oly crap, I'm blind.

Gunner tried opening his eyes again, but quickly determined that wasn't the smartest idea he'd ever had. His head throbbed with a distinctive *thump, thump, thump,* and felt like somebody decided to use his skull as a conga drum. Still, it didn't take a rocket scientist to figure out a blindfold covered his green eyes. *What the hell?*

His head felt fuzzy, his memories jumbled and indistinct. Last thing he remembered, he'd gotten off the plane at Louis Armstrong International Airport, after flying back from Dallas, helping his teammate with a case. And he'd flown coach, dammit.

Carpenter's private jet was grounded in Dallas, out of commission after the attempted hijacking of his partner, Nate Blackwell and his girlfriend. It would stay grounded until the police had enough time to scour it from cockpit to tail rudder, gathering evidence to toss Roger Dawkins behind bars for the rest of his hopefully miserable life. Though the way the justice system worked, chances were equally good he'd end up a guest in a locked psych ward, 'cos the guy was certifiable.

Focus. What do I hear? Smell? Let's figure out where I am.

1

If his military training taught him anything, it made him a damned fine tracker, teaching him to use his assets. It honed him into one of this country's finest killing machines, because he could find anybody, anywhere.

His first impression, the one that overrode the rest, was dampness. It hit with a tang of mold and mildew that seemed to coat the back of his throat. Someplace nearby there was either a leaky pipe or standing water. It didn't have the brackish twinge of brine he associated with salt water, so he figured it wasn't near the ocean or the swamp—at least not close enough.

He tried moving his hands, jiggling his wrists. All his fingers worked when he wiggled them, but his arms were stretched taut behind his back. The feel of cold metal encircled his wrists. *Handcuffs*.

He was sitting, that much was certain. Knees bent, his ankles were attached to chair legs, anchoring him to his seat, but whatever bound him to the chair, it didn't feel like rope. Too smooth. Whoever took him, they'd been smart to secure his hands behind him, but stupid to think tape would hold him to a chair for long. Even duct tape. There were a half dozen ways to snap the stuff without breaking a sweat, and he'd used them all.

Memories started coming back, slow at first, then in a kaleidoscope of vivid colors. Of him, standing at the airport, searching for a cab. Somebody bumped into him. A stunning blonde dressed in all black. He remembered the look on her face, the hint of regret in her eyes.

The rest was pretty muddy. Two hulking bozos manhandled him into the back of a vehicle—maybe a van or an SUV—but not much else. From his slow reaction time and foggy thought process, obviously, he'd been drugged.

Huh. He huffed out a long breath. Why the hell would anybody want to snatch him? Not money, he didn't have enough for anybody to care. His boss would pay if a ransom demand surfaced. Hell, what was he thinking? Carpenter wouldn't shell out one red cent. He'd call in C.S.S.'s elite team and come in guns blazing, riding to the rescue. Then he'd bill Gunner for services rendered.

Right now, that sounds like a mighty fine plan.

The silence, wherever the hell he was, felt deafening. No ticking clock. No sounds indicating animals or humans nearby. No breathing, except his own.

Man, he hated working blind. He could tell something more than the blindfold alone obscured his vision, because he was encased in total blackness. With a standard blindfold, tiny slivers of light still managed to make their way through. A cloth tied around the head stretched across the bridge of the nose, and caused tiny gaps where light could penetrate the total darkness.

Meant he probably had some kind of covering over his head. His gut tightened at the thought. His lungs drew in a deep breath, and he fought the feeling of suffocation. It was psychosomatic, all in his head, but that didn't help the disconnect between his brain and his lungs. He'd been breathing freely the whole time, but the thought of some-thing covering his entire head? Tightening his hands into fists, he tried to focus on slowing down his breaths, finding an inner calm, the way he'd been taught in the marines.

Fighting the panicked feeling threatening to swamp him, instead he concentrated on moving his feet, tugging against whatever held him to the chair. He could feel the thick chair legs, square shaped based on the sharp edges digging into his calves through his pants.

Sucking in another deep breath, he realized his mouth wasn't taped shut. Whoever snatched him was definitely racking up the stupidity points, though it was good news for him.

He froze at a soft scraping noise on his right, and slumped forward against his bonds, deciding to pretend he was still unconscious. Unless it was a rat scratching somewhere close, it sounded like somebody was coming. Two sets of footsteps, both heavy. *Not the pretty blonde, then. Too bad. I wouldn't mind a little payback for that stunt at the airport.*

A hand shoved against his chest, forcing his shoulders against the chair back. He kept his body limp, head hanging low, waiting to see what they'd do.

"Dammit, the drugs should've worn off by now."

I was right, that sneaky bitch drugged me. Must have happened when she touched my hand.

Whatever encased his head was yanked off, and warm humid air hit his skin. *Gotta still be in the South. No place else has this miserable heat.*

Hands fumbled with the knot at the back of his skull, yanking the blindfold free none too gently. It felt like they'd taken a chunk of hair with it.

He kept his head drooped against his chest, though he

cracked his eyes open the tiniest bit, letting them adjust to the light. Not that there was much. What little he could make out looked like some kind of enclosed garage space. He didn't think his act would fool them for long, but it was worth a shot.

A rough hand grasped his chin, forcing his head up. "I know you're awake. Time to talk."

Rolling his neck, he heard the joints crack and pop, reminding him of that breakfast cereal he ate as a kid. Dang, how long had he been out to get so stiff?

"Hey, fellas, what's with the whole Manchurian Candidate reenactment?"

He watched blank looks cross both men's faces. *Heathens.*

"What?"

"Never mind. Why am I trussed up like a Thanksgiving turkey?"

"Boss needs answers, and he says you've got 'em."

"Yep, I'm a regular fount of information." *Good going, yank the tiger's tail.*

"So, you're a smartass."

Gunner chuckled. "No, just a well-educated ass."

A well-delivered backhand across his face proved his barb had hit its mark. Sometimes keeping the bad guys off balance from the start gave him a distinct advantage.

"Stop. We ain't supposed to rough him up. No marks on the body, remember?"

Gunner didn't like the gleam in his eye as the guy rubbed the knuckles of the hand he'd used to smack him.

But, he didn't like the sound of the second guy's words either. *No marks on the body? Doesn't sound like they plan on letting me skip along my merry way when they're done asking questions.*

"You Wilson Everett?"

Gunner kept his lips zipped. It sounded strange, hearing his real name. He'd gone by Gunner for so long, both while in the military and in civilian life, to hear it spoken by thug number one raised every instinct to high alert.

"Want my rank and serial number too?"

"When's the last time you heard from Margaret Callahan?" Thug number two stood about a foot behind his buddy, a K-Bar in his hand, cleaning his fingernails. Gunner wasn't impressed. Guy obviously never served a day in the military, or he'd show more respect for his weapon.

"Ain't got a clue who you're talking about—what was the name again?"

"Mr. Everett, we don't have time for games. Margaret Callahan, previously from Beaumont, Texas, currently residing in Pasadena, Texas. It's…important we find her."

"Have you tried Google?"

Blood trickled from the corner of his mouth right after a fist met his face. *Dang, that hurt.* He swiped at it with his tongue, feeling the split lip. Tilting his head to the side, he spit blood onto the cement floor.

"One last time, Mr. Everett. Where is Margaret Callahan?"

Gunner felt the duct tape peel away from his pant leg. He'd been surreptitiously working at it ever since these two buffoons strolled into the room with their Rambo tough-guy act. Please—these two idiots were the worst kidnappers he'd ever met, and he'd become acquainted with more than his fair share working with Carpenter Security Services.

"Okay, I'll be straight with you, since you asked so nicely. I do remember a Margaret Callahan. Haven't seen or talked to her in years though. I haven't got a clue where she's at."

With an almost silent pop, the tape came free from the other chair leg. Gunner maintained his relaxed posture, though inside he was gearing up. He'd only get one chance, one shot at taking down these two yahoos. Whoever hired them must have run an ad in *Mercenaries R Us* or some other piece of crap soldier of fortune magazine, because no way these two were professionals.

"I'm sorry to hear that." Thug number one motioned for his friend, who stepped closer, a wicked grin spreading across his face. Whew, if he wasn't mistaken, he also had a really bad case of garlic breath. Maybe not being able to breathe hadn't been so bad after all.

"Well, it's sure been nice chatting with you fellas, but I'm ready to go." He jerked his head toward the cuffs, and both men chuckled.

"Sorry, my friend, you're not going anywhere." Thug number one pulled out his cellphone and hit a programmed number. "He's not cooperating. Looks like we're gonna need you, Doc."

Uh oh. I really don't like the sound of that. Doctors usually mean talking's over and the drugs are coming out. Sodium pentothal I can handle, but if it's one of the newer generation stuff, I'm up the creek.

"Guys, we don't need a doctor."

"Apparently we do, Mr. Everett, unless you've changed your mind…"

"I can't tell you what I don't know!" He laced his words with an edge of panic, and moved his feet a little farther away from the chair legs. No way in hell was he letting somebody shoot him up with some half-assed truth serum, especially since he was already telling the truth. He really didn't have a bloody clue where Maggie was.

"Our information says otherwise. It's imperative we find Ms. Callahan, and we've exhausted all other leads. The only loose end is you."

Thug number two twisted the knife in the low light, and Gunner watched prisms of color glint off the blade. Bully Boy might not show a lot of respect for his blade, but the damn thing still looked bloody sharp.

"Doc's gonna make you talk." Number two smirked at his own words. "By the end, you'll be screaming, begging to tell us what we want to know."

"Listen, you two-bit, pockmarked imbecile. I can't tell you what I don't know. I haven't seen or talked to Margaret Callahan in almost ten years."

The first guy cocked his head, studying him intently. "So, you do admit you know her?"

Gunner shrugged, feeling the metal of the handcuffs slide against the back of the chair. He hoped they weren't attached in any other way, because he couldn't wait much longer to make his move.

"I know a Margaret Callahan. Lost touch with her long ago. I went into the marines, and haven't seen or spoken to her since. *Comprende?* We lost touch."

A door leading from inside the house opened with a slight squeak. A tall cadaverous man with long grayish hair pulled back in a greasy ponytail walked through, carrying a red plastic lunch box.

Seriously, the guy couldn't even deign to carry a regular doctor's bag? Well, I guess it's better than a Hello, Kitty one.

As he approached, Gunner braced his feet against the concrete floor, muscles in his thighs bunching. Two against one odds had been better. Three against one? Not so great. Hopefully these idiots didn't have any real military training or he was screwed six ways to Sunday.

"Hello, Wilson. I understand you haven't been very cooperative."

"Send the blonde out here, and I'll show you how cooperative I can be." Gunner gave the doctor a lecherous wink.

"I'm afraid that won't be possible. She outlived her usefulness."

Crud. Gunner was pretty sure he understood exactly what the good doctor implied. He couldn't help wondering if anybody'd ever find her body.

The doctor strode out of his line of sight, and Gunner turned, watching him place the lunch box on top of a beat-up avocado green washing machine in the corner of the room.

Thug number two chuckled when the doctor pulled out

a hypodermic needle and a vial containing a clear solution. There didn't appear to be a label attached. Time was up. He couldn't wait any longer, because if they shot him up with whatever the hell was in that vial, he was a dead man.

Lunging forward, he sprang from the chair, and spun, kicking out with his right leg and catching thug number one across the jaw. The sound of it breaking echoed loudly in the garage. Without pausing, he barreled forward into the second guy, ducking low to avoid the arc of his knife blade. Damn, it was tough keeping his balance with his wrists cuffed behind his back. He adjusted his stance, because he couldn't afford to make a mistake now.

Tucking into a roll, he pulled his cuffed wrists beneath his ass, and shoved his legs through his linked arms. Ah, hell yeah, that was better, now he had a little more maneuverability.

Sweeping his leg wide, he took out number two's knee, heard the popping sound as the joint dislocated. He smiled in grim satisfaction when his head bounced against the concrete floor.

Ouchie. That had to hurt.

Two down, one to go.

The doctor stood with his back pressed against the wall, between the washer and the door leading back inside the house, eyes wide and filled with fear.

"Just you and me, Doc."

"Look, Wilson...I mean Mr. Everett. I'm only doing my job."

"Gotta tell ya, Doc, your job sucks." He advanced toward the thin male, who held his hands up, one still clutching the hypodermic. Like hell was he letting Skeletor dose him with whatever was in the needle.

"Doc, you want to walk outta here, I suggest you drop that." He nodded toward the needle. Within seconds, it hit the floor, rolling a few feet away. The red lunch box sat forlorn, it's plastic case a mocking sight against the avocado green washer.

Gunner wrapped a hand around the doctor's throat, holding him in place against the wall, and looked around the garage. On the top shelf above the dryer was a roll of duct tape, probably the same one they'd used to tape him to the chair. Not a bad idea.

"Okay, Doc, here's the plan. You're going to take that roll of tape, and secure our friends here. With his foot, he kicked the K-Bar away from thug number two, who'd been reaching for the weapon, and pressed his foot against the downed man's wrist.

"Stay down, idiot."

The doctor nodded eagerly, and Gunner eased up on the pressure around his throat. "Make sure it's good and tight, because if they get loose, you'll be paying the price."

Within minutes, both thugs were bound, hand and foot, lying on the cold concrete.

"Now it's your turn, Doc. Secure your legs to the chair, and make sure the tape is good and tight."

He watched while the doctor did exactly as instructed, wrapping the duct tape securely around both legs, from knees to ankles.

"Now lean back in the chair and put your hands behind you." Gunner walked around and took the roll out of the doctor's right hand, and wrapped more tape around and around before threading it between the spindles on the back of the chair. This guy wasn't going anywhere anytime soon.

Tearing off another strip of tape, he slapped it across the doctor's mouth, his eyes imploring above the dull silver strip. Then he did the same thing to the two goons lying on the floor, trussed up like fine Christmas geese. Kinda felt good to smash the tape across their mouths, he had to admit.

He knelt and picked up the discarded K-Bar. Having his hands on a weapon seemed like a good plan, since he didn't know if he'd be running into any more wannabe mercs as he left.

Standing, he looked around, memorizing each detail of the enclosed garage, not that he was likely to forget it.

Reaching into the doctor's pocket, he pulled out his cellphone and headed toward the door. Opening it a crack, he listened, but didn't hear any movement. Remembering the squeak from earlier when the doc had come in, he slid the door open only enough to squeeze his body through, and pulled it shut, hearing the muffled curses of his former kidnappers. Hopefully, they'd think twice next time before messing with a military man.

Once a marine, always a marine.

The door led into a kitchen, which hadn't seen a remodel in at least thirty years, the avocado green appliances and mustard yellow countertops a dead giveaway to that bygone era. Man, the previous owners must have loved those green appliances—or they were just too cheap to replace them.

Across the room, on the far side of the kitchen, was a door to what he hoped was the backyard. Jalousie glass filled the door's center, the old-fashioned kind with the hand crank handle to open. Right now they were closed, and it was impossible to see what lay on the other side, and he didn't want to risk them making noise if he tried to open them.

With his back pressed against the wall, he listened, but heard no sign of another person in the house. But these guys weren't sharp enough to run this operation alone, and who knew if or when their boss might show up?

Tucking the phone into his pocket, he glanced left and right, and eased across the space on silent feet, and out the door.

The afternoon sky was beginning to fade into pinks and violets and oranges, when he sprinted around the side of the house. Pulling out the doctor's cellphone, he started snapping pictures of his surroundings. Probably wouldn't do a hell of a lot of good, because chances were all three would be long gone before the cops showed up. The duct tape wouldn't hold them for long, and he needed to beat feet as far away as possible before they got free.

Two mid-size nondescript sedans were parked in the driveway, one an older model. He tried the door handle, chuckling when it opened beneath his hand.

Looks like my luck's turning around.

Within seconds, he'd hotwired it and drove away, dialing nine-one-one, and using the speaker phone. He really hoped nobody spotted the handcuffs still attached to his wrists. Steering with his hands below window level, he tried keeping them out of sight.

The next call was to his boss, Samuel Carpenter, because he needed the team to get started and figure out what the hell was going on—and why somebody was willing to go to such extraordinary lengths to find Maggie Callahan.

Chapter Two

"You have any idea why these guys were looking for this Margaret Callahan?" Carpenter leaned back in his chair, fingers steepled beneath his chin.

Gunner had abandoned the stolen car down by The Brewery, and called a friend with keys to unlock the handcuffs, and take him the rest of the way to the office, but not before e-mailing the photos to Carlisle and ditching the *borrowed* cell phone. He was still pissed he hadn't been able to find his phone at the house.

"No clue."

"Gotta be something serious if they were willing to drug you for information."

"Ya think?" Gunner propped his feet up on the coffee table in Carpenter's living room. Andrea handed him a cup of coffee, and he smiled his thanks. He was still pissed he'd lost almost a whole day to whatever they'd drugged him with, and he spared a brief moment of thought to the blonde he was pretty sure was bayou bait now.

"Might want to let Remy know, on the QT, about the woman who drugged me. The quack posing as a doctor said she'd outlived her usefulness. Got the feeling she'll be turning up in the morgue."

"What else do you remember?"

"Boss, how many times are we going to go over this? Woman bumped into me at the airport, and dosed me with something. Next thing I know, I'm coming to in a garage, tied to a chair. Two Rambo wannabes came in, and started asking questions about Maggie."

Andrea's whole body perked up at his words. "Maggie? So you know Ms. Callahan?"

Damn it. Smooth move, Sherlock.

"Knew her a long time ago. Haven't seen or spoken with her in years."

"And you have no clue how to find her?"

He stretched out his arm along the back of the sofa. "Last time I saw her was in Beaumont. I'd kicked around there for a year after high school, doing odd jobs and day labor stuff. Had no clue what the hell I wanted to do with my life. Enlisted in the marines and was shipping out in a couple of weeks when I met her."

"Whirlwind romance?" Andrea smiled at his grimace.

"Less than a whirlwind, more than a wham-bam, thank you ma'am."

"Ouch."

"Cops find anything at the address?" He needed to change the subject about his non-relationship with Maggie Callahan. Lifting his cup, he took another sip of his coffee.

"Place was empty. No cars, no people." Carpenter smirked before adding, "No red lunch box."

Gunner waved his happy middle finger at his boss, who chuckled in response.

"They did, however, find a hypodermic needle which had rolled beneath the washer. Cops are speculating junkies were using the place, since the house was unoccupied, and I couldn't exactly dig deeper without arousing suspicion."

"Wish I could have kept the phone for Carlisle, but figured they'd try and track the GPS signal, and didn't want to lead anybody back here—though if they knew enough to find me at the airport, they probably know where I work and live. But I wasn't about to bring trouble to your doorstep."

"I've got Jean-Luc and Gator checking with the locals, seeing if there's any word on the street about anybody asking questions about you. Carlisle is trying to find Ms. Callahan's last known whereabouts."

Stefan Carlisle was the best computer expert in the business—on either side of the law. He'd worked with him for the last several years, both in Dallas as well as here in New Orleans after they relocated. There wasn't anything the man couldn't do with a laptop and internet connection. If Maggie was anywhere on the grid, Carlisle would find her. People didn't realize how much information they used. Data always leaves a trail, no matter how careful you are. Footprints on the web are a real thing.

"Whoever's looking for her wasn't at the house tonight, or if they were, I didn't spot them. I get the feeling somebody big is calling the shots. Thug number one said the boss had questions and I had the answers. What I can't figure out is why they thought I'd been in touch with Maggie."

At the brief knock on the front door, Andrea popped up from the arm of the chair, where she'd been sitting beside

Carpenter. Stefan Carlisle walked in, carrying his ever-present laptop.

"Got anything?"

"A whole lotta nothing." Carlisle shoved the wire-rimmed glasses up on the bridge of his nose, and opened the computer. "Margaret Elizabeth Callahan disappeared from Pasadena, Texas, a little over three weeks ago. Before that, she was working at EryX Pharmaceutical."

Carpenter's brows rose at the mention of the company's name, though Gunner didn't recognize it. Then again, he wasn't one of the wealthy movers and shakers. He did what he liked to call the grunt work. And he was damned good at it.

"That's interesting." Carpenter stood and walked across the living room, to lean against the fireplace. Gunner always called it Carpenter's *thinking spot*. A thoughtful expression crossed his face.

"There's been scuttlebutt lately about a breakthrough, with EryX at the forefront."

"What's so special about EryX?" Gunner couldn't keep the curiosity out of his voice. When he'd known Maggie, she'd been working at a bar just outside Beaumont's city limits, working evenings, and going to college during the day. A couple years older than him, it had been kinda fun to spend his nights with somebody who could carry on a conversation more relevant than the typical high school cheerleader.

"Pharmaceutical company. Big enough to make a buttload of money, but not one of the huge pharma groups."

"Weren't they working on something to do with sleep medication?" Andrea plopped down into Carpenter's abandoned seat, one leg tucked beneath her.

"FDA turned down their initial request, claiming they needed more clinical trials and additional documentation. If I remember correctly, Somnolett had a few rather nasty side effects, and the company planned to reformulate it."

"Seems like a lot of trouble for a sleeping pill, you ask me." Gunner couldn't imagine spending a crapton of money on medication for going to sleep. A stiff belt of whiskey before bed usually did the trick for him.

"You'd understand if you found yourself going weeks without getting a good night's sleep. People get desperate, looking for anything to help." Carlisle shrugged at his eye roll.

Andrea joined in, looking at Gunner. "Things aren't as simple as they were twenty or twenty-five years ago. Everything today is nonstop go, go, go. We work longer hours, have added stress not only from jobs, but from family and social activities. It can be difficult, oftentimes impossible, to get your brain to shut off long enough to fall asleep, much less get a full seven or eight hours."

Carpenter chuckled. "Says the woman who snores like a freight train five seconds after her head hits the pillow."

Andrea grabbed a decorative pillow and threw it at her fiancé, who caught it one-handed, tossing it back with a grin. She wrapped her arms around it, and hugged it to her chest.

"I have a friend, somebody I used to work with. She tried everything to get a good night's sleep. Meditation, yoga, aroma therapy. Even hypnosis. Nothing worked. The incidences of depression increase dramatically with sleep deprivation. She's tried over-the-counter sleep aids, as well as prescription. Some things work for a short time, others are useless."

Gunner got what she was saying, but figuring out what Maggie had to do with EryX and more importantly why he'd been grabbed off the streets in an attempt to find her held his main focus. Honestly, he didn't give a rat's patootie about any drug. Maggie though? That he cared about—a lot.

"Carlisle," Carpenter moved over and lifted Andrea like a rag doll, reclaimed his seat, with her in his lap, "let's have somebody from the Austin office head down to EryX Pharmaceutical in Houston. Subtly ask about Ms. Callahan. Maybe we can get a lead—where she's gone, or why she disappeared in the first place."

"I'll go." Gunner immediately stood, ready to catch a flight to Hobby.

"No, you're staying put."

"Boss, I can be there—"

"You've got a job to finish here, remember?"

"Don't worry, Gunner. We'll find your friend, and if she needs help, she's got it." Andrea's calm smile eased the knotted lump in the center of his chest.

"Thanks." He turned to Carlisle. "Anything on the info I sent you?"

"Burner phone, so no record. I can tell you it was bought at a Walmart in Slidell three days ago. I checked the CCTV cameras at the airport, and it was a dark SUV with stolen plates. No record of the police recovering it yet."

"Great. In other words, we've got nothing."

"Hey, we've solved cases with less to start with." Carlisle skimmed his finger across the mouse on his laptop. "The house is listed on the MLS as a rental property. The owners live in Arkansas. It's currently listed as available—so probably not much there. The cops took fingerprints, but I doubt they'll prove useful."

"Okay, people. Meeting's over. Carlisle, keep digging. Gunner, try and remember anything pertinent about Margaret Callahan." He tapped the tip of Andrea's nose. "And you, check with your brother and find out what he knows about Eryx Pharmaceutical. He keeps a closer eye on that kind of thing than I do."

She narrowed her eyes at him, before giving him a quick kiss on the cheek. "Goody, I get to call my brother."

Gunner walked out the front door with Carlisle, and held out a hand to stop him. "I appreciate you helping with this. Maggie was important to me at one time, and I'd hate to think she's in any kind of danger."

"Don't sweat it. I'll keep you posted."

With that, Gunner headed upstairs to his apartment. He needed a shower to get rid of the filth from the grungy basement where he'd been held, and a little quiet time to think about the girl he'd left behind.

Chapter Three

Maggie Callahan stood in the pouring rain, her hair plastered to her scalp, the cold droplets running down her face and onto her chest. She was in the last place she ever expected or wanted to be, but she didn't have a choice. Somewhere along the line, her life had taken a crazy-ass left turn, and here she was standing on Canal Street in New Orleans, staring up at a multistory brick building, terrified to walk through the glass front door.

Because one step through that door and her whole life would change—forever. She huffed out a laugh. Like her life wasn't already screwed.

I can do this. Hell, it's been almost ten years. He probably doesn't even remember me. Not like we had anything monumental, just two stupid kids who didn't have a clue what life was really about. Thank goodness he never knew how I felt about him, or I'd have been humiliated. He was ready for a whole new life, and didn't need me dragging him down.

"Ma'am, can I help you?" A pretty blonde woman stood framed in the doorway, holding the glass door open in silent invitation.

"Sorry. I was working up the nerve to come inside." Maggie pushed a sodden mass of hair out of her eyes and smiled at the other woman.

"Well, we don't bite. Come on in." She held the door wider, motioning Maggie inside. Taking a deep breath, she forced one foot in front of the other, until she stood inside the gorgeous reception area, with its high ceiling and ultramodern furnishings.

"Here." The woman handed her a towel, and Maggie took it, nodding her thanks. When she'd started out driving last night, she'd had no clue a monsoon would be moving through the area. It had taken her most of the night, driving straight through the nearly eight-hour trip.

"There's a restroom right over there if you'd like to freshen up." The receptionist pointed toward a door to the right. "Do you have an appointment with anyone in particular?"

Maggie took a deep breath before answering. "I don't have an appointment, but I'd like to speak with Wilson Everett, please."

The other woman's eyes widened at the name. "Of course, ma'am. If you'll give me your name, I'll let him know you're here."

"Just tell him it's Maggie. Maggie Callahan."

With that, she headed for the restroom. One look in the mirror above the sink had her gasping. Talk about a train wreck. She'd expected the black circles beneath her eyes, after all she'd been driving all night. But add in the wet, straggly hair, and the nearly transparent cotton dress—there was no way she wanted to meet Wilson again looking like an escapee from *The Rocky Horror Picture Show*.

Fortunately, the hand dryer was one of the hot air blower types. She rotated the nozzle until it pointed at the front of her chest, blasting hot air onto the material plastered against her skin. It was a slapdash effort at best, but even partially dry had to be better than drowned rat chic.

A quick tug of a brush through her hair was the best she could muster. She'd already been in here too long. The receptionist had had plenty of time to call him.

Would he even remember her? The few weeks they'd had together were etched in her mind, time she'd never forget for a variety of reasons, but maybe they hadn't meant anything to him other than scratching an itch before shipping out with the marines.

A soft knock sounded on the door, and the receptionist, or who she thought that was, stuck her head through the small opening in the door.

"Everything okay in here?"

Maggie plastered a smile on her face, feeling like she was about to meet her executioner. She tried to swallow past the lump in her suddenly too-dry throat.

"Fine, thanks. I'll be right out."

"Okay." With a quick smile, the other woman was gone. Maggie tugged at the fabric of the faded cotton dress. She hadn't even bothered to change, knowing every minute wasted meant more problems she'd have to clean up. And she was so tired.

"We who are about to die salute you," she told the woman in the mirror, executing a mock salute before heading to the door.

Pulling it open, a gasp escaped at the sight of the man standing in front of her.

Wilson. He'd changed. She'd expected it, but the reality was overwhelming. He seemed bigger and broader, his chest and arms covered with muscles that hadn't been there when she'd known him before. Obviously, the military had been very good to him. His face was different, more mature, his cheekbones more defined and angular. He wasn't handsome, not in the way magazines and the press portrayed men today. No, he looked like a warrior of old, a knight prepared for battle, ready to risk everything for his beliefs. His eyes were still green, a light jade shade that she'd always envied, surrounded by dark lashes. His sharp blade of a nose added to the overall masculine look, and his medium brown hair was cut almost military short, close to his scalp. No, not the ideal of perfection, but then she wasn't looking for perfect.

She wasn't the timid maiden in an ivory tower waiting for the handsome prince to ride to her aid. Hell, no. She wanted the dragon, breathing fire, vicious and primitive. The protector of his clan.

She just hoped once she told him everything, he'd be willing to be the uncivilized warrior and protector she needed, because if not, she was dead.

Chapter Four

"**M**aggie."

He couldn't believe she was here. In New Orleans. In his office. She'd changed, matured. When he'd known her, she'd worn her light red hair short around her face, with tiny curls that would fly around her cheeks when she moved. Now it hung in thick waves down over her shoulders. Though he couldn't see, he'd guess it fell halfway down her back. Her whiskey-colored eyes were surrounded by light-colored lashes, drawing him into their depths. He'd teased her that he could get drunk on her eyes. She didn't have a cute little button nose, but one that fit in proportion with the rest of her face, and her full lips were the same. Ones that always drew him in for kisses—kisses he'd never wanted to end.

"Hello, Wilson."

"Gunner. Everybody calls me Gunner now."

He watched the corners of her lips tug upward, obviously remembering the conversations they'd had, in bed, about how he couldn't wait to get a nickname. Everybody in the marines got one, he'd proclaimed, and he'd wanted a strong, memorable one. He'd been named after his grandfather, and while he'd loved the old coot, he couldn't stand the name.

Especially after that Tom Hanks' movie with the stupid volleyball. It took forever for the teasing and ribbing about that to die down.

"Gunner. I like it."

"Come on, let's go to the conference room. We can talk there." He placed his hand on the small of her back, and led her to the elevator. She'd been caught in the rain, it was obvious, but he could still smell the faintest whiff of the gardenia perfume she loved.

Within minutes, he got her seated at the huge conference table, and closed the double doors, wanting a little privacy. As soon as Stephanie mentioned Maggie was there, his heartbeat had raced like an adrenalin-junkie about to skydive without a parachute. Telling her to inform the boss Margaret Callahan was downstairs had been next on his list. He hoped Carpenter took a few minutes before barging in, because he really wanted to get a handle on why Maggie was here, and who the hell was hunting her.

"It's been a long time." He clasped her hand, stroking along the skin, feeling its softness before noting the chill bumps spreading along her arms. Damn, caught in the rain, and with the air conditioning blasting, she was probably freezing.

He reached across the table for the phone.

"Stephanie, could you bring a blanket or a sweater to the conference room for Ms. Callahan? She's freezing."

"Right away, Gunner."

Maggie rubbed her hands along her bare arms. "You didn't have to do that. I'll be fine."

"Sugar, you're cold and wet. Can't have you catching pneumonia."

There was a brief tap at the door, and Stephanie walked in, a dark blue blanket draped over her arm.

"Here you go, Gunner. I'll bring in some hot tea in a few minutes. Lemme know if you need anything else." He heard the unasked question in her voice, but ignored it. Hell, he didn't have any answers anyway.

He draped the blanket over Maggie's shoulders, watching her snuggle beneath its warmth. Couldn't help noticing the dark circles beneath her eyes, and the paleness of her skin. He wondered if the shaking was all from the cold, or maybe something more.

"Want to tell me what brings you all the way to New Orleans?"

Start off with something simple he'd been taught when questioning a suspect—though Maggie wasn't a suspect. Gently lead the person to the actual point of why they were there. He wasn't sure when or even how it happened, but since being with Carpenter Security, he'd become the client whisperer.

She inhaled a shaky breath, and he picked up her hands again, rubbing them between his. It felt like he was holding icicles.

"I'm not sure where to start."

"Try the beginning." He gave her a reassuring smile.

She laughed. "Still a smart-ass."

He shrugged. "Some things never change. Let's start with something easy. Whatcha been up to since the last time I saw you?"

"Let's see. I finished school, got an associate's degree in business, and I'm working on my master's, specializing in forensic accounting."

"Wow, that's amazing and kind of intimidating. You always were good with numbers. I still can't add two dimes and a nickel and come up with a quarter."

"But he's damned good at figuring out the important stuff."

Damn. He'd been so engrossed with Maggie, he hadn't noticed Carpenter slip into the room. Maggie spun around in her seat, staring at the tall blond man leaning against the doorjamb.

"Maggie Callahan, meet Samuel Carpenter, my boss, and head of Carpenter Security Services."

Acting on instinct, he moved to stand behind Maggie's chair when Samuel walked the few feet separating them.

"Pleasure to meet you, Ms. Callahan."

"Please, call me Maggie."

He smiled, and Gunner knew it was his boss's charming, put-people-at-ease smile, the one that never failed. Yet with his hand resting on Maggie's shoulder, he felt the fine tremor running through her, and again had the impression it wasn't just from the cold.

Carpenter took the seat Gunner had abandoned, leaning toward Maggie and intruding into her personal space. "Ms. Callahan, you're obviously a very hard lady to find. I know, because there are a lot of people searching for you."

"What? They've already been here? I've got to go." She

struggled to stand, but Gunner made that impossible, keeping his hand on her shoulder.

"Shh, take it easy, sugar. Nobody's going to get to you here. This is probably the safest building in the city. Hell, the state."

"This was a mistake. I need to…"

"You need to tell us what's going on, so we can help." Carpenter looked at Gunner, a silent inquiry in his eyes. He shook his head, because he hadn't had a chance to find out what the hell had her so spooked.

"I was just telling Wil…Gunner that after I graduated with an associate's degree in business, I went to work for EryX Pharmaceutical. I started in Human Resources, but before long, I'd been promoted to administrative assistant to the Vice President of Marketing and Sales."

Carpenter nodded, though he didn't interrupt. Gunner knew his boss was almost as good at reading people and getting them to talk as him—almost. Maggie had finally stopped trembling beneath his fingers, but he was loathe to move away from her. Something deep down put him into protective mode the second he'd seen her, and that instinct hadn't backed off.

"I knew it wasn't a long-term job. Forensic accounting is what I'm studying now, because I'm good at puzzle solving, and numbers make sense, at least to me."

"Glad they do to somebody." Gunner shut up when Carpenter shot him a glare.

Maggie chuckled. "He hasn't changed, always has to pipe in with some witty comment."

"You think he's witty? Everybody around here thinks he's a brick shy of a full load."

Maggie laughed, and the sound was like magic. She looked lighter for the first time since she'd walked out of the restroom downstairs.

"Anyway, as I said, I wasn't looking for this job to be permanent, but it paid well and I had lots of time to study. My boss didn't mind if I hit the books at my desk, if things were slow."

"Nice perk. But something happened recently, didn't it?"

Trust Carpenter to ease her back on track.

She nodded, tugging the blanket closer around her shoulders. "The boss had left for the day, and I'd stayed later, because it was a federal holiday, and most of the people were off. I'd agreed to come in and catch up on a couple of things, to give us a jump start for Tuesday. I was packing up my books, and heard voices outside, in the hall. I guess they didn't realize anybody was still there."

He squeezed her shoulder, lending his silent encouragement. Whatever had her disappearing and on the run had to be huge. The Maggie he remembered wasn't the type to shy away from anybody.

"What were they saying, sugar?"

"First, you need to understand, I don't know who these men are. I didn't recognize the voices, and I never got a look at either one. I don't know why, call it gut instinct or sheer stupidity, but I walked over to the door and listened. They were talking about the FDA turning down approval of Somnolett for a second time."

Carpenter perked up in his seat. "I didn't know they'd applied for a second patent. I knew about the first one. The FDA said it warranted further testing and clinical trials, though personally I don't think they have a shot in hell of getting it through. Nasty rumors about side effects."

"Apparently, things didn't go well with the second application either. The FDA demanded more testing, something about a double blind study—at least that's what these guys were talking about."

Gunner definitely didn't like the sound of this. Drugs were big business in the United States and meant billions of dollars once they were approved for sale and distribution. But it also meant billions of dollars of loss if they didn't pass the rigid restrictions demanded by the Federal Drug Administration.

"Did they mention what kind of side effects?" Carpenter probed gently. Gunner was pretty sure he didn't want to hear the answer. He'd known more than a few fellow marines who'd been on the receiving end of some pretty nasty stuff. Unfortunately, Uncle Sam sometimes looked the other way when it came to some of those so-called experimental drugs.

Maggie's forlorn sigh filled the air. "Yeah. The study group contained twenty-five people, both men and women. Several of them are dead."

Carpenter sprang from his chair cursing a blue streak, and even Gunner straightened at her words. That was a damned high rate of deaths, especially for such a small sampling group.

"Son of a bitch! No wonder they didn't report it to the feds. No way in hell they'd allow it to get to market."

"It gets worse." Her quiet voice froze Gunner's blood.

"Worse?"

"I heard one of the guys say they've already sold the formula. Another company has started production of the drug overseas, and they're planning to sell it, without FDA clearance."

"Can't do it." Carpenter raked his hand through his blond hair until his usually impeccable cut stood straight up.

"Mr. Carpenter, do you have any idea how much money is made on medications sold on the internet?"

"Hell, yeah, sweetheart. I worked for the DEA for years. I know exactly how that crap gets funneled into the U.S. It's too damned easy. Not to mention all the people who fill prescriptions in foreign countries and bring them back home with them."

"Then you know with or without FDA approval, people are going to get their hands on this drug once they know it exists—and with the right advertising, people will know."

Carpenter began pacing across the front of the conference room. It was a familiar sight to Gunner, he'd seen the man do it more times than he could count. Usually meant his brain was processing all the information, and coming up with a plan.

He stopped abruptly and turned to Maggie. "That still doesn't answer the question of why somebody's after you, Ms. Callahan."

Maggie smoothed her hands along the front of her skirt

before standing, the blanket puddling along the back of her chair.

"Because I waited until the men left. Then I hacked into the company server—and, yes, I know I can be arrested for computer espionage—copied everything I could find on Somnolett, the supposed reformulation or second generation of the sleeping medication. Unfortunately, everything is encrypted, and I haven't been able to crack it yet."

"You mean…"

Maggie nodded. "I have the study results they want hidden from the FDA."

"They'll still be able to use the formula, because it's already changed hands." Gunner stood at Maggie's back, and bit back a groan when her hand clutched at his.

"From what those men were saying," her voice cracked on the last word, "I think there may be more than falsified study protocols. I think they're killing everybody who took part in the double blind study."

Chapter Five

"Stephanie, round up everybody and get them here now," Carpenter barked into his phone.

Maggie sat down and tugged the blanket back around her shoulders, and fought the need to ask Gunner to wrap her in his arms. He'd grabbed another chair, scooted closer, and she smiled at his nearness, a spiral of warmth and calmness seeping deeper in her chest.

She'd told them everything. When she'd first overheard the men talking outside her office, she'd considered grabbing her stuff and leaving anyway. Until she fully understood what they were talking about. While she might not know a tremendous amount about pharmaceutical testing procedures or standards, she'd learned a hell of a lot about sales and marketing, and knew any new sleep aid hitting the market was going to sell a gazillion dollars of product. While weight loss medication was the hottest trend at the moment, and billions of dollars were funneled into research and development from all the major pharmaceutical companies, insomnia remained right there at the top, too. There were tens of millions of people diagnosed with sleeping disorders, of which there were a variety of disorders just waiting for the next big thing. Living with the daily stressors of the twenty-first century, more and more people were diagnosed every day.

"Okay, Maggie," Carpenter parked his hip against the edge of the conference room table. "You pretty much disappeared off the grid three weeks ago. Wanna tell us where you've been?"

"Pretty much everywhere. I took as much money as I could from the ATM, and started driving. I needed time to think, figure out who I could trust with this information. Never stayed in one place more than a single night and moved on."

"Smart. They're hunting for you."

Her stomach did a flip-flop motion as Carpenter's words sank in. She'd been stupid, thinking she could stop them. Sooner or later they'd find her, and she'd end up another crime statistic, buried near the last page.

"How do you know that? Maybe they already gave up and…"

"Sugar," Gunner's hand closed around hers, "you've uncovered a conspiracy within Big Pharma that could cost your company potentially billions of dollars. And you've got evidence of a major cover-up that's costing people their lives. There's no way they're not coming after you to get that information back."

"Plus, they snatched Gunner to try and find you." Carpenter added.

"What!" Maggie spun around and stared at Gunner. "Somebody kidnapped you?"

"Amateurs. Didn't have a clue what they were doing. I

got away slicker than a greased pig at the county fair."

"But...but..."

"Shh. They didn't hurt me, and I couldn't tell 'em a thing, because I really didn't know where you were. Not until you showed up on my doorstep, like a gift from heaven."

"This is all my fault. But, how did they connect me to you? We haven't seen each other in years."

"No clue, but we'll figure it out. In the meantime, we need to take a look at the information you took from EryX Pharmaceutical."

She shook her head. "I don't have it with me. It's hidden. I figured the safest thing would be to put part of it in another place and only keep a portion of it with me. That way, if they found me, or got their hands on one piece, it was only part of the whole."

"Very smart." Carpenter stood when Carlisle walked in the door followed by Jean-Luc. He pointed to Carlisle and his laptop. "This is Stefan Carlisle. He's going to become your new best friend. I need you to tell him everything you've told us. *Everything*. Don't leave anything out, even if you think it's not important."

"What did you do with your laptop, honey?" Gunner's hand squeezed her shoulder. "Carlisle is a wizard with computers."

"Gone."

Carlisle's head popped up. "Gone? What do you mean gone? Like not in your possession anymore?"

"I mean fried, as in the hard drive is at the bottom of the

river."

Carlisle looked at Carpenter with a laconic grin. "Nothing I can do about that, boss."

Carpenter pinched the bridge of his nose, and Maggie could feel the tension rising in the room.

"Maggie, you said you got part of the list of people participating in the Somnolett trial. We need those names."

"Does this mean you believe me?"

"Yeah, I do."

Shoulders slumping, Maggie relaxed for the first time since she'd walked through the front door of Carpenter Security Services. But, now came the hard part. Proving she wasn't crazy.

"Carlisle, you've already run a check on me, right?" No doubt that had been the first thing Carpenter ordered when she'd walked into his offices. At his nod, she continued. "What did you find?"

His eyes slid to Gunner before he answered. "Maggie Callahan, age thirty-one, birthdate February twenty-second. Rental apartment, one bedroom, one bath, in Pasadena, Texas. Attended community college and received an associate's degree in business. Working part-time on obtaining your Master's degree in forensic accounting, which you should finish this summer. How much more do you want? I can give you clothing and shoe sizes if you'd like." The last was said with a wink.

Maggie chuckled. "I don't think that'll be necessary. Can you get into my medical files?"

"Hang on a sec." She watched his fingers fly across the

laptop keyboard, marveling at his skill. She might type that fast on the number keypad, but no way could she make a keyboard sing the way he did.

She winced at his frown. "Gimme your primary care's name."

"Dr. Ronald Malcolm. In Houston." Reaching up, she tucked a lock of her still damp hair behind her ear, a small shiver ran through her.

"Hmm. Interesting." Carlisle paused to stare at her, his scrutiny intense and questioning, before going back to his typing.

"What's interesting?" Gunner stood behind her, and rested his hands on her shoulders.

"Dr. Malcolm's records show Margaret Callahan was referred to a psychiatrist. His consultation shows your gal has some pretty severe mental problems. Manic depressive with auditory and visual hallucinations, along with delusions." He whistled. "Those are some pretty heavy meds you're on, Ms. Callahan."

"I'm not on any medication. Not even aspirin."

"According to your medical records, you've been taking very high doses of antidepressants and antipsychotic meds. Prescribed two years ago. You were also hospitalized at that time for almost a week—end of November. You've missed your last two appointments, too. The latest refill hasn't been filled, so there's a notation that you are possibly off your medications, and could be a danger to yourself or others."

Maggie turned to face Carpenter. "This is the other reason I need help. Somebody is setting me up, trying to make me look insane. I've never been sick or hospitalized in my life. The worst I've ever had was a broken arm in elementary school when I fell off the monkey bars."

Her head hurt, remembering the shock of finding out her records had been tampered with. An even bigger shock— finding the pill bottles in her apartment. Prescriptions showing her name and dosage in bold black print. She wasn't lying when she said she didn't take medication. The feeling of lack of control on anything stronger than Tylenol bothered her.

"Right off the bat, I can spot the modifications in your chart, though whoever did them did a decent job. Didn't cover their tracks all that well, but at a cursory glance, it'd pass muster." Carlisle lifted his hands from the keys at Gunner's snarl.

"You're saying somebody tampered with her confidential medical records to make it look like she has a mental illness?" The outrage in Gunner's voice soothed her on a primitive level. Too bad this wasn't the end of what she needed to share.

"There's more."

"Of course there's more," Gunner muttered under his breath. "Nothing about this whole situation sounds simple."

"I found prescription bottles in my apartment, tossed in the back of a kitchen drawer. They'd been filled in my name, and a number of the pills were missing—making it look like I'd been taking the meds, but didn't finish the prescription. I couldn't figure out where they came from, not until the pieces of the puzzle started coming together."

"Puzzle?" She turned toward the dark-haired man who'd been silent throughout everything. He'd been introduced as Jean-Luc somebody, Carpenter Security's second-in-command.

"That's what I've been calling it, because each clue has been like a puzzle piece, fitting into place to reveal the whole picture. The first was overhearing the two men outside my office."

"Then securing the list of test subjects," Carlisle added, and she again felt his scrutiny, watchful and assessing. She'd felt his curiosity from the start, and somehow instinctively knew he believed her, which was more than she could have expected. Even to her own ears, the story sounded unbeliev-ably farfetched.

"Knowing people died while on the study? I'll admit it, I got nosy and looked up the obituary of the first person on the list. It didn't show much, the usual date of death and next of kin. I'm pretty good with a computer." She grinned at Carlisle. "Not in your league, but I manage to get around on the web. I dug a little deeper and found out the medical examiner listed the cause of death as an accidental overdose."

"Which would fall in line with a patient having commit-ted suicide." Carpenter lounged in his chair, his head thrown back, staring at the ceiling, fingers intertwined resting on his stomach. She could practically hear the wheels spinning around inside his brain.

"So I checked the next name on the list. Her cause of death was listed as a subdural hematoma caused by a fall. Again, an accidental death—but why did the two men claim they'd been killed?"

"Where's the rest of the list, Maggie?" Carpenter asked the question softly, still looking at the ceiling. Though his posture was casual, she had the distinct impression he was wound tight, ready to spring. Throughout everything, he'd been pleasant and charming, but she wasn't a fool. Beneath the societal veneer, he was a lethal weapon, ready to obliterate anybody and anything in his path.

"I don't have it. Never did. What I have is only a partial. Remember, I told you what I pulled off the EryX's server was encrypted. It was only through a process of elimination I even connected these two people to the list—and I could be wrong. It's an educated guess on my part. What scares me is that the study is still ongoing. They haven't canceled the clinical trials."

Several people at the table cursed. Not that she blamed them. People were still in danger, and if what they said was true, Gunner was too.

Carpenter turned his steely gaze on her, and she almost flinched at the anger she saw simmering beneath the surface. "Give me everything you've got with you. Carlisle has some damned fine code-breaking software. Maybe he can figure out exactly what EryX Pharmaceutical is trying to hide." He strode over and picked up her hands, kneeling down beside her chair. "Maggie, I know you're scared, and you've got a right to be. But you did the right thing coming to Gunner. He's a good man, and he's got a good team here backing him. Trust him—and trust me. We'll get to the bottom of whatever EryX Pharmaceutical is up to, find out who's behind it, and make sure they're prosecuted. We'll get justice for the innocent, and keep you safe. I give you my word."

His words rang with a promise, and she nodded. Coming to find Gunner had been the right choice—the only choice.

"Okay, everybody, get busy."

Gunner held out his hand. She stared at it for a second, before she placed her's in it, and he led her to the door. "Come with me, and let's get you a hot shower and some dry clothes. It's been a long morning."

Honestly, it had been an exhausting three weeks, but for the first time in a long time, she had something she'd been missing.

Hope.

Chapter Six

G unner opened the door to his apartment before placing his hand on the small of Maggie's back and ushering her forward. Was it a little bit vain that he wanted her to see how far he'd come from the callow youth she'd known? A lot of years had passed since they'd seen each other, yet he cherished the memory of the brief time they'd spent together for a lot of reasons.

"Gunner, this is beautiful."

He looked around, trying to picture it through her eyes. Not a whole lot had changed since he'd moved in. When Carpenter Security moved its headquarters from Dallas to New Orleans, he'd been one of the first to agree to relocate. There'd been nothing holding him in Dallas except his job. Plus, one of the perks of moving to New Orleans was a rent-free apartment.

Carpenter owned the whole building. Apparently it belonged to his grandfather, and he'd inherited it and renovated the entire thing, from the studs out, restoring the brickwork to its former glory while integrating all the modern conveniences to bring it into the twenty-first century.

"It's home."

"Well, it's a beautiful place. Sure beats my little one bedroom in Texas." She walked across the dark hardwood, and he watched the sway of her hips beneath the floral cotton dress. The fabric had dried, leaving a transparency she probably wasn't aware of, but he definitely appreciated the view.

"You drove all the way here. Is your luggage in your car?"

"What there is of it. I didn't have a lot of time to pack. Basically left with the clothes on my back. I picked up a couple of things on the road." She smiled at him, the same smile she'd given him the night they'd met. "Don't worry, I'll be fine."

She sat on the butterscotch-colored sofa, sinking into its cushions, and leaned her head back. The entire place was a study of contrasts. Warm colors mixed with ultramodern pieces of chrome and glass, he liked the eclectic feel. She blended in like she belonged, and he felt a warmth unfurling deep in his chest.

"Hungry? I can whip up something quick."

Eyes widening, she asked, "You cook?

Her words brought back another memory, one when they'd first gotten together. After a night in her bed, he'd awoken early, deciding to make her breakfast in bed. After all, he'd done his best to wear her out the night before.

Unfortunately, that full-of-himself nineteen-year-old kid hadn't known how long to cook scrambled eggs, and they'd ended up black and extra crispy around the edges. That along with the blackened toast which he'd ruined were the best offering he could give.

Maggie had raced into the kitchen when the smoke alarm blared from the smoke-filled room, leaning against the door wearing only his shirt and a grin.

Funny, they'd never finished that breakfast.

"I learned. Got tired of eating out all the time, or grabbing a fast-food burger. It gets old after a while. So I took a couple of classes. Found out I like cooking."

She watched him with those big whiskey-colored eyes, studying him for an eternity before responding. "I'd love something to eat."

Holding out his hand, he helped her from the sofa, and led her to the kitchen counter, where three empty barstools sat, and pointed to one.

"We can talk while I'm cooking."

Pulling a carton of eggs from the refrigerator, he also grabbed a package of cheese, some ham, and mushrooms. Reaching under the counter, he pulled out the butcher block cutting board, and went to work on the ham and veggies, cutting them into bite-sized pieces. He whisked the eggs until they were light and frothy, and added all the other ingredients into a bowl.

Heating the skillet with a dollop of butter in the bottom, he poured in the egg mixture.

"If you want to help, there's bread there," he pointed toward the corner of the counter, "you can make the toast."

She hustled around the peninsula counter and popped slices of bread into the toaster, then turned and watched him. He could almost feel her eyes on him. Knew she could see the changes from when he'd been a gangly youth of nineteen to the man he was now. Though having her eyes on him caused his body to have another distinctly physical reaction, one he hoped she didn't notice, as he shifted his stance.

Another minute and he had two plates heaped high with a breakfast scramble, the cheese all melty and gooey, and the toast golden brown and loaded with butter. The real stuff too. Ms. Willie didn't allow any of that processed junk. Didn't matter it wasn't her kitchen. She dropped by often enough with goodies, and he didn't mind indulging her.

"Coffee?" He asked, setting the plate in front of her.

"No, thanks. Just water, please."

They ate a couple of bites before he asked, "Maggie, why didn't you write?" He'd made sure she knew how to reach him before he deployed.

"Wil…Gunner, you were just starting out, and needed a chance to spread your wings, find out who you were meant to be. You'd never have done that if you'd felt tethered to somebody back home."

"That's not how I felt, ever. I knew what we had was temporary, at least the physical part, but I thought we'd had a friendship starting—and then it was gone." He could still remember the hurt when every week passed and there weren't any letters or calls, until he stopped waiting. *Because the disappointment hurt too much.*

"We did. I felt it too. But you needed to be free to explore every aspect of your new life, one that I wasn't going to be a part of." She waved her fork around, indicating his apartment. "Obviously, you've done well. You've got a great place, good friends, and a job you obviously adore. Seems like I made the right choice."

He wanted to come back with one of those one-liner smart-ass remarks he always used, but he couldn't. Not with Maggie.

"I'm still trying to figure out how EryX Pharmaceutical knew there was any connection between us. It doesn't make sense they'd grab you."

"Well, they seemed pretty insistent that I knew where you were. Said their boss had questions. We need to have Carlisle check into your boss at EryX Pharmaceutical. There's probably no connection, but you never know."

"I honestly can't see Mr. Davidson knowingly being part of this whole fiasco. He's the sweetest man. An introvert, he's never had a confrontational word with anybody, plus he's getting close to retirement."

"So he's older?" Why didn't that make him feel any better? All he could picture was some old sugar daddy wanting to hand Maggie the world on a silver platter. Wine and dine her and give her all the finer things that he'd never be able to afford, not even on his more than generous salary.

"Actually, he's only in his forties, but he inherited quite a bit of money when his wife died. It left him heartbroken. He promised her if anything ever happened, he'd use the money to travel around the world, seeing the sights, and living every moment to the fullest."

They ate in silence for another few minutes, Gunner going over what she'd said. Wondering again how they'd made a connection between them, when they'd only had a brief liaison years ago and hadn't spoken since.

"I keep going back to the two men in the hallway, out-side your office, sugar. You said they didn't know you were there, right?"

She nodded. "I stayed longer, until I knew they'd both walked away. Remember, I'd come in on a holiday, so there was only a skeleton crew there."

His mind raced. "How'd you get to work?"

"What?"

"Did you drive? Take the bus?"

"I...drove to work." He could see the exact moment she got it.

"And where'd you park?"

"The company parking garage." She smacked her hand against her forehead. "They must have seen my car still there, and knew I was in the building, or figured it out somehow." She tugged on her hair. "I'm so stupid. We have to use a key card to get anywhere in the building. If they had access to the records, they'd see what time I keyed out, and know I was still there."

He picked up their empty plates and loaded them in the dishwasher, and grabbed a cloth and wiped off the counter-top.

"That's my guess. They probably aren't sure whether you heard anything or not, but better safe than sorry. If they can discredit you, make you look crazy, nobody's going to believe your story. I mean, it's pretty convoluted to begin with."

Maggie stared at the floor, refusing to meet his eyes.

Somehow, he remembered she did that when she was hiding something, because she had a very expressive face, and anybody with half a brain cell could tell when she was lying.

"Maggie, look at me." When she just shook her head, he walked around the counter, and spun her barstool around until she faced him. Stepping closer, between her knees, he cupped her chin in his hand, forcing her head up.

"Tell me." His voice held a coaxing quality, because he knew better than to order her. She could put the S in stubborn.

"I called in sick the next day—Tuesday. Going over everything in my head, and looking at the files I'd downloaded—not that I could get into them or anything. I didn't have any of the passwords. So I went in to work on Wednesday morning, like nothing had changed. When I got home, I found my apartment trashed. The whole place was ransacked. Every drawer was dumped on the floor. Kitchen cabinets, bathroom cupboards ripped off the hinges. Even my dresser. They went through my underwear, for heaven's sake."

"You reported it to the police, right?"

"Of course I did. At first, I thought it was a robbery, although nothing was taken. It wasn't until I started connecting the dots that I realized it must have been the two men I heard."

"You're sure they work for EryX Pharmaceutical?"

She threw her hands up. "I don't know. I told you, I never saw their faces. But why else would they have been in the building if they didn't work there? Either somebody let them in or they had key card access."

He reached forward and cupped her cheek. "That's what we're going to figure out, and keep you safe at the same time."

Her eyes widened at his touch, the pupils dilating to swallow up the golden brown. A hint of a flush painted her cheeks, and he couldn't help himself.

He kissed her.

Chapter Seven

The feel of his lips on hers was both shocking and welcome. A short inhalation of breath parted her lips and he dove in, deepening the kiss. Her lids drifted shut and she relished the sensations racing through her, feelings she hadn't felt in a long time.

She looped her arms around his neck, threading her fingers along his scalp, feeling the softness of the short hair. When they'd first met, his hair had brushed his shoulders, dark as midnight without a hint of curl. Now he kept it military short.

Cupping the back of his scalp, she leaned in, her tongue stroking against his, loving the feeling and the raw power of his kiss. The sweetness was there, in its unhurried strokes, but she could feel the restrained desire, the urge to unleash the wildness they'd once shared.

She pulled back from the kiss, and opened her eyes to find him staring at her, his breath a ragged caress against her cheek.

"Maggie…"

She stopped him with a fingertip against his lips. "Don't apologize. We both wondered, and now we know."

At least she knew. The chemistry from their brief youthful interlude was still there. If they allowed it, the raging inferno would burn hot and fast, devouring everything in its path like a forest fire. She couldn't allow it, couldn't let him get close enough to break her heart—again.

"Carpenter will let us know once they've found out anything. Carlisle is good. It won't take him long to start going through the names and matching them up against obits or medical records."

"I wish I'd been able to get the whole list. Maybe there's a back door into the mainframe. If they haven't changed my password…"

"No."

Her finger met the middle of his chest. "You got a better plan?"

"We're working on it. Carpenter's already got a couple of guys from the Austin team headed for EryX, and they'll start snooping around your old office. Check out your apartment. See if they can spot anything."

Maggie couldn't believe what she was hearing. She might have come to them for help, but she wasn't going to sit on the sidelines while everybody else dug in and did the heavy lifting. That wasn't part of her nature.

"What can you tell me about the two guys? I know you didn't see 'em, but did they have any kind of accent? Did they sound like locals?"

She knew he deliberately changed the subject, and she let him—for now, though they weren't done. Not by a long shot.

"I didn't notice any kind of accent. Though they didn't

seem like they were running things, more like they were lower on the totem pole, and didn't mind getting their hands dirty."

His jade green eyes sparkled and he grinned. "Wonder if they are the same two yahoos who tried to question me."

How in the world was he so nonchalant about being kidnapped. She didn't know much about his job, other than he worked for Carpenter Security, but surely their employees didn't go around getting snatched off the streets all the time, especially by hoodlums with guns.

"How can you be so casual about being kidnapped?"

"Ain't the first time, sugar. Probably won't be the last. I'd much rather they take me than the client I'm assigned to protect." He chuckled before adding, "You remember anybody around your office named Doc?"

"Probably more than you can count. Everybody there working in R&D was a doctor."

"You'd recognize this guy. Tall, cadaverous, full of his own self-importance, but ready to piss himself when he's confronted by somebody bigger and badder than him."

She thought about all the guys in white coats who came through the doors of her office on a routine basis, dealing solely with her boss. He might have been a VP of sales and marketing, but he kept well-informed of everything pertaining to new drugs, because that's where the money was. One face stuck out from the rest that matched Gunner's description.

"There is one. Dr. Mueller. Reminded me of a tall, skinny Boris Karloff. Never deigned to speak with me, except to ask if the boss was in."

"That's it! Boris Karloff. I knew he reminded me of somebody, but couldn't place it at the time. Plus I was kind of busy—fighting for my life and all." He chuckled and Maggie joined in, though she wondered how he could laugh about something so awful.

Gunner pulled out his cell and called Carlisle.

"Busy here."

"Get unbusy. Might have made a connection to the good doctor who wanted to shoot me full of truth serum. Maggie says it sounds like Dr. Mueller. Works at EryX Pharmaceutical."

"Got it. Lemme call you back in a couple minutes."

He hung up without another word. Gunner wasn't worried. He knew Carlisle would have an answer, or at the very least a photo of the elusive Dr. Mueller to compare with his own personal nemesis.

"Carlisle will call us back in a few, and we'll know if Mueller is the same guy."

Maggie shook her head. "This just keeps getting deeper and deeper. I'm afraid if we dig too far, we're going to uncover the whole company is a mirage or a front for organized crime or something equally dastardly."

"Hate to tell you, sugar, but it wouldn't be the first time, and probably won't be the last. Pharmaceuticals are big business, especially now with supposed affordable healthcare. When money is involved, people forget all about things like morals and scruples. All they see are dollar signs and yachts and mansions. Who cares if the little guy gets screwed. There are plenty more waiting in the wings, dying for their chance to make a few bucks."

He watched her wrap her arms across her chest, and rub her her hands along them. She was still in the clothes she'd arrived in, and they'd been sopping wet.

"Want me to grab your bag, so you can change? Maybe grab a hot shower?"

"A shower would be great. But I left what little I brought with me in my car." She grabbed her purse and dug out a set of keys. "I'll go get it."

Gunner took the keys from her. "I'll get them. Where'd you park?"

"About three blocks north. It's in a parking area behind a bakery. I didn't want to leave it on the street."

"Good thinking. What make is it?"

"An old Oldsmobile Cutlass. Dark green with Arkansas plates, though probably more rust than paint. One bag in the trunk."

Without thinking, he reached up and ran a thumb along her cheek, feeling the softness of her skin beneath his hand. Her eyes closed and she leaned into him, and he felt humbled by her trust.

"The shower off the master bedroom is the nicest. Go ahead and jump in. I'll leave your bag on the bed, so you'll have your stuff when you're finished."

She opened her eyes, the brown color having darkened from the whiskey hue to a deeper brown, one that he remembered though he hadn't seen it in forever, and thought he'd never see again. The change in hue happened when she felt desire. He swallowed, knowing he needed to get out of there, before he did something they'd both regret.

"I'll be right back. Make yourself at home." He strode for the door and never looked back. Because if he had, he'd give in to the urge to sweep her off her feet and carry her straight to his bed, and keep her there.

Too bad. It sounded like a really good idea. He took a deep breath, and headed for Maggie's car.

Chapter Eight

S he was a fool. Standing in front of the windows in Gunner's apartment, she wondered again why she'd come here. Not that she had anyplace else to go. It had become apparent that no matter how far she ran or how fast, somebody always found her.

Two nights after she'd grabbed her cash and her laptop and ran, she'd checked into a nondescript motel in a small town outside Oklahoma City. The kind of place a family on the road might stop while watching their pennies, but not a dump either. Several semis were parked in front, and she'd figured it would do for a day or two, while she tried to make sense of what she'd uncovered.

The motel had ground level rooms only, the kind with the doors facing the parking lot with peepholes to see outside. Though she'd have preferred one of the multi-floor hotels, she had to watch her funds, and this was cheap and fairly clean, and not in the middle of a big city.

It still wasn't enough, though. Two thirty in the morning, she'd been awakened by a noise at the front door. Watched in horrified silence as the knob jiggled. Somebody turned it left and right.

She'd made sure the deadbolt had been on, but knew one

good kick to the door and it would cave in, probably frame and all. They weren't meant to keep out people desperate to get in.

She'd snatched up the phone and dialed the front desk, claiming somebody was trying to break into her room. It felt like an eternity passed before she heard somebody yell from across the parking lot, and heard footsteps racing away.

The night manager assured her this kind of thing never happened, when she checked out an hour later. Probably didn't, she mused, but most people weren't on the run for their lives.

Though she had no idea how they'd found her, she didn't take any chances, and the next morning she'd sold her car, and grabbed a bus ticket, headed anyplace that was farther away than the day before.

She'd been doing the same thing for the last couple of weeks. Riding the bus during the night, headed in any direction she could buy a ticket, and sleeping during the daylight hours.

Every other spare moment was spent scouring the files she'd taken from EryX Pharmaceutical. Most of them had to do with the clinical trial of Somnolett.

Hearing those men talking about the adverse effects of the drug, and the people participating in the trial dying raised all kinds of red flags in her mind.

She'd been stupid. It had taken her a full twenty-four hours before she'd realized they could track her cellphone. Chalk it up to being terrified, but she'd ended up tossing it and buying a burner phone. One that couldn't be traced.

The next problem turned out to be her laptop. Somehow, and she still wasn't sure how, they'd used it to figure out where she was, even after she threw away her cell.

In desperation, she'd ended up at an office supply store, and printed out everything she had on Somnolett, and the clinical trials, and made multiple copies. Downloaded the files on thumb drives that she purchased. E-mailed copies to herself at e-mail addresses that she created after she'd started running.

Took every precaution she could think of—and still they found her. Every single time. She'd finally taken the battery out of the laptop completely, and hidden part of the list in a bus station locker in a little Podunk town in Tennessee.

A set of the printed documentation went into a storage locker she bribed the manager to let her rent without any ID. That had taken a huge chunk out of her cash.

She made up packets from the information, containing portions but not all of the data. If she was caught, whoever had her wouldn't have access to the whole list.

But she needed one place, one person, who she trusted enough to turn over everything to—and that had been Wilson. Though they hadn't spoken in years, there wasn't a single person she could think of who she'd trust with her life except him. Even when she'd known him years earlier, she knew on a gut-deep level, he'd always be somebody she could count on.

It hadn't taken long to find him. A Google search showed his military career, and that he now worked for Carpenter Security Services. There'd even been an article about the company relocating to New Orleans.

She'd bought an old junker, and drove like a bat out of hell, straight to New Orleans. Shown up on his doorstep, bringing danger in her wake.

"I'm so sorry," she whispered. "I never meant for this to happen."

A phone rang, and she noted Gunner must have left it on the coffee table after he'd called Carlisle. Walking over, she looked down and saw the caller ID said it was Carlisle. She hesitated a moment, then swiped her finger across.

"Hello."

"Ms. Callahan? Where's Gunner?" Though Carlisle's question wasn't couched as a demand, she knew he wouldn't give up without an answer.

"He went to get my suitcase from my car. He should be back soon."

"Okay." There was a long pause, as though he were deciding whether to tell her anything else. "I'm texting him a picture of Mueller. Have him take a look and see if it's the same guy he called about."

"I'll do that. Thanks for getting it so quickly."

"Just doing my job. Have him call me back." With that he hung up, and she heard the door open. Gunner walked in with her small overnight bag.

"Got your stuff. We'll have to move your car to a better spot later." He raised a brow at the phone in her hand.

"Carlisle called. He texted you a picture of Dr. Mueller. Wants you to call him back."

Setting down the bag, he walked over and she handed

him the phone. Watched his face when he looked at the photo.

"Yep, that's him. One mystery solved."

"And opens the door for a lot more. I still can't figure out how they knew about you."

"That's a good question, and we'll figure it out, but in the meantime, I need to let Carpenter know that Mueller is one of our guys. Though I'm pretty sure he's not the one calling the shots. No backbone."

While he texted, she picked up her bag and headed for the previously promised shower. It had been a long night, and the day hadn't been any easier.

"I'm going to head downstairs for a bit." Gunner walked up behind her, stopping her with a hand on her arm. "I'll lock the door on my way out. Keep it locked and don't answer it for anybody except me. Got it?"

"Got it." She gave him a mock salute.

"Smarty pants." He chuckled, heading for the door, leaving her alone once more.

"Have you gotten the list of names from her yet?"

Those were the first words to greet Gunner when he walked through the doors to the conference room. Carpenter stood with his back against the giant whiteboard, waiting not so patiently for Gunner's answer.

"Not yet. It's been a little crazy. At least we got Mueller's name. He's definitely the "Doc" from the garage."

"I hacked into his cellphone records, with the info on the

phone you *borrowed*," Carlisle grinned, "and he's already ordered a replacement. Shipping it to the Ritz in downtown New Orleans." He chuckled. "I can't believe our bad guy was stupid enough to use his personal phone and not grab a burner—what a moron."

"The Ritz? Somebody's got deep pockets. That place costs a fortune." Gunner looked around when he heard Nate's voice, noting the phone was on speaker.

"We brought Nate up to speed. He and Sheri will be here in a couple of days—with my plane, right?"

"I promise, boss, the second it's released from evidence, it'll be fueled and winging its way back to ya."

Andrea poked Carpenter in the side. "Give him a break. It's not his fault a crazy man tried to crash your plane."

"Well, I have to blame somebody, and he drew the short straw."

"No fair. I wasn't there to draw any straws." Nate protested. "I was busy fighting for my life."

"Maybe next time you'll check the cockpit." Carpenter winked at Andrea, who blushed.

"Can we get back on target here?" Gunner flopped down into a chair, and swiveled around, sparing a glance for each person in the room.

The elite team. Carpenter's A-team of experts, the ones he'd handpicked. They'd worked their way up through the company, each one a standout in their field, with specialized skillsets.

Other than Nate, who was still in Dallas, every member of the elite team was present. Jean-Luc was the second-in-command, directly beneath Carpenter in the company hierarchy. They'd known each other from childhood, and Gunner knew there was some history there that neither man spoke of, their unshakable loyalty to each other was unquestioned. Andrea had joined the team recently, after they'd worked a case together, bringing down a drug smuggler and arms dealer. Stefan Carlisle had been with C.S.S. as long as Gunner. The man was a certified genius, and there wasn't anything he couldn't do with a computer. No data was secure if Carlisle wanted it. Sometimes Geek Boy was downright scary in his pursuit of information, but he was invaluable to their group, and a good friend. Stephanie might not work out in the field, but she was another valuable asset, and had relocated with the company when they'd moved from Dallas to New Orleans. Gunner was pretty sure the company would collapse around their ears if Stephanie ever walked out.

Even Gator Boudreau was present for today's meeting. Though not officially a member of C.S.S., Gator was Jean-Luc's father and there was pretty much nothing that happened in or around New Orleans that Gator didn't know about.

The only person missing was Ms Willie. And he was pretty sure she'd show up any minute, loaded down with something delicious. The woman was a walking marvel when it came to culinary delights. She'd been the housekeeper slash nanny slash bodyguard for Samuel Carpenter when he was growing up—although he hadn't known about that last one. Not until recently, when it was revealed that Ms. Willie was a former MI-5 agent. Though only a few people knew that information and it was kept on the Q.T.

"Couple of fellas pulled a body out of the swamp this morning. The police are swarming all over their camp. Best they could tell, it was a woman. Blonde."

Gunner knew deep in his gut the blonde would turn out to be the same one from the airport—the one who'd drugged him and started this whole debacle. What were the odds it might be another blonde dead in the bayou?

"Which leaves us trying to figure out who our two Rambo wannabes are. Do they work for EryX Pharmaceutical? Or are they hired muscle—lousy muscle, but still…" Gunner tossed out his thoughts, wanting to hear what the others thought.

"Well, I looked at the footage from the airport security cameras." Carlisle muttered. "I gotta tell you, their video sucks. I've seen better quality at a mom and pop convenience store."

"Fine, bad pictures, got it. What about the two mooks?" Nate's voice was filled with humor. Everybody on the team knew Carlisle was bloody picky about anything electronic. He expected nothing less than perfection, and couldn't understand why everybody didn't have the best of the best. Of course, when your boss is a billionaire and provides you with top-of-the-line equipment, you might be a tad spoiled.

Tapping a couple of keys, Carlisle turned the laptop around, and Gunner watched as he walked out of the airport. Saw the pretty blonde bump into him. Noted the split second when his knees began to buckle, and the black van pulling up to the curb.

Two men wearing dark shirts and jeans hopped out of the back the moment the door slid open. Within the briefest moment, they'd positioned themselves on either side of him, and half dragged, half carried him to the open door and tossed him inside. From the limpness of his body, it was evident that he was out.

The blonde clamored into the front passenger seat, and the van sped away. The whole thing probably took less than sixty seconds.

"Any chance of cleaning that up enough to get the license plate?"

"Sorry, boss. I might be able to get a partial, but I'd bet good money the plates are stolen. Probably the van too."

Gunner agreed. "There was no van at the house when I got away. If it was me, I'd have either torched it or sunk it."

"Lemme ask around, see if anybody's noticed a torched van." Gator gave Gunner a nod, which meant he approved of his conjecture. High praise indeed from the older guy.

Nobody knew much about Gator, and he liked to keep it that way. All four of his sons either worked for C.S.S. or would be when they finished out their military service. Ranger had taken a few weeks off, after working a missing person case. It had been ugly, but ultimately a success. They'd found the girl before it was too late, and Ranger had found the love of his life.

"I've got the facial recognition program running the two guys, though it's going to take longer, because I don't have adequate pictures of either perp."

"I know you'll work your magic, bro." Gunner reached across and fist-bumped Carlisle, who twisted the laptop back around and started typing.

Every head in the room turned at the sound of the door opening, and Gunner jumped up from his chair to help Ms. Willie wheel in the cart loaded with food. She'd gone all out, making enough to feed an army. Well, maybe not quite that much, but Carpenter's army put away a hell of a lot of grub.

There were platters filled with sandwiches, piled high with roast beef, turkey and ham. Bowls of chips, including his own personal favorite, the barbecue ones. Another huge platter contained brownies, which Gunner knew would be homemade from scratch and the chocolate would melt in his mouth. Ms. Willie had the magic touch when it came to sweets, and every single member of Carpenter's team had begged her to marry them.

"Ms. Willie, you are a lifesaver." Carpenter walked over and gave the older woman a hug.

"It's no trouble, Mister Samuel."

"Aw, no fair. Somebody tell me what she brought so I can live vicariously through you." Nate's voice sounded like a pouty little boy, though Gunner knew he was teasing. Mostly. Nate ate like his stomach was a bottomless pit.

"Here you go, mate." Carlisle snapped a picture and Gunner knew he'd sent it to Nate.

"No! Brownies. Ms. Willie…"

"Don't worry, Mr. Nathan. I'll make sure to have something special for you as soon as you get home with Ms. Sheri."

Gunner pulled Ms. Willie aside, while everyone else loaded their plates and started eating. That was one of the nice things about working together with this group. Carpenter didn't mind the casual atmosphere, because he knew that the second the elite team went into action, they were on the job, ready and focused.

"Ms. Willie, I've got a guest upstairs. If you wouldn't mind, I'd like to fix up a plate for her, and introduce you. Maybe you can sit with her for a bit, until we finish up here?"

"Her?" A smile tugged at the corners of her lips, but she didn't fool him. Ms. Willie probably already knew precisely who Margaret Callahan was, and why she was here. She might be retired from MI-5, but the woman still had a few fingers in the business, and stayed on her toes.

"I'll explain everything, though I'm sure Mister Samuel's already filled in the details."

"Of course he has. The covered plate on the bottom of the cart is for your young lady." Ms. Willie's British accent came through strongly, though it still took a little getting used to. Before they'd discovered her connection to MI-5, she'd barely had an accent, and what she did have was pure Texan. A little bit of the Texas twang still bled through from time to time.

"And you wonder why you're my hero, Ms. Willie." He watched the blush spread across her cheeks at his words.

"Go on with you, Mr. Wilson. Let's go meet your young lady." Ms. Willie was one of the few people who still called him by his real name. She'd insisted that it was a fine upstanding name, and that he should be proud of it. So while he might be Gunner to everybody else, with Ms. Willie, he'd always be Wilson.

"Be right back," he called over his shoulder, though he doubted anybody would miss him. They were too busy shoving all of Ms. Willie's great food into their pie holes.

Carrying the plate in one hand, he escorted Ms. Willie to his front door, and softly knocked.

"Maggie, it's me."

The door swung inward, and she stood silhouetted in the sunlight pouring in from the bank of windows. She'd obviously had her shower and changed, because now she wore a pair of jeans that fit her just right, hugging her curves. The hips that he'd caressed every single night. A deep purple T-shirt emphasized her breasts, and the color was a perfect foil for her reddish gold hair. It lay in waves around her face and over her shoulders.

"Hi." She held out her hand to Ms. Willie, ignoring him. "I'm Maggie."

"Wilhelmina McDaniels, but everybody calls me Ms. Willie." Before he could open his mouth, Ms. Willie had enveloped Maggie in her arms, smoothing a hand over her hair.

"You poor dear, you've had a rough time, haven't you? Mister Wilson, put that plate on the table and get Ms. Maggie a glass of milk to go with her meal." Turning her back to him, Ms. Willie led Maggie to the small table set up by the kitchen. Round, it was big enough to seat two comfortably. He followed behind like a trained puppy, and set the plate on the table.

"You didn't have to go to all this trouble."

"No trouble, dear. I fixed some food for my boys, and made up an extra plate. It's nothing fancy, just sandwiches and chips."

He met the older woman's eyes over Maggie's head, and mouthed "thank you," and finished pouring the milk. Maggie would be safe with Ms. Willie here. The former MI-5 agent was a master at getting people to talk. She might be able to get Maggie to open up and remember something she hadn't mentioned. It was worth a shot.

"Maggie, I have to head back down and finish up the briefing. Ms. Willie's going to keep you company for a bit, until I get back. If you need anything, let her know and she'll get me."

He couldn't stop himself. He leaned forward and brushed a kiss against the top of her head, breathing in the scent of citrus from her shampoo. Catching Ms. Willie's eye, he motioned for her to call him and then headed for the door, pulling it shut behind him.

Damn, he hoped they figured out what was going on with the clinical trial before too much longer, because being around Maggie was beginning to feel too good. He had a sneaking suspicion if she stayed, that too good feeling would grow into something he was reluctant to face.

Chapter Nine

Maggie dug into the food with gusto, not realizing how hungry she was until after that first bite. Ms. Willie kept busy in the kitchen, wiping down the countertops while Maggie ate. She had to admit the brownie was the best part of the meal. The gooey frosting was perfect with the moist cakey dessert. No way that came from a box mix.

"That was delicious, Ms. Willie. Thank you."

As she shoved the last bite into her mouth, Ms. Willie plopped into the chair across from her. She nodded toward the empty plate. "Want some more?"

"Goodness, no. I'm stuffed. Everything was wonderful, especially that brownie. Mind sharing the recipe?"

Ms. Willie smiled. "I'll write it down for you. It's a simple one."

"Trust me, Ms. Willie, there was nothing simple about the flavors of that brownie. I love to bake, but I've never made anything that tasty."

"Really? I don't run into many people these days who enjoy baking. Personally, I do it to relax. Then it morphed into feeding all my boys." She smiled fondly at the mention of her boys.

"You've been feeding all the men from Carpenter Security. That seems a monumental task for one person."

"It's a labor of love, dear. I never had children of my own, so I've adopted them as my surrogate kids. Though they do keep me on my toes."

"Well, all I know is, if I baked like that, I'd look like the Hindenburg, from sampling all the goodies."

Ms. Willie leaned forward. "Confidentially, between you and me, for a while there I ate way more of my own baking than was good for me. Added an extra fifty pounds, without even realizing it." She winked. "I've lost forty of them since moving to New Orleans with Mister Samuel. Still have another ten I want to lose, but they're being bloody stubborn."

Maggie grinned at the thickening British accent. The fire glinting in the older woman's eyes convinced her more than her words that the woman was a force to be reckoned with. And the stubborn set of her jaw when she mentioned those last ten pounds—there was no question in Maggie's mind that she'd accomplish her goal, and heaven help anybody who stood in her way.

"Now, Ms. Maggie, since Mister Wilson is one of my boys, why don't you tell me how you know him." She shook her finger at Maggie, the corners of her lips curving upward in a grin that belied the action. "Don't leave out a single detail. That boy keeps his emotions bottled up tight, covering them up with a sarcastic mouth, but he doesn't fool me. He feels things more deeply than any of my boys." Her expression turned serious in a flash. "I won't see him hurt. Not by anyone."

"I would never hurt Wilson—I mean Gunner."

Maggie noted the change in Ms. Willie's expression when she stumbled over Gunner's proper name. Noted the distinct sparkle in her eyes. She didn't doubt for a minute that Ms. Willie was a born nurturer, with the heart of a grizzly protecting her cubs. And she couldn't help wondering how many people had felt that momma grizzly's claws?

"I'm not sure how much Gunner's told you. We met almost ten years ago. I was waitressing in a bar outside Beaumont part-time while attending college. He'd enlisted in the marines and was getting ready to head out to boot camp in San Diego."

Ms. Willie didn't say anything, simply nodded, but Maggie knew she was listening intently, absorbing each word, every kernel of information about *her boy*. She wondered if Gunner knew how lucky he was to have this feisty fighter in his corner?

"We spent a very…intense couple of weeks together." Emotions swamped her, swift and strong, nearly choking her with the memories she'd thought hidden away.

"You fell in love with him." It wasn't a question.

Why deny it? It was the truth. She nodded. "We were young, and he needed to get away from South Texas. Needed a chance to find himself, and become the man he was always meant to be. I couldn't take that chance away from him—so I let him go."

"And you've regretted it ever since, haven't you?" There was clearly sympathy in the other woman's gaze, but also a wealth of understanding. So much so, Maggie's eyes clouded with tears.

Ms. Willie's hand covered hers. "You know deep in your heart you made the right decision. I've always believed if two people are meant to be together, fate or kismet or whatever you want to call it, will bring them back together no matter how many years or miles have kept them apart."

She gave a watery chuckle. "Well, I don't know about that. We haven't been in touch in years, but when I needed help, he was the person I thought of."

Ms. Willie patted the hand she still held. "That's because he's a good boy. Now, I'm a very good listener, besides being a buttinsky, so why don't you tell me what exactly brought you looking for Gunner?"

Maggie started talking.

Chapter Ten

"The first three names on Maggie's list all check out. One died from a brain aneurysm, though wasn't hospitalized at the time of death. M.E.'s report shows nothing to indicate it was in any way considered anything but natural causes."

"That doesn't mean she isn't telling the truth. Records get changed all the time," Gunner protested.

"The second name," Carpenter continued as though Gunner hadn't interrupted, "was killed in a car accident. Head on collision with a semi. Again, the medical examiner found no evidence of anything other than alcohol in the patient's system. It's a long shot, and it might be classified as a suicide, although without corroborating evidence, it's just supposition."

"Still, it's unusual for two deaths from the same study group. How far apart were these deaths?" Jean-Luc tapped his fingers on the tabletop, in a rhythmic pattern.

"Fifteen days."

"The third name on the list passed away in her sleep. No evidence of foul play according to the autopsy. Again, nothing to indicate that Somnolett caused anything abnormal."

Gunner didn't like the direction this was heading. As far as he was concerned, Maggie was telling the truth. The first three names on the list didn't die of natural causes or from accidents. At least not accidents that weren't helped along by a little outside intervention, and he said as much.

"Believe it or not, Gunner, I agree." Carpenter stared at him, the intensity of his gaze piercing. "I can't think of a single clinical trial for any drug having this high a percentage of mortality. It's strange that nothing has shown up on any blood tests."

"Boss, unless the state labs are looking for specific drugs, they probably only did routine screening for the usual suspects. Arsenic, cyanide, and narcotics. They wouldn't be looking for something that's within a clinical trial. Shoot, they probably wouldn't have the formula to find it anyway." Carlisle barely looked up from his computer. "Think about all the poisons that never get caught, because they have to be looking for a specific agent. Take antifreeze for example."

"Makes sense." Gunner remembered reading or hearing about that someplace. "Wasn't there a case where they killed a bunch of people with succinylcholine because it couldn't be traced?"

"Yep."

Carpenter stood and walked around the desk, easing down the laptop's cover, slow enough that Carlisle could get his fingers free. "We've got three. That still leaves us with eight more deaths to investigate, not counting the fourteen people still alive."

Chapter Eleven

G unner plugged the address into the GPS as Maggie read it off the printout. The drive was going to take a while, and they'd be in the car together for at least five or six hours, barring any unforeseen traffic snarls. It was a long time to spend with somebody you hadn't seen for years.

He turned on the car stereo, hitting one of his favorite playlists. Most of the time, he'd have country singers crooning in the background, singing about lost loves, but today seemed more like a smooth jazz kinda day. The soft wail of a saxophone wove enticingly through the speakers. He glanced over at Maggie, wondering what she thought of his choice. A small smile curved the corners of her lips, her fingers drumming along her thigh in time with the beat. Looked like he'd made a good choice.

"What's your gut telling you, Gunner?" She posed the question during the break between one song and the next. "I know my story is unbelievable. Major drug companies don't go around bumping off the people participating in their drug trials. They have them sign confidentiality agreements for a reason. Plus, they've got a battalion of lawyers to keep anybody from denigrating their products."

"Honey, I hate to say this, but big businesses will do

anything to keep their bottom line in the black. EryX Pharmaceutical wouldn't be the first company to squelch bad news in the most permanent way possible."

She wrapped her arms across her chest. "I hate this. I hate that I overheard those two men talking about killing people, and nobody seemed to give a damn. Selling a drug shouldn't be more important than a person's life."

He agreed, but he also knew the darkness and corruption that greed created. Even the best people could be persuaded to do things they'd once never have condoned, all because they chased the almighty dollar.

"Maybe the first few deaths were exactly what the coroner's report stated, accidental or natural causes. Look on the bright side—we might get to Leland Jackson's house and he'll greet us at the door, hale and hearty."

"Well, I'd much rather that than the alternative." She leaned her head back against the headrest and closed her eyes. He had a hard time keeping his eyes on the road, when he'd rather be looking at her. There had been changes since the last time he'd seen her, but the years had been good to Maggie.

"I didn't want to ask before, with everybody around, but—why'd you come looking for me, Mags?"

The interior of the car was silent except for the slow rhythm of the jazz playing through the speakers. Finally she opened her eyes and swiveled in her seat, until she partially faced him.

"I know a lot of people, friends and family back in Texas that I could have called or gone to see, but I needed to be sure the person I gave this information to was above reproach. Somebody who'd listen to me and believe me without question, even if I sounded like I'd lost my mind. Somebody who'd do the right thing, even if it wasn't the easy thing. When I weighed all my options, there was only one logical choice. You."

Gunner swallowed the lump that formed in the back of his throat. Did she really believe all that—about him?

"How could you be sure about me?"

The mysterious smile that played around her lips had him gripping the steering wheel hard enough his knuckles turned white, to keep from reaching across and pulling her toward him. He shifted in the driver's seat trying to ease the discomfort that the growing erection caused, making it difficult to concentrate on the road.

"I know we were both young the first time we met, but we packed a lot of time into those few weeks we had together. Shared our hopes and wishes and dreams of the future. It might not have seemed like it, but I really did listen to everything you said. The things you believed, the core values you had, even growing up on what you called the wrong side of the tracks, they were grounded and true. When push came to shove, and I needed somebody I knew would do the right thing, the first person I thought about was you."

"I'm not sure what to say. Hopefully, I won't let you down."

Her hand reached across and clasped his forearm. "I believe in you, Gunner. Now let's go find Mr. Jackson."

The miles flew by, the scenery changing with each little town and city along the way. He stuck mostly to I-10, wanting to make the best time getting to Katy, Texas.

Following the directions from the GPS, they pulled up in front of a small boxy house. Looking around, he could see that it wasn't in the best neighborhood, though it bordered onto a fairly up-and-coming area. Jackson's yard was well-cared for and orderly, with the trees pruned and the flowerbeds filled with a variety of white and yellow blossoms.

The yard was surrounded by a chainlink fence, and the sidewalk on the city side of it was cracked and broken, with weeds growing up between the jagged spaces. Yet, the pathway from the gate to the front porch was pristine and new. It was apparent Mr. Jackson took a tremendous amount of pride in his home.

"I don't see any cars. Do you think anybody's home?"

"Only one way to find out." He opened the gate and held it open for Maggie, closing it quietly behind him, noting the gate didn't squeak and moved easily.

Reaching the front porch, he knocked on the door. No sound emanated from inside. Taking a step to the left, he looked in the window beside the front door, peering between the opening in the drapes. He didn't spot anything.

Maggie tapped his arm and he straightened. "Look at the mailbox." She pointed to the rectangular box on the other side of the front door. The lid was propped open overflowing with what looked like several days' worth of mail.

"I'm going to take a look around the back. Stay here."

"But…"

"Maggie, stay put. I'll be right back."

He ignored the mulish look on her face and the stubbornly crossed arms, and walked around the side of the house, until she was out of sight. His guts were a tangle of knots, because he had a really bad feeling—like they were too late.

The back of the house was as immaculately maintained as the front, with a detached shed and a small patio. Sliding glass doors spanned a good portion of the back wall, with white sheers obstructing a clear view inside. Walking past the patio, he peered in the kitchen window.

On the floor, right in front of the open refrigerator door lay a prone body. He'd bet it was the recently deceased Leland Jackson.

"What is it?"

Fortunately, he'd heard her sneaking around the corner, or he'd probably have jumped a foot. Instead, he frowned and turned to her with a glare.

"I told you to stay out front."

"I've never been good at following orders." She shrugged. "What did you see?"

"Enough to know we need to call the police."

"He's dead?" The color leeched from her face.

"Somebody is. We won't know who until the cops get here."

Pulling out his phone, he dialed nine-one-one and reported what they'd found, and agreed to wait for officers to respond.

Wrapping his hand around her elbow, he marched her around to the front and through the gate to the car. In less than five minutes, the police and EMTs had arrived.

Gunner succinctly explained what he'd found, though he didn't tell them why they'd come to visit Mr. Jackson—at least not the real reason. No way was he telling the cops they were checking into suspicious deaths by Big Pharma.

He was still answering questions when they wheeled the stretcher out the front door, with the body covered. It was clear to see he was dead.

"Any idea what happened to him?" He asked the officer he'd been talking with.

"EMTs said it looks like a heart attack. What was your business with Mr. Jackson?" The narrowing of the officer's eyes told Gunner he was getting suspicious.

"Just a friend. We stopped to say hello on our way through town, and didn't get an answer when we knocked."

"Good thing you went around back. Old guy probably wouldn't have been found for days otherwise. Lived alone, no pets."

Gunner pulled out a business card and handed it to the officer. Noted his eyes widen when he saw the Carpenter logo. People, especially those in law enforcement, were well aware of C.S.S.'s reputation.

"What would somebody from C.S.S. want with Mr. Jackson?" The cop tapped the business card against his notebook. Gunner knew his curiosity was mixed with a little suspicion. Understood it, because it was part of the game. But he wasn't about to tell him anything.

"Nothing business related. Like I said, we stopped by on our way through town."

"From New Orleans?" Again the side-eye from the cop.

"We've got offices all over the country, Officer…Holmes. Including Houston."

"Your card says New Orleans, so I assumed…"

"Never assume. If there's nothing else?" Gunner didn't feel an iota of guilt about deliberately misleading Officer Holmes. He didn't outright lie, but not volunteering information was a tried and true tactic. Plus, he didn't have much to add. There was no evidence that EryX Pharmaceutical was behind Leland Jackson's death. Maybe it *was* a heart attack.

Except he really didn't think so. Something about the whole scenario seemed too perfect, right down to the open refrigerator door. On the surface, it looked like Jackson had been getting something from the fridge and collapsed. He decided to wait until they had more information.

"Thanks for your help, Mr. Everett. If we have any more questions, we'll get in touch. Ma'am." Holmes nodded toward Maggie and walked away.

"They think it was a heart attack?" Maggie's voice was pitched low, so no one else could hear, but he didn't want to talk here. They needed to get someplace where he could call Carpenter and update him on what they'd found.

"Let's go. We'll talk on the way."

She settled onto the passenger seat, and he closed the door, jogging around to the driver's side. He remembered passing an IHOP a couple of miles back. It seemed like as good a place as any to grab a bite and make the call.

Pulling into the parking lot, he killed the engine and pulled out his phone. "I'm going to call the boss and let him know what we found, so he can get copies of any records from the M.E.'s office when they're ready. Then we'll grab something to eat."

"Okay."

He updated Carpenter and Carlisle on what they'd found at Jackson's house.

"I'm starving." He rubbed his hand across his stomach. "Ready to eat?"

The growling of her stomach was answer enough. He grinned. She hopped out of the car before he could walk around and open her door, and they went inside and were seated at a booth toward the back.

The waitress came, filled their coffee cups, and took their orders. He knew Maggie was about to explode with questions, but she'd been a champ, not saying anything until after the waitress had walked away.

"They think it was a heart attack?"

He nodded, taking a sip of his black coffee. He winced when she poured three of those little creamer cups into hers, plus a couple of packets of sugar. Ruined a perfectly good cup of coffee, but hey, he wasn't drinking it.

"Preliminary by the EMTs on site, but that could change when they do the autopsy."

"I know EryX Pharmaceutical is behind this. Think about how many people from the trial have died." She sat with her hands wrapped around her cup, and he reached across and unwrapped one, holding it in his.

"Honey, I know you're right. But knowing it and proving it are two different things." He squeezed her hand. "I wish we had the full list of all the people, instead of a partial, but Carpenter will have people on every name on the list. They'll be protected twenty-four/seven until we figure out exactly what we're up against."

Reluctantly, he released her hand when the waitress returned with their order. He'd gotten the steak and eggs with a stack of pancakes. Maggie had opted for an omelette and toast.

The text message alert on his phone dinged before he'd taken the first bite. Reaching for his phone, he swiped the screen, staring at the message from his boss and frowned.

"What's wrong?" Maggie put down her fork, and waited.

"Carlisle's been able to verify two more people on the list. One deceased and one in critical condition in intensive care."

"That's what, seven so far? Out of twenty-five? Gunner, they're not going to stop until everybody in that drug trial is dead." She shoved her plate away, the food untouched.

"You not eating isn't going to help." He pushed the plate back in front of her. "If you get sick, there's nobody left to help the rest of these people."

She lifted her gaze to meet his. "Yes, there is. There's you."

The knot in his stomach unfurled and he felt a warmth spread through him. She hadn't seen him in years, but she'd instinctively trusted him. Sought him out to ask for help.

And she truly believed that if anything happened to her, he'd continue fighting for these people.

"Eat."

Picking up her fork, she dug into her meal, and though he'd lost his appetite after the text, he ate until he'd cleaned his plate.

"I have an idea, but you're probably going to think I'm nuts." Maggie took a sip of her coffee, watching him over the rim of her cup. He didn't trust the twinkle in her eyes, the one he remembered always led him into trouble.

"Honey, you've been crazy since the day I met you. Hit me with your best shot."

"It's another six hours back to New Orleans, and it's getting late. My parents have a rental place near Galveston. It's empty now. Why don't we head there and spend the night?"

Chapter Twelve

H ad she lost her mind? What insane impulse had her throwing out an invitation to spend the night together?

Gunner's eyes lit up with laughter, and she knew he read her discomfort, and was enjoying every minute of it. Her and her big mouth.

"Well, that's an invitation I can't refuse."

"Don't go reading more into it than I meant, cowboy. It's a place to sleep, that's all."

"Sure, honey, we'll sleep—eventually."

How had she forgotten his wicked sense of humor? He'd always gotten the better of her when it came to double entendres and suggestive come ons.

"Sleep, as in two bedrooms."

"Darlin', you wound me."

She tossed a paper napkin across the table. "Flag on the play, unsportsmanlike conduct. Ten yard penalty."

He guffawed and heads turned to watch. He raised both hands in surrender, though she knew it was a temporary retreat at best. Nothing kept Gunner down for long.

"Come on. Let's head out. A couple hours of downtime sounds really good right now. I've got the feeling we might end up going to the hospital, to check on the woman in intensive care, but we'll wait until we hear something from the office first."

He dropped several bills on the table, and picked up the check, and headed to the front. Once they'd paid, he opened her door before walking around to the other side.

She hoped she wasn't making the biggest mistake of her life. Her first thought had been to head for her place in Pasadena, but what were the chances hired help from Eryx Pharmaceutical hadn't already tossed it, looking for clues of where she might be? The last time she'd talked to her parents, they hadn't mentioned anybody asking about her, which meant they'd left them alone—so far.

She was still hoping to get ahold of the rest of the list, or at least get a few more names. Knowing that people were dying, all in the name of big business and greed, made her even more determined to put an end to it.

Her first thought had been to go to the press. Except she didn't have enough for any reputable reporter to run with the story, and there was no way she'd pander to the tabloids. They'd run the story, but who with half an ounce of brains would believe it?

"Gunner, should I go to the press? I thought about it before, and decided against it, because I didn't have any evidence. But I can't let them keep killing people—not over money. Not to keep their dirty little secrets."

"Gotta admit, I thought about that angle too. I'd say wait. Once we've got a little more concrete facts, I bet Carpenter has some really influential reporters who'd kill for a story this big."

"Bad pun, cowboy."

He grinned. "Let's go over what we've got so far. You heard the two men discussing the drug trial participants, admitting they'd been ordered to eliminate everybody who'd been on the list, right?"

"Yes."

"My biggest question is why? Sure, money is a big part of this, I get it. But there's got to be more than just dollars in the pockets of Big Pharma. This was the second application for a patent. Even if it got turned down again, it would eventually pass muster."

"Not all of them do. Sometimes the drugs' side effects are just too dangerous. Other times it's not cost effective. Or, and I hate to say it, but there isn't a high enough need for the drug."

He'd pulled out onto the highway, and headed toward Galveston, checking the rearview every few miles.

"What's that mean, not enough need?"

"Sometimes they'll develop a drug for a specific disease, but there isn't a large percentage of the population who have that problem. It's not financially feasible to produce and market the drug, so they never finish the research and development on it. Or they've got the formula and all the trials are successful, but because it won't make a ton of money, they never even apply for the patent. Pharmaceuticals is all about supply and demand."

He shot her a glance. "That's just wrong on so many levels. You mean they have medicine that can help people or cure some lesser-known disease and they never produce or manufacture it, because not enough people have it?" At her nod, he huffed out a sigh. "Seems stupid to me."

"Me too."

They drove on toward Galveston, and she gave him directions to her parents' beach cottage. When she'd been younger, she'd loved spending the summers there. Her folks weren't rich, but they'd been left the little two bedroom place by a distant relative, and used it as a rental property. Last time she'd talked to her mom, they'd pulled it off the listing to make some repairs, so she was pretty sure it was unoccupied.

"Turn left at the next light."

She continued giving him directions, until they pulled in front of the weatherbeaten cottage. Mom was right, it could definitely use a coat of paint, and some repair work on the porch. But it was filled with happy memories from her childhood.

"Nice place." Gunner studied it through the windshield. She couldn't help wondering what he saw. To her, it was ice cream sandwiches in the heat of summer. S'mores cooked over the fire-pit in the backyard. A dash along the dunes to splash into the waves. She wanted to share that with him.

"We keep a spare key under the third tread from the door." She smiled and stepped from the car, climbing onto the porch and pulling up the loose plank. Hanging on a bent nail was the keyring she'd bought her mother as a gift when she'd been twelve.

"I'm not sure what it's gonna look like inside. Might be a

little dusty."

"I'm not picky, honey. Four walls and a roof will do fine. Well, as long as there's a bed in there somewhere."

She unlocked the door, swinging it inward. It still stuck a little when first opened. It had been doing that forever, and she pushed it with her shoulder. Inside everything looked exactly like she remembered.

Whitewashed floors with blue rag rugs before the fireplace, made from Texas limestone. The sofa and one chair had throw covers over them, a necessity with kids running in and out all day, covered with saltwater and sand. The kitchen was off to the right of the front door, small and compact, but nobody really cooked much when they were at the beach.

"Nice place."

"Thanks." Suddenly tongue-tied, she walked down the hall, with the two bedrooms directly across from each other. Her old bedroom had a full bed, covered with a white bedspread. The other had a queen-sized bed with a yellow and turquoise one.

"You can have the bigger bedroom."

He didn't say anything, simply nodded and headed back for the living room.

She followed, watching as he gazed through the front door at the waves in the distance. The wind had picked up, whipping frothy white foam along the beach.

He was alert, scanning the surrounding area. Vigilant. Even as a nineteen-year-old, he'd been like that, always watching, always ready.

"Do you think somebody followed us?"

"Probably not. I'm going to let the boss know we'll be back tomorrow." He stepped onto the porch and she allowed him the privacy, instead walking to the kitchen.

She was so tired of running. Today was the first day in over three weeks that she'd awakened after a full night's sleep. Didn't have to set booby-traps around the windows and doors.

Finding Gunner again was an unexpected but welcome reprieve. There had been too many days that she remembered him, thought about him. Wondered where he was—and who he was with.

Letting him walk away had been one of the hardest things she'd ever done, because she'd known, right from the moment they'd met, he was special. A one in a million kind of guy, but he'd needed to find his own way. Find his place in the world where he felt he didn't fit in. And she'd been right. Seeing him now, he'd achieved all the hidden potential she'd seen beneath the surface of the angry young man.

But she couldn't help wondering what if. What if she'd told him she loved him? What if she'd taken him up on his offer to go with him? So many questions, ones she had no answers for.

She wasn't foolish or naïve. When everything was over, and they'd gathered the evidence needed to shut down EryX Pharmaceutical's criminal activities, he'd go back to Carpenter Security Services, and she'd go back to the same lonely life she'd led before all this happened.

"How about a walk on the beach?" She hadn't heard him

come up behind her. Pasting on a smile, she turned.

"Sounds like a great idea." She stepped out onto the porch and headed for the worn path leading to the beach. Tall fountain grass danced in the breeze on either side of the trail, the tall white tops swaying in the breeze. She remembered as a kid thinking it looked like floating silk.

Reaching the sand, she slipped her shoes off, picked them up in one hand, and twirled in front of Gunner. "Wasn't this worth the extra hour's drive?"

His answering grin was beautiful to see. "Definitely."

Racing forward, she dipped her bare feet into the wet sand at the water's edge, feeling the familiar squishy sensation between her toes. The waters from the Gulf of Mexico were warm as they swirled against her skin.

When she looked back, Gunner was sitting further up the beach on dry sand, rolling up his pants' legs and taking off his shoes and socks. Grinning, she skipped along another few feet, loving the feel of the wind whipping through her hair. Laughing, she turned and Gunner was there, close enough she could feel the warmth radiating from his body.

"I haven't walked on the beach in years." He took a couple of steps into the water, and she watched the sea foam twirl around his ankles.

"It's been a while for me too. I let work take over way too much of my life, and forgot how nice the simple things could be."

They strolled side-by-side, spotting an occasional family with their kids, frolicking in the surf. She knew there were other cabins not too far from her family's, but not so close they intruded on the idyllic setting.

"Where'd you go after you left Beaumont?" She slid her hand into Gunner's, twining her fingers with his. "Where'd the marines send you?"

"First to San Diego. Boot camp. I've never worked so hard in my life as going through those thirteen weeks of hell on earth."

"But it was worth it, right?"

He chuckled. "I didn't think so at the time. Sleep deprived and dead tired half the time. The rest of the time I was dirty, covered in mud, running, marching, and saluting. Figured out really quick the answer to any question asked was Sir, yes Sir." He sketched a mock salute. "Pretty much was told from the beginning, if it moved, salute it."

She swung their entwined hands between them, noticing the difference in her pale hand engulfed by his darker one. "That probably didn't work so well, unless you had a major attitude adjustment. When you joined up, you were as they say, an *angry young man.*"

"You have no idea, honey. The first couple of weeks, I was basically a pain in the ass to everybody. I'm lucky they didn't drum me out. Fortunately, I met a couple of guys who straightened me out." He was silent for a long time, and she waited, knowing he had more to say. "You develop a different kind of bond with those men. It's hard to explain. They become your brothers. It's more than a flesh-and-blood kind of thing. It's a shared experience that only someone who's gone through it understands."

They continued walking, finally reaching the long wooden dock that extended out into the Gulf at least a hundred feet.

"Look," she whispered, pointing to the sky. The sunset painted the skyline in the distance with amazing swaths of color. Yellows and reds and oranges spread across the horizon, as the giant ball of orange sank lower and lower, until it winked out of sight.

"We'd better head back before it gets too dark." She didn't want to, because that meant the end to this magical moment out of time. Away from the realities of death and corruption. Here she could pretend none of that existed, and there wasn't another soul around except her and Gunner.

"Wait." Looking at him, she read the indecision in his face a moment before he leaned forward and brushed his lips against hers.

Her heartbeat raced in time to the butterflies in her stomach. This kiss was like coming home. The memory of his lips on hers was a fantasy she replayed over and over in her lonely bed. Yet this was no fantasy.

She kissed him back, putting all her pent-up longing and need into this the kiss. At her response, he deepened the kiss, taking control and command, sweeping inside her mouth when she opened beneath his touch.

Her tongue swept forward, rubbing against his, and she felt his hands slide around her, pulling her closer, and she leaned against him. She felt the physical evidence of his response.

The chemistry they'd shared in the beginning was still there, the sparks threatening to ignite a conflagration that would consume her.

Stepping back, she broke free of the kiss, drawing in a deep breath. It felt like she'd stepped off a cliff and was falling, flying, and she wasn't sure whether she'd crash on the rocks or soar above the clouds. All she knew was she wanted to find out.

"Maggie..."

She raised her hand, pressing a fingertip against his lips. "Let's go back."

He stared at her, his intense gaze missing nothing in the light of the dusky sky. Breaking their stare-down, she started the trek back to the cabin, this time careful not to hold his hand. Afraid if she touched him, she'd tackle him down onto the sand and have her way with him. And that would be a mistake, a colossal, gigantic mistake. Because if he ever found out about her secrets, he'd never forgive her.

Chapter Thirteen

G unner knew before they'd reached the well-worn trail from the beach back to the cottage, something was wrong. He froze, putting out a hand to stop Maggie. Looking up and down the beach, he studied his surroundings.

Footprints on the sand were evident, both his and Maggie's from earlier, but also others. Might have been left by other beachcombers or families, but his gut told him different.

"I'd tell you to stay here, but I know you won't. Stay behind me, and let me check things out first." He handed her his shoes.

At her nod, he started up the path, pulling out the knife he kept in a sheath at his waist. Too bad his gun was in the car. He'd stuck it in the glove compartment when they'd called the police to report Leland Jackson's death. Wouldn't have looked good to have a gun around the cops, even a legally registered one. He had his concealed carry permit, but there hadn't been any reason to court trouble.

Now it looked like trouble had found them. The first thing he noted was the car didn't look right. A second glance showed him both tires on the driver's side, front and back, had been flattened. Chances were good the other two were flat too, but he wasn't going to take the time to look.

Holding up his hand, he motioned Maggie to stay, and he crept toward the porch on silent feet, careful to avoid the squeaky board he noticed earlier that afternoon.

No lights shone from inside, but he didn't need any. He'd memorized the interior layout earlier, something he'd been taught by a staff sergeant, and it had served him well. Easing open the door enough he could squeeze through, he slid to the right toward the kitchen a few steps, and froze, listening. The utter stillness of the place probably meant whoever had been there was long gone. *Probably.*

Too bad he was the suspicious sort. Instead of giving Maggie the all clear, he crept toward the living room. The small amount of moonlight through the window glinted off the glass and illuminated enough to see the whole place had been tossed. Somebody had been here, looking for something. Might still be in the place. Good. He'd been itching for a fight all day.

The kitchen looked pretty much the same, drawers pulled out and emptied onto the floor, cabinet doors hanging open, the dishes broken. Even the oven door hung open, in a mockery of a silent scream.

His cautious footfalls on the wooden floor never made a sound as he ghosted down the hall, careful to stay close to the walls, knowing that's where they were least likely to make a sound.

The smaller bedroom resembled the other rooms, except whoever did it took things one step further, slashing the mattress with big gouges, pulling out stuffing and tossing it everywhere, with the mattress mostly hanging off the bedframe. The box spring received the same treatment, with deep cuts. End tables were overturned.

The closet door stood open, and he checked its depths. Nobody.

That only left two rooms, the other bedroom and the bathroom. He decided to leave the bathroom for last, just in case somebody decided it would be cute to hide behind the shower curtain in a macabre twist on Psycho.

The other bedroom looked the same, and nobody lay in wait. As he stepped into the hall, he heard a gasp. Maggie must have decided she'd waited long enough.

"What the hell…" Her words trailed off and he heard her footsteps heading into the living room. He'd better get the bathroom checked, before she came looking for him.

The final room hadn't been spared the ransacking assault. Nobody hid behind the shower curtain, because it had been ripped off the rod and tossed into a heap on the floor, its bright yellow color an incongruent sight.

"Gunner?"

"I'm back here." He heard her coming down the hall before he saw her. "All clear. Whoever was here is long gone."

Her body slumped against the doorjamb. "Is it ever going to end?"

Taking a step forward, he threaded his fingers through her hair, brushing it away from her cheek. "We're going to catch them, honey. Unfortunately, it looks like we're going to have to make another call to the local authorities. Luckily, we're not in the same city as before, or that would look mighty suspicious."

She nodded and walked away, her posture defeated. What he wouldn't give for five minutes alone in a room with the jerks who'd done this. If he was lucky, they'd end up being the same two yahoos who'd snatched him at the airport.

He flipped on the light switch, grimacing at the sight. It looked even worse in the bright light.

Maggie righted one of the chairs that had been knocked over, and he walked over, pulling her into his arms. Her whole body trembled, and he'd give just about anything to take this burden away from her. It wasn't fair that she'd been dragged into the middle of this mess for trying to do the right thing.

"We probably don't want to touch anything until the police have been out. Your parents will need it on record, so they can file insurance to get the place put back together."

The bewildered look on her face made him squeeze her tighter, until she collapsed into his arms, wrapping hers around his waist, her head resting against his shoulder.

They stood like that, simply holding each other for long minutes, until he finally let his arms drop to his sides. "Let me make the call, and we'll find someplace to stay for the night."

"Yeah, we can't stay here. What if they come back?"

"I doubt that will happen. They've already searched the place from top to bottom. The only reason they'd come back would be…" He trailed off but knew from her expression that she knew precisely what he'd been going to say.

"Might want to call a tow truck while you're at it. All four tires are flat. We won't be driving anywhere."

"Aw, hell, I forgot about that."

Pulling out his phone, he walked onto the porch and stood in the darkness. With the front door open, he had enough light to see, but the blackness gave the illusion of privacy.

His first call wasn't to the cops, though. It was to his boss.

"Got a problem, boss."

"What have you done now?" Carpenter's voice held a joking quality. They had a great working relationship, as well as being friends.

"Whoever's looking for Maggie hasn't backed down."

"What happened?" All business now, he could practically see the other man straighten, giving him his full attention. That was one thing about Samuel Carpenter, when he took you under his wing, he backed you one hundred percent, no matter what.

"Drove to Maggie's family cottage outside Galveston. Decided to take a walk on the beach before sunset."

"Please tell me you kissed the girl."

Gunner rolled his eyes, refusing to rise to the bait. "When we got back, the place had been trashed. Somebody was definitely looking for something, because they cut open the mattresses and box springs, dumped drawers. I'd say they weren't true professionals, because there were a lot of spots they never touched."

"Hmm. Think it's the same two goons?"

"No clue. But they're secondary. I want whoever the big boss is. The one pulling their strings."

"I've got everybody here working the case. Nate's working on it from Dallas. Good news is, Sheri's going to transfer to school here, so we aren't going to lose him back to Dallas."

That was good news. Nate was one of his best friends, and he'd hated the thought he might relocate to be with the woman he loved.

"You know, once she graduates, she'd be a pretty good fit for C.S.S. You could use a good business manager, and she'll have her master's degree." Didn't hurt to drop a hint in the boss's ear now, let him consider the possibilities.

"Ha! I already offered her the job."

"Back on track, boss. I'm gonna need a new set of wheels."

There was a pause before Carpenter asked, "What happened to my car?"

"Not my fault, I swear. Whoever trashed the place slit all four tires."

Carpenter harrumphed. "Well, at least you didn't total it—like last time."

"Again, not my fault. I'm the best defensive driver you've got. Could I help it that blonde stepped out when I was chasing the getaway driver? I can just see the headlines. Carpenter Security squashes pedestrian in high speed chase in downtown New Orleans—film at eleven."

"Smart-ass. Text me the address, and I'll get it picked up. And let me know where you'll be staying overnight, and I'll have another car dropped off. Take better care of this one, because it'll be a rental."

"I'll let you know. Gotta call the police next, and file a report, then we'll get settled for the night someplace."

"One room, right?" He could hear the smile in Carpenter's words. He was such a teenage boy sometimes.

"Yep. I'm not letting her out of my sight until we're back home."

"Not to repeat myself, but I'm gonna say it again. Go on and kiss the girl. Get it out of your system. The two of you could barely keep your hands off each other in the conference room."

"Samuel!" Gunner heard Andrea's outraged reprimand in the background.

"What? It's the truth. You saw them."

"And I remember two other people who acted exactly the same. I don't remember hearing Gunner egging you on."

That's because he'd made a point not to say anything when Andrea was within earshot. But he'd done his fair share of goading the boss to go after his girl. Oh, well, what's good for the goose...

"Gotta go. I'll send you the info. Give Andrea a kiss for me." He hung up before Carpenter could come back with one of his famous retorts.

Didn't help that the man was right. He wanted Maggie, ever since she'd opened that bathroom door and he'd seen her wet from the pouring rain and more beautiful than a woman had a right to be.

Stop. Do the job. Get her to safety, then deal with the over-whelming need to kiss her, hold her. Make love to her all night long.

Dialing nine-one-one for the second time, he reported the break-in, and agreed to wait for the officers to arrive. He turned to go back inside, only to find Maggie standing in the open doorway. He hoped she hadn't overheard the conversation with Carpenter, though from the twinkle in her eyes, she probably had.

"Cops are on the way. Carpenter's going to have the car towed. Then we'll get a ride into town and find someplace safe to crash for the night."

He'd barely finished his sentence before his phone rang. It was Carpenter.

"Boss?"

"I've got an agent not too far from you, working a case. He's going to pick you both up and take you to a safe house for the night. Name's Dean Westin. Currently out of the Austin office. Whatever you need, he'll get you set up."

"Westin. Got it. Thanks."

Carpenter hung up without another word. Gunner didn't take it personally, he knew the man had his fingers on just about every case, and was stretched pretty thin. Maybe he'd talk to Andrea about getting the boss to take a little unscheduled vacation. Bora Bora sounded good.

"That was Carpenter. He's got somebody coming to pick us up, and take us someplace safe for the night. Once we've dealt with the police report, we're outta here."

"Okay." She stepped out onto the porch, looking up at the night sky. This far away from the city, the sky seemed filled with a million stars. It would have been nice to build a fire in the fire pit, and sit with his arm around Maggie, watching them. Instead, he had to deal with cops for the second time in less than twenty-four hours. Not one of his better days.

The crunch of gravel announced the arrival of the cop car. He led them through the scene, answering their questions.

Finally, they left, telling them there had been a couple of break-ins down the beach.

Headlights gleamed in the darkness, heralding the tow truck, followed by a silver Ford F-250 pickup. Gunner watched in silence as the tow truck hooked a long chain to the front of the car, attaching two giant metal hooks around the front axle. The driver hit a switch and the winch slowly pulled the car up the tilted bed of the tow truck. Once anchored in place, the bed lifted, and the driver secured the car, had him sign the release forms, and drove away with Carpenter's baby on board.

When he turned back to the porch, Maggie and a tall stranger stood illuminated in the light shining through the front door.

"You Westin?"

"Yep. Carpenter sent me." The tall stranger had a couple of days of scruff on his chin and light brown hair that curled along his neck. And he was standing way too close to Maggie. Apparently, the other guy was good at reading people, because he grinned and took a step to the side, holding up a hand in a nonthreatening motion. Grey eyes the color of a thundercloud stared at him, a definite twinkle in their depths. Darned if he hadn't seen those eyes before, but where? He'd figure it out, given enough time. If there was one thing he was good at it was puzzles, and the man standing before him was a walking enigma.

"I've got a safe place for you to stay the night. Sam said you'd be heading back to New Orleans in the morning."

"That's the plan." No reason to share any unnecessary information with the other man.

"You ready, ma'am?" The gruff tone from moments earlier disappeared into a smooth Texas drawl, and Gunner watched a hint of pink tinge Maggie's cheeks.

"Let's get out of here." She switched off the lights and pulled the front door closed, locking it with the key from earlier, and sticking it in her pocket. Gunner wondered if that was deliberate, so as not to reveal its hiding place to this stranger. Smart girl. It was something he'd do.

Westin opened the door to the pickup, and Maggie slid across the seat. Gunner climbed in beside her. He'd be damned if he'd ride in the bed of the truck and leave her up here alone with Westin. He might work for Carpenter, but as far as Gunner was concerned, the boss hadn't given Westin any seal of approval.

Westin climbed in the driver's seat, and headed toward town. Once they hit the city limits, with its brighter lights and motels on every corner, Gunner expected him to pull into one of them. Instead, Westin continued driving through the city and turned off into one of the subdivisions of a new development. The billboard advertising the homes for sale rated the prices as mid to upper four hundred thousand.

The truck twisted and turned through the streets, past the model homes, finally coming to a stop in front of a corner lot.

"Home, sweet home. At least for tonight." He tossed a keychain to Gunner. "Place is all yours. Refrigerator and pantry have been stocked, enough for a couple of days anyway. Should tide you over until you head back."

He climbed out of the truck and went around to the bed, pulling out two duffle bags. Gunner walked around to the back, and Westin tossed him one.

"Clothes for you and the lady. Andrea gave me sizes, so hopefully everything will fit."

This guy knows Andrea?

"Who's the other bag for?" Gunner had a feeling in the pit of his stomach he knew the answer, but asked anyway.

Westin grinned. "Me."

"No reason you need to stay."

His nonchalant shrug punctuated the sentence. "Got nothing urgent pending. Finished testifying on a case early this morning. Was headed back to Austin when Sam called. Another day or two here on the Texas coast isn't a hardship."

Maggie climbed out of the truck and headed for the front door, not waiting for him. Gunner cursed under his breath and sprinted after her.

"Where do you think you're going?"

"No sense me sitting in the car while you two idiots have

your pissing contest. Might as well go inside and get comfortable." She held her hand out for the key.

"Let me check it out first." He glared at Westin, as he strolled up the walkway. "Keep her out here."

"My pleasure," he murmured, winking at Maggie.

Gunner let the remark slide and opened the door. Flicking on the lights, he looked around with appreciation. The boss had great taste in safe houses. But he didn't have time to sightsee, he needed to make sure everything was secure.

A quick survey of the house revealed no intruders, and he motioned for the others to enter.

"Wow." Maggie eyed the twenty-foot high ceilings with awe. Her footsteps were light against the shining hardwoods. "Nice digs."

Westin dropped his bag by the front door, tossed his cowboy hat on top, and strolled past them. "Anybody hungry? I'm starving. Missed lunch."

"I could eat." Maggie followed him into the kitchen, with Gunner bringing up the rear. Three steaks were pulled from the refrigerator, the packages tossed onto the granite counter.

"It's a little late to fire up the grill, but I can still fix a mean steak. What kind of fixin's do you like with it?"

"You cook the steak, I'll handle the sides." Maggie opened the pantry and peered inside its cavernous depth. "Shouldn't be a problem with all this."

Gunner definitely felt like a third wheel, sitting at the kitchen island without a thing to do except watch the others puttering around the kitchen.

"I'll be back," he said before stalking to the back patio. Might as well call in, give the boss an update.

"Hey, boss. Car's been towed, cops have been updated. By the way, who the hell is this Westin guy?"

Carpenter gave a sputtering laugh. "Giving you a hard time, is he?"

"He's an arrogant S.O.B. Can't keep his eyes off Maggie." *Oh, hell, did I say that out loud?*

"Don't worry, you can trust him. He'll have your back."

"If you say so."

"I really wish Maggie had been able to get more of the list. Trying to piece this together with no clear-cut identification is taking longer than I'd like."

Gunner ran a hand through his hair before glancing through the back door. Maggie was laughing at something Westin said, her head thrown back. He gritted his teeth. He'd better get back in there fast, before Westin turned into Mister Grabby Hands.

"Carlisle not having any luck getting into their mainframe?"

"The mainframe's not the problem. Apparently, they're not keeping the trial results on it. He's working backward, checking IP addresses to see what other computers have accessed the mainframe, and working on getting into those. It's long and tedious, but I'm sure he'll figure it out."

Gunner was sure too. There wasn't a computer built that Carlisle couldn't hack—at least not yet. Hopefully, this wouldn't be the first.

Another glance through the back door showed Westin

twirling Maggie around, and dipping her. The faint strains of music wafted through the slightly open door. What the hell?

"Gotta go. I'll call tomorrow." Without another word, he hung up, storming back into the kitchen. The soft strains of *You Look So Good In Love* came from Westin's phone, sitting on the island.

"Dinner almost ready?"

Maggie and Westin eased apart, not looking in the least bit guilty. Yet, the knot clenching in the pit of his stomach told him more than words he needed to stake his claim. Make it clear to the other man in no uncertain terms Maggie wasn't some prize in a game of tug-of-war. She was his.

"Gunner, will you grab some plates and silverware from the cabinet?" Maggie turned and walked toward the wine fridge, her hips swaying enticingly. If Westin didn't stop looking at her, Gunner might make it impossible for him to watch her. Two black eyes should do the trick.

He set the smaller table in the breakfast nook, seeing no point in using the formal dining room. Maggie filled three wine glasses from the bottle of red she'd chosen, and Westin carried a platter brimming with steaks to the table. Baked sweet potatoes oozing with cinnamon and butter, and steamed broccoli finished out the menu.

"Looks good," Gunner grudgingly admitted, spearing a steak for himself. The others loaded their plates and dug in. He hated to admit it, but Westin made a mighty fine steak, perfectly medium rare, just the way he liked it.

"Oh, this is so good." Maggie's eyes were closed as she chewed, and Gunner stopped eating to watch her. He remembered putting a similar look on her face, when they'd been making love. Pictured again the way she'd toss her head back, and close her eyes. And the little moan that caught in the back of her throat.

He shifted in his chair, and damned if he didn't see Westin doing the same. *Don't go there, buddy. You don't want to poach on another man's girl. Especially mine.*

His fork stopped halfway to his lips when he realized— she wasn't his girl. And hadn't been for a long, long time. The thought felt like Thor's hammer striking a blow straight to his heart.

"Gunner, are you okay?" He jerked at the sound of Maggie's voice, and shoved the piece of steak into his mouth, chewing, though it now tasted like shoe leather.

"Fine," he muttered after he'd swallowed. "Thinking about everything that's happened today."

"Did Mr. Carpenter find anything new?"

Westin chuckled. "Shoot, darlin', I don't think I've ever heard anybody call him Mr. Carpenter. All I've ever heard was Carpenter or Samuel."

"You call him Sam." Maggie took a sip from her wine, watching the other man over the rim of the glass, and Gunner noted the single drop clinging to her lip. Resisted the urge to lean across the table and lick it away, kiss her and never stop.

"Sam and I have a…complicated relationship."

Now that, Gunner could believe. There was something about Westin, an underlying familiarity that niggled at the back of his mind, a feeling he was missing something just out of reach.

"Carlisle's not having much luck." How much could he say around Westin? There was too much on the line, including keeping Maggie safe, for him to screw up.

Westin leaned back in his chair, resting his hands across his stomach. "Sam filled me in on your case, and what Ms. Maggie here uncovered." He winked at Maggie before continuing. "I've got a question for you, darlin'."

Maggie laid her knife and fork onto the side of her plate, and leaned forward, her attention focused on the other man. "What?"

"These people in the testing group or study or whatever you call it, it's all anonymous, right?"

"Yes. From what I've been able to find out, from a friend who went through testing a cancer drug, all the participants are put into what's called a blind study. They're assigned an identifier or number, known only to the people overseeing the study."

He scratched his chin, and again Gunner was hit with that sense of deja vu that he'd seen Westin before. It was really starting to bug him. Maybe in Dallas?

"Okay. Some of the participants are given the drug, right? And others are given a placebo, to test the efficacy of the drug and or its side effects?"

Maggie nodded. "From what I've been able to determine, that's right."

"Where are you heading with this, Westin?"

"Somebody is killing people in the study. Is there any way of knowing which ones got the actual drug, and which ones the placebo?"

Gunner's gaze shifted back to Maggie, waiting for her to answer, since he didn't have a clue.

"Somnolett is apparently part of what's known as a double blind study. In that neither the physician nor anybody else knows who is receiving the real drug. The drug is prepared and sent to be administered, and only by matching the participant's identification number and the number assigned to the drug at the company level, i.e., the pharmacist who formulated it, knows."

"That seems overly complicated." Gunner was beginning to figure out Westin's train of thought. "Makes it almost impossible for anybody outside EryX Pharmaceutical to track or follow up without going through the company—who can skew the data any way they want."

"Confidentiality is key with medical cases, Gunner." Maggie turned to him, her face animated. "With all the HIPPA laws, rules have gotten even tighter."

Westin stood and picked up his empty plate. "Thanks for the great dinner. I'm going to think about everything we've talked about. Maybe I can come up with a different angle, but it sounds like Carpenter's got things pretty well covered." He laid his plate in the sink and turned. "I'll keep an eye on things. Get some rest. I'll see you in the morning."

Without another word, he walked out of the kitchen and disappeared.

Gunner picked up his glass and finished the wine, before standing and taking his plate and Maggie's to the kitchen.

Reaching for the dish soap, he began filling the sink with

hot water. He heard Maggie step up behind him. "Let me do that."

"No. You cooked, I clean up." He turned his head, and noticed her shoulders were drooping. It was late, and she'd been going since early morning.

"Why don't you head upstairs? Grab a shower, and try to get some sleep. I'll check on you after I finish up down here."

"Okay." Her footsteps moved quietly away, and he braced his hands on the edge of the sink. Willed his aching body to stand down, give her time. She'd been through hell the last few weeks, and didn't need any more pressure in her life.

Finishing up the dishes, he glanced out the kitchen window and noted a solitary shadow sitting on the back porch, recognizing it as Dean Westin.

Probably a good idea to grab a couple hours of shut-eye before he had to spell the guy. Flicking off the lights, he headed down the hallway into his room.

And stared at the empty, lonely bed. It was going to be a long night.

Chapter Fourteen

M aggie stepped out of the shower, one towel wrapped around her head, and another around her body. The hot water had felt good, getting clean even better.

Whoever had packed the duffel, probably Westin, had been thorough. It included clothing plus shampoo, conditioner, toothpaste, a new toothbrush, and deodorant. All the comforts of home, even if they weren't her brands. She couldn't afford to be picky.

Pulling the towel from her hair, she shook it free and squeezed the water from it. When she looked up, she gasped. Gunner stood in the open doorway of the bedroom, his gaze intent—and hungry.

Warmth pooled deep inside with an answering hunger. Not that it surprised her. Every time she looked at him, she wanted him. But she wasn't a fool. Giving in to temptation when she was twenty-one was one thing. She'd been young and carefree, and had the whole world ahead of her. All too quickly she'd learned life tended to throw curve balls when you least expected them. She'd been pelted with her fair share. It was too late to try and change what used to be.

"Hi."

He stepped further into the room, closing the door behind him with an audible click. His hair was damp, as if he'd already taken a shower. The top several buttons on his shirt were undone, and offered little glimpses of his chest with each step forward.

"Wanted to check on you. You need anything?"

Just you.

"I'm fine." The words came out husky, and she felt heat flow into her cheeks. *Smooth, Maggie, real smooth.*

"I'm directly across the hall, if you need anything. Westin's taking first watch."

"Do you think anybody followed us?"

"Doubtful. But better safe than sorry, as my granny used to say." His warm callused hand cupped her cheek before threading his fingers into her hair. She laughed, the towel clutched in her hand.

"What's so funny, babe?"

"When I showed up at your office, I looked like a drowned rat, dripping wet. Here I am again, my hair a tangled damp disgrace."

The heat in his gaze almost singed her. "You know what I see?"

She shook her head slowly, breath held in anticipation.

"I see a beautiful woman, all soft and warm. Fresh and clean and—I want to do all kinds of wicked things that'll make you end up back in the shower again—with me."

"Really?"

"Honey, do you have any idea how hard it's been to keep my hands off you? From the moment you opened that bathroom door at C.S.S., it's taken every ounce of willpower to keep from snatching you up and heading for the nearest bed." His eyes flicked toward the king-sized one not two feet away.

She took a tentative step forward, dropping the towel to the floor that she'd been clutching, leaving her clad only in the one she'd wrapped around her body.

"Honestly? I want the same thing."

Gunner closed the space between them, yanked her into his arms, and stole her breath with an all-consuming, soul-shattering kiss.

Pressed against his body, her breasts pinned the terry-cloth between them, which left her hands free. She twined her arms around his neck, angling her head to deepen the kiss. His tongue stroked against hers, and she tasted the minty toothpaste he'd used, as well as Gunner's unique flavor.

He pulled back, his lips playing across hers, nibbling and teasing, before diving back for another soul-stealing kiss. Finally, she pulled free, breathing out a long sigh.

Meeting his questioning gaze, she debated for all of a second before giving in to all six feet two of walking temptation molded against her.

"Make love to me."

As if those were the words he'd been waiting for, Gunner's fingers went to the tucked-in corner of the towel and tugged.

It pooled on the floor at their feet, and she stood before him, naked and unashamed.

His gaze was a burning visceral thing, as it swept across

her, and she watched his expression. Afraid she'd read disappointment or disgust in his eyes.

"So beautiful." The words were soft, barely above a whisper, but she felt them to the depth of her being. Could read the hunger searing her in his perusal. A thousand butterflies fluttered within her stomach, and she felt like a young girl with her first beau.

When Gunner took her lips again, Maggie opened herself to the flood of sensations, unable to resist the erotic pull between them. It burned hotter than a raging inferno. Strong arms slid around her, pulled her body closer. The roughness of his shirt abraded her nipples, causing them to bead into sensitive peaks.

Moaning into his mouth, her tongue swirling against his with a desperation she hadn't felt since—forever. Together they were combustible, gasoline to a flame, and the explosion was glorious.

There was no denying the man could kiss, and she succumbed to the pleasure rushing through her at his touch. Her teeth tugged on his lower lip, welcoming the intimacy of his mouth. Hands reached upward to cup his face, angling him just right to plunge deep inside. Their tongues twined around, in and out, in a mating dance.

Yanking free, breathless, she rested her forehead against his shoulder. She couldn't meet his eyes, afraid of what she'd read in their depths. His fingers tangled in her hair, tugged gently and forced her head back to meet his gaze.

Without speaking, he bent forward and took her lips again. This kiss was long and slow and deep. The iron bands of his arm pressed her deeper into his embrace.

The desire coursing through her was unlike anything felt before, and she loved it. The sensations drove her to want more.

With a smooth movement, he walked her backward until the back of her knees hit the mattress. His hands freely explored her back, never breaking their kiss. His tongue traced against her lower lip, nipped at it and then laved away the slight sting. It slid inside her mouth, to tangle with hers, and she met him stroke for exquisite stroke.

He pulled back with a groan. Staring into his eyes, his pupils were dilated and the color deepened with the unbridled desire she read in their unguarded depths. A desire matched only by her own. One fingertip traced across her lower lip, and she trembled. Breaths soughed in and out, her chest rising with each inhalation, drawing his gaze to her breasts.

One hand reached out, and her breath caught at his touch against her skin. He leaned forward again, his breath a warm exhale against her cheek. She couldn't resist trailing her tongue along the side of his neck, pressing nibbling kisses beneath his jawline before tugging his earlobe between her teeth for a quick nip before soothing away the hurt with a brief kiss.

When his mouth covered hers again, pleasure surged through her. He took the kiss deeper, wilder, holding nothing back. By the time he pulled away, she trembled in his arms. Her nails dug into his shoulders, needing something to keep her grounded, because she felt light as air, desire bubbling through her veins. Needing him to make her feel whole again.

"You have no idea how much I want you, Maggie."

"I want you too." Her eyes closed as he laid her gently on the bed, feeling the softness shift beneath her. Reaching up, she twined her arms around his neck, pulling him down into her kiss. He braced his arms on either side of her, caging her body in his strength and she let out a little hum when his forearm scraped against the side of her breast.

She was on fire, every need focused directly at her core. Heat and moisture pooled between her thighs, and she marveled that he'd gotten her so hot and bothered with something as simple as a kiss.

Still the kiss went on and on, a perfect dueling of tongue and lips and teeth, each striving to bring pleasure to the other. It wasn't enough. Didn't come close to easing the torment her body felt. Her hips pushed back against the mattress and he followed, cradled between her thighs, notched against her and she felt his firm hardness against her dampened core.

Her hands fisted in his hair, and he pulled back enough to stare into her eyes. She knew he could read the desperation, the overwhelming need, because he smiled. No, it was more than a smile. It was triumph.

She placed her palms against his chest, not trying to hold him back, but simply to touch him. "Stop teasing me, Gunner. I want you."

Reaching up, she grasped his shirtfront and yanked. Nothing happened. Every single button remained fastened and she frowned. It wasn't fair. In the movies it looked so simple to rip the guy's shirt open in one yank.

Obviously reading her expression, he chuckled, pulling the shirt tails free of his jeans before gripping the front and ripping. The buttons pinged against the floor, and he peeled the torn pieces off, revealing his muscled chest to her heated gaze.

Lifting her up off the bed, he pulled her against him, and she wrapped her legs around his waist. Her arms slid around his neck and she undulated against him, needing to get closer. The feel of his jeans against her sensitized skin was an exquisite agony.

This Gunner was so different from the boy she remembered. He was a man with a man's appetites and needs and she wanted him so badly her body quivered. His hands moved to her hips, held her in place against his rock hard erection while he played with her breasts, sucked and licked, moving from one to the other. Hot breath blew against the tip and he chuckled when it tightened even more.

"I need you inside me." She heard the demand in her voice and inwardly cringed. Gunner was the only man who could turn her emotions on their head without a single word. All he had to do was touch her and she melted like warm butter.

"I need you." His hand trailed down her belly, and she quivered beneath his touch. Without thought, her thighs opened, spreading for him as he licked and kissed his way down her body. When his fingers slid between her wet folds, she felt warmth blossom in her cheeks, knowing he could feel how wet she'd become. He groaned against her skin, trailing damp kisses against her stomach.

A sizzle zipped through her when he swiped his tongue across her abdomen. She couldn't hold back the cry that escaped when he plunged one finger deep within her heated core.

"That's what I need, sweetheart. Let me hear how much you want me." She met his intense gaze. The hunger she felt was echoed in his eyes. Agonizingly slow, his finger withdrew, and he added a second, the slightest sting of pain quickly easing as he stretched her. It had been a very long time, and as much as she wanted him to go faster, she was grateful he took the time to make sure she was ready for him.

His fingers plunged deeper, all the while his thumb circled that little bundle of nerves, toying with it, and her head rolled back against the mattress.

Maggie couldn't breathe. She was close, so close she could taste it. Her heart pounded faster when she felt his body settle over hers. One hand reached down and in seconds she felt him positioned at her core.

Then he stopped.

"Are you sure, hon? Because once I'm inside you, I won't want to stop. Tell me to stop now or…"

"Don't you dare!"

Within seconds, he'd stripped off his jeans and slid on the condom he pulled from the back pocket. With a single thrust, he plunged deep, sliding with ease through her silken folds. His growl of approval was sweeter than any symphony.

Wrapping her arms around his neck, she held him close

as he stroked within her, pulling all the way out only to rock deeper with each thrust.

"You feel so good, babe. Tell me if I hurt you." His voice was deep and guttural with each word. "Tell me you want this."

Maggie stared at his gorgeous face, his rock hard body, and felt the beginnings of her orgasm building. Could he doubt how much she wanted him?

"Need you…"

She didn't want to hold anything back from him. Tonight might be all the time she'd ever have with Gunner, and she intended to make enough memories to last a lifetime. Though he controlled each thrusting movement, she saw the strain it took for him to go slow, make it good for her, etched across his face.

He wasn't as in control as he wanted her to think. She could see it, and it made her love him more. Filling her, invading every inch of her, her body felt stretched almost to the point of pain.

She wanted everything he had to give and more. Craved it like an addict needed her next fix. She watched his face, memorizing every nuance, every emotion, every grimace as he tried to hold onto his control.

Tears pricked her eyes, and she willed them away. Because she had no idea how she'd be able to give up this man. When the danger was past, they'd go their separate ways once again. He made her feel brave, stronger than she really was, and somehow she'd find the strength to walk away. No matter how much she'd regret it in the bright light of day.

"Ah, Maggie, I need you." The words came out as a strangled groan, and she felt his hand slip between their bodies and rub against her clitoris. Her body coiled with need and coalesced into a giant ball of pleasure exploding through her.

Pushing upward, she took him in deeper. She wouldn't accept less than all of him. She wanted everything he had to give. Gave over to her wild side, biting back her scream as she bucked beneath him.

The circling around her clitoris continued, as Gunner continued pounding into her, and she felt herself climbing higher and higher. When he pinched her clit, she felt her body explode, starlight and fireworks bursting behind her eyelids as her body arched into his, an undeniable rush of sensation washing through her in wave after wave of pleasure.

Pure ecstasy coursed through her veins. Her body shuddered beneath the impact of her orgasm, and she gave herself over, let it take her.

She moaned as his hands tightened on her hips, holding her still as he came. Felt him pulse within her, prolonging her orgasm. His body stiffened before he slumped against her, his whole body limp.

Long moments passed before he rolled to his side, and dragged her against him. She snuggled close, resting her head against his shoulder.

"That was..." Maggie stopped because there weren't words to describe what just happened.

"Yeah, it was." Gunner dropped a soft kiss against her

forehead, before climbing off the bed and disposing of the condom. Flicking off the lights, he crawled back into the bed, pulling her close against him, and breathed out a contented sigh. "Get some sleep, sweetheart. Tomorrow's going to be another long day."

He reached down and pulled the blankets over them, tucking her against his side once more.

Before drifting off to sleep, Maggie couldn't help wondering how she was going to survive without Gunner in her life, because being in his arms again, even for one night, had unlocked the secret she'd buried deep inside.

She was still in love with him, and always would be.

Chapter Fifteen

Who the hell thought it was a good idea to have Westin tag along on the trek back to New Orleans? All Gunner's plans for a leisurely drive back home, with Maggie cuddled against his side went up in flames when Westin announced at the breakfast table that he was driving.

One phone call to Carpenter later, and damned if the man wasn't sitting in the driver's seat, wearing an irritating smirk. The vibe he'd gotten from Carpenter during the call still had the little hairs on the back of his neck doing the *cha cha*.

He made the routine follow-up call to the police, not expecting anything, so he wasn't disappointed when they'd announced nothing had been discovered at the cabin. Fingerprints were taken, but because the place was a rental for most of the year, the chances of getting a hit were slim.

"I heard Carpenter set his elite team members up with their own apartments at the New Orleans headquarters. True?"

"Yep."

Westin let out a whistle. "Nice. I haven't seen the new digs. Looking forward to it."

"The apartments are beautiful," Maggie added, patting

Gunner's thigh lightly. "At least Gunner's is. It's the only one I've seen."

Take that, asshat. Maggie's off limits.

"Andrea told me all about Sam's penthouse and the rooftop deck. Maybe I can get her to show me around while I'm in town."

"Only if you want to carry your teeth home in a little plastic sandwich baggie, because Carpenter will hand 'em to you if you approach Andrea."

Westin turned to face him. "So it's like that, is it?"

"Oh, yeah."

"Good to know."

Westin turned his attention back to the road, and Gunner's thoughts returned to the case. The faster they could close it, the sooner he could get Maggie out of danger. To him, that was priority number one.

"I've been thinking." Maggie stared straight ahead, watching the road. "There has to be a way to draw out the two guys from EryX Pharmaceutical. We have to assume they were employees, because security there is locked down tight, even on a holiday. You have to use a keycard to access every room, especially the laboratories and places with confidential information—like the study group trials."

"We already thought of that. Carlisle is working with a guy he's worked with before who's also an expert at computers, and they're accessing the security system at EryX Pharmaceutical. Going through every person that logged in or out of there on the day you overheard them. Unfortunately, they have a very sophisticated system and it's taking longer than either one of them expected to get through."

Maggie tapped a finger against her lips before continuing. "I'm positive I'd recognize their voices again if I heard them."

"If Carlisle…"

"Not if, when. It doesn't pay to underestimate Stefan Carlisle's skills, Westin. Never seen a computer yet he can't crack."

Gunner watched the other man's lips curve up in a grin.

"Gotcha. *When* Carlisle gets into EryX Pharmaceutical's security program, I'm sure we can set up a scenario where you can listen in on the gentlemen in question, and make a positive ID."

"Hmm. That'll work. We can round them up and make them talk." Maggie had a decidedly wicked glint in her eyes as she winked at Gunner, and he couldn't hold back his laugh.

"Honey, kidnapping is against the law."

"So is what they're doing. I'd like to apply a little friendly persuasion to the mix, make them spill their guts."

"Damn, Gunner, she's a vicious little thing, ain't she?"

"You have no idea." *And she's my vicious little thing, and I mean to keep her.*

The radio played quietly in the background, the strains of *Jose Cuervo* filling the cab of the truck. When the chorus began, Maggie started belting out the lyrics at the top of her lungs, and so off key he was afraid his ears would start bleeding. Instead, he joined in, adding his bass. Westin shot them both a look like they were crazy, before he added his tenor to the mix, and they sang along with the radio the rest of the way to New Orleans.

The minute they walked through the front door, Stephanie told them Carpenter wanted to see them upstairs. Looked like Westin was gonna get his wish about seeing Carpenter's place.

They rode the elevator to the top floor, where Gunner knocked on the door. Andrea opened it, her face wreathed in smiles.

"Welcome home, guys." Her gaze drifted to Westin, and she let out a squeal. "Dean!"

Westin opened his arms wide, and she plastered herself against him. "Samuel didn't tell me you were coming."

"Now, darlin', would I pass up the chance to see your pretty face?" Her smile was wide enough Gunner thought her face would split. Obviously, she knew Westin, a lot better than he'd implied.

"Come in. Samuel's on a call, but he'll be right with you. Want something to drink?" she called over her shoulder, heading for the kitchen.

"No, thanks, we're good." Gunner kept his hand on the small of Maggie's back, leading her further into the living room. Though the penthouse apartment was similar to his, it far exceeded his place in size, the living space alone nearly doubling his. It had the same exposed red brick, original to the building, with a large fireplace against the far wall. He spotted Samuel standing out on the small balcony, the phone to his ear, and couldn't help wondering if it was about their case.

"Well, knowing Ms. Willie and her uncanny ability to know whenever we have people here, chances are good she'll be showing up any minute with food." Andrea glanced toward her fiancé, and he smiled at her. His eyes met Gunner's, and he gave one brief nod before turning his attention back to his phone call.

"How was Texas?" Andrea curled up in one of the big chairs, her feet tucked under her. "I love it here, but sometimes I miss the Dallas-Fort Worth metroplex."

"Things were…eventful."

"Ohhh, details. Gimme details." Andrea rubbed her hands together like an eager kid waiting for her bowl of ice cream.

"Mr. Jackson was dead." Maggie's soft voice announced.

"Ah, hell, honey, I'm so sorry."

"We found his body in the kitchen of his home. The first responders suspected a heart attack." She paused and Gunner squeezed her hand, and she threaded her fingers with his. "We'll know more after an autopsy, but if I was a betting woman, my money would be on EryX."

The sound of the sliding glass door punctuated her words, and Carpenter sauntered across the living space. He inclined his head to Maggie, ignored Gunner, and turned to face Westin.

"I knew I'd get you here one way or another."

"Couldn't resist the chance to check out your fancy new digs, bro."

Bro? What the hell? Gunner looked at Carpenter and Westin, noting the differences—but also the similarities.

"Ah, hell, no. There are two of you?"

Andrea giggled, her hands across her mouth. Carpenter didn't say a word, quirked his brow in that way that drove Gunner crazy.

"Same father, different mothers."

"I'm the black sheep of the family," Westin added. "The illegitimate bastard nobody wanted." The harshness of his words was belied by the mischievous smirk on his face.

"Do. Not. Start. That. Again." Well, look at that. Carpenter's face had taken on a decidedly mottled red tone. Westin better be careful, or he'd get to see what an on-the-warpath Samuel Carpenter looked like.

"If anybody is a bastard, it's the man who fathered us."

"You'll get no argument from me, Sam. My mother had the misfortune of falling for him hook, line, and sinker. He stuck around long enough to knock her up, and then took off looking for the next woman good enough for the Carpenter name."

The tension in the room ratcheted up with each word. It didn't take a Mensa member to determine that there was a lot of unresolved issues between the two brothers.

And didn't that just boggle the mind—Carpenter had a brother. Gunner knew about his sister, the one who'd died of a drug overdose. She'd been the reason he'd gone to work for the DEA in the first place.

"Stop it, both of you." Andrea hopped to her feet, standing between the two men squared off facing each other. She laid a hand on Carpenter's chest, patting it gently, her actions seeming to soothe the savage beast.

Gunner turned and whispered to Maggie, though he made sure it was still loud enough for both men to hear. "One of them's bad enough. Not sure I can handle two of 'em. Wanna run away with me?"

She grinned. "Naw, I'd rather watch the show. Don't suppose you've got any popcorn?"

"No, no. Please, tell me she's not just like him? That's one smartass too many in this room." Carpenter flung himself down into the chair Andrea had vacated, pulling her down onto his lap.

Westin eased back onto the sofa, next to Maggie. "You have no idea. Wait until you hear her sing."

"Hey!" Maggie punched him in the arm.

"Okay, children, can we get back to business? Gimme a rundown on what happened."

"Went to check on Leland Jackson, test subject RUX-1274. When he didn't answer his door, I walked around back and looked through the window. Saw him lying on the floor and called nine-one-one."

"No visible signs of foul play?"

"Nothing. First responders thought heart attack. I couldn't really tell the cops why we were nosing around, so we might have to go through a backdoor to get the autopsy report."

"You okay, Maggie?" Andrea half rose from her seat, but Carpenter pulled her back onto his lap.

"I'm fine. Thinking about the possibility that EryX

Pharmaceutical did this—and I worked for them."

Before anybody could respond, a brisk knock on the front door sounded, and Gunner's stomach rumbled. *Must be Ms. Willie.*

Sure enough, she bustled through the door, her face beaming and her hands filled with a tray loaded with napkin-covered plates. She stopped when she spotted Westin, and drew in a sharp breath.

"Mister Dean, oh it's so good to see you again."

He stood to help her with the tray, but Westin was quicker, taking it from her hands and passing it to Carpenter.

He pulled Ms. Willie into his arms. "You know I couldn't come to New Orleans without seeing my special lady, now could I?" He lifted her off the ground, spinning her around in his arms. "Although some of you seems to have disappeared."

"Oh, put me down. Let me look at you." She cupped his face between her hands. "How long has it been?"

A flash of what looked like guilt crossed his face, but was quickly disguised behind his grin. "Much too long. When are you going to leave this surly group and come work for me? I'll pay you double whatever this louse pays you."

"Hush now. I'm retired and aim to stay that way."

He saw the look that passed between Carpenter and Westin, the silent communication. Whatever their differences, both men adored the British woman who'd practically raised Carpenter. There was a story there. Maybe one day he'd pry it out of one of them.

"I brought a few snacks. Something sweet for Mister Samuel. Brownies for Mister Dean—though give a woman a little warning next time. And for you, Mister Wilson, I made those ham and cheese roll-ups that you like."

Carpenter set the tray on the coffee table and the napkins covering the plates went flying in every direction as they were yanked free. Andrea and Maggie looked at each other, then at the three men digging into the food like they'd been stranded on a deserted island and this was their first meal after being rescued.

"You better grab something fast, or there'll be nothing left. Trust me, I learned that the hard way." Andrea snatched a brownie off the plate.

Maggie grabbed one of the ham and cheese things and took a bite, and immediately reached for another. She wasn't about to lose out on the best thing she'd tasted in ages. Gunner started to reach for the extra one in her hand and she pulled it back with a growl.

"Mine. Get your own." He grinned, because he understood exactly how she felt. It was how most people reacted when they tasted Ms. Willie's cooking for the first time. He couldn't wait until she tasted the woman's pot roast. She'd think she'd died and gone to heaven.

Carpenter leaned back, his loaded plate in his hands. "Okay, everybody's eating. Now tell me what's new."

Talking between bites, they filled her in on what happened with the study participant and at Maggie's parents' cabin, and the slashing of Gunner's tires. Gunner didn't think it was necessary to tell her about making love to

Maggie the night before, though from the sparkle in Ms. Willie's eye, and the fact that he sat as close to Maggie as he could without having her actually in his lap, she'd probably already figured that out.

"Has Mister Stefan had any luck getting past their security?"

"He's close. Hopefully by this afternoon, he'll have the list of people that worked on the Monday in question, and we can narrow down our two blabbermouths."

Maggie sat quietly by his side. Too quietly. He could practically see the gears spinning in her head.

"What are you thinking about so hard, hon?"

She started when he tapped her arm. "Oh, sorry. I was just thinking. There's a girl I worked with at EryX. We went to school together." She stopped talking for so long, Gunner wanted to shake her, and say *spit it out already*. But he waited, knowing she'd tell them when she'd worked it out in her head.

"What if I could get you access to a keycard for EryX? Is there any way we could duplicate it? Mine's been deactivated, I'm sure, but I could go back inside and…"

A chorus of no's erupted.

"I'd say yes, absolutely yes, to getting a keycard for EryX Pharmaceutical. But, sorry, sugar, you aren't going anywhere near there."

"But…"

"No. Carlisle can duplicate the card and go onsite. If he can get access to the computer there, it would make things a hell of a lot easier."

"I'll go with him." Westin scooted forward on the sofa, resting his forearm on his knee.

"No, I'll go."

"Sorry, big guy," Westin added with a smile, "but you need to stay here and guard your gal. Carlisle is the brains, and I'll be the muscle."

Gunner wrapped his arm around Maggie's shoulders, and she let him, actually leaning a bit closer. He hated that Westin was right, but he had a point, because he didn't want to let Maggie out of his sight—not until everything was over.

"So, Maggie, how are we going to get this card?"

Chapter Sixteen

Carlisle swiped the phony keycard into the security scanner, and held his breath. He was ninety-nine point nine percent sure it would work, but there was always the slightest chance—*ah, there we go*. The light blinked green and he pressed down on the handle, and eased the door open. Dean Westin stood close behind him, and slid through the opening on silent feet.

It had been a while since he'd been out in the field, though he hadn't forgotten everything he'd been taught. The schematic he'd downloaded to his laptop showed them exactly which hallways to follow and when to turn left or right.

By his calculations, he'd have to scan the card four times before he finally reached his destination. Maggie's friend, Caitlyn, had come through for them, putting her job at risk. If they ever caught onto the fact that her identification had been tampered with, she'd definitely be fired, or worse, prosecuted. But once they'd explained the bare minimum to her, she'd been more than willing to take down the corporate giant.

They'd come in right after the mass exodus of people at the five o'clock hour, leaving only a skeleton crew working.

Now if they could just avoid the cleaning crew, they might actually make it all the way to their destination.

Caitlyn's office was directly across the hall from Maggie's. Maggie's friend worked for the vice president of research and development, which meant he'd have all the pretty little details about the drug somewhere in his office. All they had to do was find it.

He and Westin started to round the final corner, but Carlisle held up his hand, freezing at the sound of laughter not far from where they stood. After what seemed like hours, but actually was only five minutes, he heard the welcome sound of the elevator dinging its arrival.

Hearing the doors whoosh closed, he slipped around the corner, motioning for Westin. One last swipe of the keycard and they were in.

Flicking on the light, he immediately went to the computer and logged on with Caitlyn's password.

"Why don't you take a look in the boss's office while I see what I can find here."

Westin walked away without a word, and Carlisle went back to his treasure hunt. Using Caitlyn's password only got him so far. With a thin cable, he attached his laptop to her system and began typing.

This felt familiar, like sliding into his own skin. Computers and programs made sense to him in a way nothing else did. There was a structure and order to the chaos, and he was very good at spotting when something wasn't right.

Like now. There was a big dark gap where files should be. A whole block of information had been deleted.

Fortunately, nothing was ever deleted completely. There were always ways to get information back if you wanted it bad enough.

And he wanted this information. His fingers flew across the laptop keys, digging deeper into the black hole.

A file named RUX formulaic study number one reappeared and he downloaded it to his system. RUX number two quickly followed. When he hit RUX study number three, he decided it was time to make a call.

It was answered on the first ring. "Gunner, put Maggie on the phone."

"Hang on."

"Stefan? It's Maggie." She sounded breathless, and he really didn't want to think about what he might have interrupted.

"How many study groups did RUX do?"

"There was a study group for the first formula, the one that the FDA didn't give an approval for. RUX two is the only other one I know about." He heard her indrawn breath. "Why? What have you found?"

"I'm looking at three deleted folders. Studies for RUX one, two…and three."

"I never heard of a third study. As far as I'm aware, there were only the two formulations of Somnolett."

"Tell Gunner somebody deleted a ton of files. I'm going to recover everything I can and we'll head out. Gotta go."

He hung up before she could ask any questions, because he knew she would. That's all they seemed to have right now, lots of questions without answers.

More and more files were undeleted and he transferred them to his laptop. Playing a hunch, he made a separate folder and copied all the information he'd collected from the previously deleted files, storing them for later retrieval. Nobody would notice it—not unless they knew what they were looking for. Then he quickly and efficiently deleted the files—though he'd be able to recover them again if he had to.

Westin came out of the back office, a couple of file folders clutched in his hand. "Found these hidden in the back of a locked file cabinet. From the way they'd been secreted away, I figured they might be useful."

Carlisle didn't even bother looking at them, he simply tucked them into his laptop bag. He reached for the cord to disconnect from Caitlyn's office computer when something caught his eye and he paused, studying the file name.

RISKVSREWARDRATIO.DOC

Westin peered over his shoulder. "Now that looks mighty interesting, don't you think?"

Funny, this file hadn't been one of the deleted files he'd recovered, but something about it made him download it anyway. Best to play it safe. He didn't want to have to come here again.

Reaching into his pocket, he pulled out a thumb drive and stuck it into Caitlyn's computer, and uploaded the files he'd brought with him. Might as well install a backdoor program, in case he had to get in again. He doubted anybody would notice it. Not unless they did a full system scan.

"Let's go."

He walked toward the door, when he saw the knob turn. Shooting a glance at Westin, he nodded toward the back office and both men raced through, closing it almost all the way, but leaving it cracked enough he could peer through.

"I'm telling you, she doesn't want anything to do with your sorry ass." A whiny male voice stated as the door swung inward. A tall, thin man in a security guard's uniform stopped and looked around. "See, she isn't here."

"But the lights are on." A second man, short and pudgy with coke-bottle glasses elbowed his way past the other man, a single white rose in his hand. "She's gotta be here. I checked the system and her keycard's in use."

"Look around, dummy. Do you see her?" tall and skinny asked. "She probably walked out with somebody and forgot to key out."

"Maybe she's in the bathroom—I'll wait."

"Dude, you can't stay in here. The office door was locked. She's gone home for the day."

Carlisle almost snickered at the lovesick puppy dog look on the pudgy guy's face.

"I'll leave the flower on her desk, with a note."

"Right. And she'll have you written up by the boss for stalking her, and for entering her office without authorization. Do you want to get fired?"

"Fine. I'm clocking out. Want to go get a beer?"

"Gimme ten minutes to secure the floor and we're outta here."

Carlisle exhaled and gave a thumbs' up to Westin when the other two flicked off the lights and locked the door.

They'd give them their ten minutes to leave, then make their way out and back to New Orleans.

Frankly, he couldn't wait to get out of this place. Knowing what he knew, it gave him the heebie-jeebies.

"Remind me to give Caitlyn the four-one-one on her stalker."

Westin nodded. "Yeah, I get the feeling he's not the type to take a polite no for an answer. He'll smother her with affection until she either gives in or has to file charges."

Carlisle gave himself a mental reminder to delete any record of Caitlyn's keycard being used. The last thing they needed was to draw unwanted attention to somebody who'd done them a solid.

No help for it—he'd have to let Westin drive back, because he couldn't wait to get his hands on those files—especially that last one he'd found. He had the feeling they'd just hit the motherlode.

Chapter Seventeen

Maggie studied the chart she'd taped to the wall. Everything she knew so far was outlined, graphed, and documented on the pages.

The partial list of names was the first sheet. So far they had eight names out of the original twenty-five. The next listed all the people whose deaths had been confirmed. Six of the eight, including poor Mr. Jackson.

She chewed on her nail, while she studied the spreadsheet, looking for any kind of pattern. Something to tie everything into a neat little package.

She kept going back to the two names they'd identified as test subjects. They'd been unable to contact either one yet.

But the six they'd documented as confirmed study cases, taking Somnolett, all were dead.

"What have you got?"

Gunner walked up behind her, passing a cup of hot tea around her shoulder. She smiled her thanks, and took a sip.

"Trying to see if there's a pattern. Six of the eight names we've discovered so far are all dead. No deaths the same, though we don't have a cause of death on Mr. Jackson yet."

"Carlisle's hoping he'll find something in the files they got last night. He said to thank your friend."

"I will. Hopefully, they'll never catch on to what she did, or she'll lose her job." Her gut knotted at the thought of what else might happen, if Eryx Pharmaceutical caught onto the fact Caitlyn had betrayed them.

Gunner slid his arms around her waist, pulling her against his body, and resting his chin atop her head. "Okay, six deaths, all in different parts of the country. All different physicians administering the study drug. Have I got that right so far?"

She nodded, taking another sip of her tea. "From what I've been able to piece together, participants in the studies are all part of a larger pool of patients. Some get placebos and some the actual study drug. In some cases, there can be more than one drug being administered, or a drug cocktail. Again, some patients will get one of the drugs, other patients will get the second drug, and some will get the combination of both."

"That sounds dangerous."

"It can be, but that's why it's always done under a physician's supervision, and patients have very close followup and a variety of tests performed during the trial, looking for any side effects or warning signs."

Gunner loosened his arms and took a step toward her collage of papers. "Okay, let's work with what we've got. The first six, all dead. Who was first?"

She touched the first name on the list. "Beth Andrews. Forty-six years old. Mother of two. She was one of the first people entered into the study. Died in a car accident six weeks ago."

Gunner pulled open a door and rummaged around, before pulling out a package of highlight markers. He highlighted her name in yellow, and then wrote next to it in ink—car accident.

"Okay, who's up next?" He waited patiently with another colored marker, this time green.

"Donald Grant. Age…thirty. Single, no children. Started on the protocol also six weeks ago."

Gunner ran the highlighter over his name, and paused waiting for her to give the cause of death.

"Suicide. He overdosed on prescription painkillers."

"Hmm." He noted it down, and waited for her to give the next.

She went through each of the remaining four names, right up until they got to Mr. Jackson's. He put a big question mark next to his.

"Okay, so we've got a car accident, two suicides, a stroke, a mugging turned deadly, and a possible heart attack. None of these amount to murder, hon."

"I know." Doubt coiled deep inside. "Am I crazy? I know what I heard, but…"

"I believe you, sweetheart." The fierce pride in his eyes filled her with wonder and something else, a warmth that made her tingle to the tips of her toes. Even after all the years they'd been apart, losing contact and going on with their lives, he still believed in her and trusted her.

"Thank you." Whispering the words, she walked forward until she could wrap her arms around him, leaning her head against his chest. Felt him embrace her. Felt the safety she'd been craving without even knowing it.

He took a step back at the knock on the front door, and the immediate loss of warmth assailed her. Not in a physical sense, but it was there just the same. He paused long enough to tug on a strand of hair curling along the side of her face, before heading to the door.

Carpenter and another man she didn't recognize stepped through. Tall and dark, he was an obvious fit for the rest of what she'd come to expect for Carpenter's team.

"Gunner, you remember Sebastian Boudreau."

"Hey, Bas."

The other man nodded but remained silent. Maggie's gaze swept back and forth between the three men. Carpenter with his cool blond good looks and air of sophistication, which hid a will of iron. Gunner with his tough exterior of solid steel and bad attitude, who was a big softie inside. But this new man, whom she'd never met, had the little hairs on her arms standing at attention. He was like a stiletto blade, silent and deadly—and you'd never see him coming until it was too late—unless he wanted to be seen. There was an edge to him that made her shiver.

"Bas has some news."

Gunner walked back and pulled Maggie against his side, and instantly that feeling of safety and security returned. "Might as well sit for this."

"Samuel asked me to look into the last two names on your list." Sebastian Boudreau's deep voice was colored with a slight Cajun accent that slid across her skin like melted chocolate. Which matched the warm cocoa brown of his eyes—eyes that lit with an inner fire when he smiled at her.

"What'd you find?" Gunner rested his arm along the back of the couch, his hand playing with the loose hair sliding against her shoulder.

"Louella Birch is a very spry seventy-three year-old with an indomitable will of steel. Rarely sleeps a wink, which is why she agreed to undergo the protocol—because no other sleeping agent has been able to touch her problem."

Maggie scooted forward on the couch, her hands gripping the cushion. "You said is—she's still alive?"

Boudreau smiled and immediately Maggie was reminded of a tiger, silently waiting for its prey to move one step closer.

"As of twenty-four hours ago, she was alive and kicking. And pretty damned pissed when I showed up on her doorstep asking about Somnolett. Said it's the first time in twenty years she's gotten a full night's sleep, taking Somnolett."

"You've got somebody guarding her?" Carpenter's nod answered Gunner's question, and Maggie gave a sigh of relief. At least one of the people was still okay.

"Which leaves us with Glenn Hetrick. Twenty-eight-year-old stockbroker. Killed yesterday afternoon when he fell off the fire escape of a sixth-floor walkup."

Her heart sank with each word. They'd been too late to save another one. Her head spun with the list of maybes. Maybe if she'd gone to the police, they'd have believed her. Maybe if she'd found Gunner sooner, they could have stopped EryX Pharmaceutical sooner. Maybe, maybe, maybe...

"Maggie and I were going over everything," Gunner pointed toward their setup, with the highlighted names. "Might as well add Hetrick to the list."

They all moved over to the wall, and Gunner highlighted Hetrick's name and added the cause of death, and she stepped back, studying the pages. There was an underlying connection there, she could practically see it beneath the surface, but it eluded her, and didn't that just make her damned unhappy?

"Seven people out of how many—twenty-five? Those odds are definitely skewed. We're talking a matter of weeks. I'd get it if this happened over a longer period of time, months, even years apart. But weeks—and all in the same group study protocol for the same drug? No way it's a coincidence." Boudreau's eyes narrowed, his focus straight and sure, staring at the list of highlighted names.

"Carlisle's been able to pull four more names from the data he gathered last night. One of them's in Fort Worth, so I've got Nate checking it out, since he's still there." Carpenter ran a finger down the sheet, pausing at each color.

"Each person, other than the two suicides, died from what would be considered normal circumstances." He tapped his finger against the first suicide. "How'd you commit suicide?" It sounded like he posed the question to himself, though Gunner answered anyway.

"Overdose of prescription pain pills."

"Hmm. How about the other suicide victim?" He stepped closer and peered at the written answer. "Ah, self-inflicted GSW. Convenient."

"Does this smell fishy to anybody else, or just me?" Boudreau began pacing behind them, a look of concentration painting his countenance.

"You mean how none of them involved another person kind of fishy?" Gunner nodded. "I mean, sure, a lot of people die at home unattended, but seven deaths, and none of them were witnessed, at least not first-hand."

He grabbed up a file folder off the table, and began leafing through the pages. "Take our MVA. The police report said she skidded on wet pavement and rolled over an embankment. No witnesses, no other cars around."

Maggie caught on to where he was going. She picked up another folder. "Apparent stroke. Lived alone, no witnesses. Body wasn't found for two days when they didn't show up for work."

Carpenter and Boudreau each picked up a folder and saw the same pattern. Each of the seven people had died alone. Even those that had families hadn't been home at the time of the demise. And not a single one of them died in a hospital, and had been seen by their physician for the preceding forty-eight hours.

"That has to be part of this," Maggie said, her excitement building. "All of these people were under a doctor's care, and having routine weekly or biweekly checkups. It's part of all the study protocols in the beginning. Mandatory screening, blood tests, etc."

She saw the instant Carpenter got it. "If they're under a physician's care, and died under normal or routine circumstances, like these," he waved at the files, "there wouldn't be an autopsy. Especially if the physician signed off on having seen the patient within twenty-four to forty-eight hours prior to death."

"Did any of them have autopsies?"

Chapter Eighteen

They needed a break. Mentally, physically, and emotionally exhausted, Gunner knew Maggie had to be at her breaking point. They'd been working on the Somnolett case for days without finding anything significant.

A night out, putting everybody and everything behind them, if only for a couple of hours, sounded like the perfect recipe.

He wanted to show her the city he'd come to love and call home. Though he'd only been here less than a year, he'd become immersed within the city's cultural melting pot and found a place where he belonged.

Tonight, he'd wine and dine her, do a bit of the touristy stuff. Show her Jackson Square and some of the places everybody recognizes, but he'd also take her to the hidden gems, those places where the locals gathered. The real heart of the French Quarter.

"I'm ready." Maggie's voice drew him like the proverbial moth to her flame, and indeed she was all things warm and sultry, just like the city.

The vibrant red dress hugged her curves like a lover's embrace, highlighting all the things he'd come to adore about her. Her glorious red hair was pulled back into an elegant up style, and he itched to dig his hands into it, pull the pins out and spread it out across her shoulders. Though it looked lovely, he wanted his wild, wanton princess, and hopefully he'd have her before the night was gone.

Small diamonds winked in her ears, the light catching and reflecting the sparkle, though they dimmed in contrast to her smile, which began as tentative, but grew into the sultry come-hither seductive smile of a siren, luring her prey. And he was a very willing victim. Black heels and a black clutch completed the outfit, and she did a little spin, allowing the flirty folds along the hem to whirl around, exposing enticing glimpses of her glorious legs.

"Wow. You look stunning."

"Thanks. You look pretty great yourself."

Instinctively his hand went to the tie, and he was glad he'd decided to make the extra effort, though the blasted thing would probably end up in his pocket before the night was half over.

Before he could utter another word, there was a soft knock on the door. He frowned. Didn't matter who it was, he was not working tonight. This was his time with Maggie.

"Sir, Mr. Carpenter sends his regards, and that I'm at your disposal for the rest of the evening." Etienne Boudreau, the youngest of the four Boudreau brothers stood there, dressed in a chauffeur's uniform, and though he was straight-faced, the laughter in his eyes threatened to derail all Gunner's plans. Trust Carpenter to think of everything, right down to having a member of Carpenter Security drive them around, and act as an unofficial bodyguard.

Taking the elevator, they emerged into the lobby and Gunner spotted the black SUV parked directly in front of the building, recognizing it immediately as Carpenter's private car. He'd ridden in it before, and knew it was tricked out with all the bells and whistles, including bulletproof glass and puncture resistant tires.

Etienne opened the rear door, and waited as Maggie slid across the seat. "What's going on?" he whispered to Boudreau. "Since when do you play chauffeur?"

"Boss's orders. Consider me an extra bodyguard for the lovely Ms. Callahan." Boudreau shot a glance into the car's interior. "Gotta say, you are one lucky bastard, Everett."

"I'm aware. We've got reservations at Antoine's."

"Swanky. Pulling out the big guns, I see."

"Shaddup, Boudreau, and drive."

Gunner climbed in beside Maggie and squeezed her hand. This night needed to be extraordinary, because nobody deserved it more. She'd been amazing, handling every curveball thrown their way with aplomb. He still couldn't believe everything she'd been through in the last few weeks. What it must have taken. Scared and running, unsure where to go or who to turn to? He thanked his lucky stars that she'd turned to him. And that he had the resources to help.

"This feels surreal." Maggie's hand slid along the edge of the seat. "With everything that's happened, going out for a special evening seems—decadent." She peeked up at him from beneath her lashes, and he had to swallow at the sexy smile she gave him. "Deliciously, wantonly decadent."

"I live to fulfill your every wish, hon."

"We'll see," she whispered. "I have a very vivid imagination."

The SUV pulled up in front of Antoine's, and Boudreau came around and opened the door. Gunner helped Maggie alight from the car.

Met at the door, they were led to their elegantly appointed dining room, and greeted by their waiter.

"Mr. Everett, it's so good to see you again."

"Thank you, Henri," Gunner replied. "This is my good friend, Miss Maggie Callahan."

"It's a pleasure to meet you, Ms. Callahan. Welcome to Antoine's. It is an honor to take care of you this evening."

Gunner pulled out Maggie's chair and ordered a bottle of wine. Within moments, Henri was back, pouring the wine. Gunner ordered the Oysters Rockefeller, which was one of the house specialities.

"This place is amazing."

"It's a New Orleans icon. Everybody who is anybody has eaten at Antoine's." He watched her take a sip of her wine, her eyes widening at the taste. Henri would be getting a big tip, because he certainly knew his way around a wine list.

Over dinner they talked about everything but the case. That had been his only caveat before they'd left. No work talk. Tonight was a night for new beginnings. A night filled with only pleasurable experiences.

Though he'd thought about lingering over dessert, he wanted to have Maggie in his arms, and he'd promised her dancing. He could remember a night they'd spent together, so long ago, when he'd parked his old rust bucket on the edge of the lake, and they'd danced under the moonlight to the music from the car stereo. That memory had gotten him through a lot of long lonely nights in his bunk in Iraq.

A quick text to Etienne had the SUV brought around and they headed toward Benny G's, a club he'd discovered a few months ago. Tucked away on one of the side streets, it was a favorite place for people who loved swing dancing and the classics. The music was a mixture of old classics like Benny Goodman tunes, hence the club's name, as well as slow ballads. There was a live band who played nightly, and the dance space was big enough you didn't feel like you were about to get an elbow to the face with every turn.

The soft strains of *As Time Goes By* wafted on the breeze as the door opened, and Maggie clasped his hand. Bodies filled the dance floor, swaying to the sultry rhythm, and a woman in the center of the raised dais sang the words. He loved the atmosphere of the place, a throwback to an almost forgotten era, and apparently a lot of other people did too, because the place was gaining a reputation for being *the* place to go if you wanted to dance. Maybe he was getting old, but the nightclub scene didn't do much for him anymore.

"Shall we?" He gestured toward the other couples circling around the center of the club. A smattering of tables and booths were scattered around the outer perimeter, and the lights burned low, jarred candles on each table adding to the allure.

"Absolutely." She smiled at him, extending her hand.

He took it, sliding his arms around her, and pulling her

close. She leaned into him, her head resting on his shoulder, as her arms twined around his neck.

This was what he'd been waiting for all night. A chance to hold her in his arms, letting their bodies speak without saying a word aloud.

The song ended to a smattering of applause, and the band segued into *Secret Love*, the old Doris Day classic.

The irony wasn't lost on him. He'd kept his feelings for Maggie bottled up all those years ago, when they'd both been young and foolish, never telling her how he felt. He'd loved her with a youthful infatuation. Time and distance eventually allowed it to fade, but it never completely obliterated his feelings. Yet the moment he saw her again, all those emotions rushed to the forefront, and he'd tumbled. Head-over-arse, right back into love with her.

With everything going on, now wasn't the time or the place to say anything. Hell, it might never be the right time or place, and he'd keep his secret love a secret, like the song. Didn't mean it wasn't true. Every beat of his heart proved that fact.

They danced for over an hour. Maggie surprised him with her moves, and the woman definitely knew her stuff. And that red dress—it was perfect for dancing, giving enticing flashes of skin when she spun with the music.

It was getting late when they finally left Benny G's, and walked the few blocks toward Jackson Square. He'd called ahead and left a message with one of the men who ran the carriages, an old buddy from boot camp, making arrangements for a little surprise for Maggie.

"Really!" Her voice was filled with excitement when she saw where they were headed. "How'd you know I've always wanted to do this?" Strolling up to the horse, she ran her hands along its neck, and patted its velvety nose, grinning at him. He felt a million feet tall. He hadn't known it was something she'd wanted to do. It had just been a romantic gesture, but he was really glad he'd listened to his gut instinct.

Helping her up into the white carriage, he handed her the dozen red roses his friend left on the seat, and watched as she buried her nose in the blossoms. The smile she gave him made every ounce of effort worthwhile, and he'd do it again in a heartbeat, just to see that look in her eyes.

The horse clopped along under the light of the full moon, its hooves beating out a rhythm that blended with the soothing jazz filling the air.

"This city really is amazing." Her head rested on his shoulder, as she gazed up at the stars. The moon was nearly full, and the heat from earlier in the afternoon had dissipated. A slight breeze from the river brought the briny tang to the air, adding an underlayer of richness.

"I've grown to love the grand lady since I've been here. Glad I agreed to relocate with Carpenter when he moved things from Dallas to New Orleans."

"It's funny, I never had the urge to move away from South Texas. My family's there, and I've been there my whole life. Yet seeing all this makes me wonder if I've made a mistake, stagnating in place."

Gunner brushed a brief kiss against her forehead. "I

think we make our choices for a reason. Whether to stay or to go—each one holds positives and negatives. It's what you do with those choices that makes all the difference."

She lifted her head to stare into his eyes. "What about your choices? Are you happy with the ones you've made?"

"For the most part—yes. Do I have regrets? Absolutely. Are there things I'd change, if I could go back? Some. Would I do it all again—yes, I think I would."

She snuggled back against him, as the carriage continued its circuit. They were taking the longer scenic route, so they had plenty of time. Time he'd spend holding her close. He draped his arm across her shoulders, scooting over a little more to get closer.

"What would you change?" Her voice held a wistful quality, a note of something he couldn't quite identify.

"Leaving you." The truth popped out before he could halt it.

"What?" She straightened, and immediately he missed the feel of her pressed against him. His words had surprised her, eyes wide in shock.

"I've always regretted leaving you, Maggie. Wondered what our lives would have been like if I'd stayed in Texas instead of shipping out with the corps. Or if I could've talked you into going with me."

Her hand tightened on his, trembling. "I wondered that too. Asked myself a thousand times, what things might have been like if I'd said yes and gone with you. Played a million scenarios in my head. We might have made it, but more than likely we'd have been one of the statistics. Young couples who start out with so much promise, but implode under the pressures."

"I know. I'd like to think we'd be one of the lucky ones, but I was a very angry man back then. Hell, I wasn't even a man. I was a kid with a chip on his shoulder and mad at the world. Luckily, I've grown up a lot since then." He chuckled softly. "Well, I like to think I've matured, but if you ask the other guys, they'll tell you I'm still a smart-ass."

She giggled. "Some things never change. Once a smart-ass, always a smart-ass."

"Hey!" The sound of her laughter was pure joy, and he joined in. "What about you? Any regrets?"

"Probably more than you'd care to hear about."

"Try me."

A soft blush colored her cheeks. "I always wanted to be an artist."

It was his turn to be surprised. "An artist, huh? What medium?"

"Painting." The blush got a little deeper, and he couldn't resist running his finger down her cheek.

"Why the interest in painting?"

"I remember going on a field trip in school. We went to the museum, and I was fascinated with the art. I loved wandering through the exhibit. I kept getting in trouble for lollygagging behind the group, because I studied each one, looking at the brush strokes and the blending of colors. It just…fascinated me."

"Hate to say it, but I'm a total Philistine when it comes to art. I'm more into just sticking black and white photos on the wall."

She gave his arm a playful punch. "You heathen!"

Tugging her back against his side, he tucked her head against his shoulder, the roses still clutched against her chest. They'd come back around to their starting point soon, though he didn't want their night to end.

"It's almost midnight, Cinderella."

The teasing look in her gaze was mixed with a sensuality that made him almost swallow his tongue. "Does the night have to end?"

"No. But the carriage ride does. Then we'll go some-where with a little more privacy."

"Um-hmm." She stretched upward and brushed a kiss along the underside of his jaw. "I'd like that."

The carriage drew to a stop back where the ride had begun, and Gunner placed his hands around Maggie's waist, lifting her down, the sound of her laughter filling the evening air. He gave his buddy a generous tip, and he texted Etienne to pick them up.

Pulling her close, he kissed her under the moonlight, feeling her lips part beneath his. The magic of the night had him hopeful that things would be even better when they got home.

Right up until the air around him echoed with the sound of a gunshot.

Chapter Nineteen

The black SUV skidded to a stop with a squeal of brakes, and Etienne Boudreau jumped from behind the driver's door, flinging open the rear door. Gunner shoved her through, his body wrapped protectively over hers.

"Was that a gunshot?" Boudreau's foot hit the gas with enough force, the SUV shot forward, flinging her back against the upholstered seat. She still hadn't caught her breath, everything happened so quickly. Thank goodness for Gunner's quick reflexes. He'd shoved her back against the panels of the carriage, shielding her with his big body, until the SUV pulled up.

"You see the shooter?"

Gunner shook his head. "No. Who the hell takes a shot like that in the middle of one of the biggest tourist spots, even at this late hour? There are dozens of people out there!"

"I called nine-one-one. Doubt they'll find anything, but maybe they'll get a shell casing or something."

Maggie's gaze ping-ponged between the two men, who completely ignored her.

"Gunner?"

"Yeah, sweetheart?"

"Your friend owns that carriage, right?"

He nodded before reaching for her hand. "Yeah, he's a buddy I met in San Diego—boot camp." His intense gaze studied her face closely. "Why?"

"You might tell him to have the police dig the bullet out of the wood to the left of the wheel."

Right where she'd been standing. The squeezing sensation in the center of his chest increased with the realization he might have lost her.

"You heard it hit?"

"Saw the hole too." Her hands reached up and clasped his face. "Don't. I'm okay. I'm not hurt."

He inhaled a long breath. "I might have lost you."

"Not gonna happen, big man. I'm not going anywhere." *Not ever, if I have anything to say about it.*

"Damn right, you're not." He tapped Etienne on the shoulder. "Call the boss, tell him what happened, and that we're on our way in. Tell him about the bullet," she could hear the catch in his voice before he continued, "and see if we can get the caliber. Might be able to see if it was somebody playing amateur hour or if they've hired a professional."

She swallowed, really wishing she could overlook his last statement. Because if they'd hired somebody to take her out…

"Stop thinking about it. We'll get you back to my place and lock it down like Fort Knox. Trust me, nobody gets into Carpenter's building unless they have a bloody engraved invitation."

Etienne looked in the rearview mirror, and she could

read the concern in his gaze. "Don't worry, Ms. Maggie, we're gonna take good care of you. Now, you two hang on, and I'll get you there PDQ."

With that, he stomped on the gas hard, and the SUV leapt forward, racing through the streets. Good thing it was getting late and the traffic was light. And that there weren't any cops around, because she knew he was breaking all kinds of laws.

Almost before she could blink, they were pulling up behind the Canal Street building. She hadn't even realized they had anything behind the place, but there was a large area of concrete and gravel, where several cars and pickups were parked. The back façade of the building looked much like the front, although there were outdoor fire escapes leading to each floor. There was also a large metal door that looked like it would take a Mack truck to get through.

"Come on, sugar, let's get you inside." Swinging the door open, Gunner helped Maggie out while Etienne entered a code into the panel beside the door.

"I'm going to head over to N.O.P.D. Let the boss know I'll call Remy Lamoreaux, see if he can get on top of things right away."

"Thank you for all you've done, Mr. Boudreau." Maggie held out her hand, and he brushed it away to pull her into a hug. It startled her for a second, since she wasn't expecting it. Just as quickly, he stepped back, grinning at her.

"Don't worry, Ms. Maggie. You're part of the family now, and we take care of our own."

With that, he climbed back behind the wheel, waiting

long enough to make sure they were inside, before driving off.

Her head was still spinning. Everything had been beautiful, the night enchanted. All her plans for spending the night in Gunner's arms, in his bed, making love, went up in flames with a single shot.

And she wasn't stupid. They were shooting at her. As far as she knew, nobody was after Gunner. Which meant it had to be EryX Pharmaceutical. They weren't going to stop until they'd covered their tracks and destroyed any evidence, and anybody who could cause them problems. Including her.

She'd been the one to stir up the hornet's nest, and she'd have to be the one to end it. Except she didn't think EryX would accept anything less than her complete and utter destruction, because they'd never be satisfied with just her word that she wouldn't leak any of their questionable practices to the press—or to the government. Because they'd be shut down in a heartbeat, costing billions of dollars to their stockholders, not to mention all the patients counting on the drugs manufactured by EryX Pharmaceutical.

"It's never going to stop, is it?"

"Yes, it will. With everybody working on finding the rest of the patients in the trial, we'll shut it down. I don't care how high up the ladder we have to go, we're going to cut off the snake's head."

"What if it turns out to be more like a hydra, and every time you cut off one head, two more pop up in its place? I thought I was doing what was right, trying to save lives and stop the corruption. Instead, all I've done is endanger you and the rest of your team."

"Stop it. None of this is your fault. If anybody's to blame, it's the greedy corporate bastards who only see dollar signs, without any consideration of what it takes, as long as they show a profit and gain more of the almighty dollar."

"What's that bible verse say—the love of money is the root of all evil? I hope I never come to value money more than people, and the things that matter."

With his hand on the small of her back, Maggie followed the hallway from the back of the building until they reached the reception area, where the lights were blazing.

Stephanie sat at the reception desk, and sprang from her chair the second she spotted them. "Everybody's in the conference room, waiting for you."

"Thanks, Steph." He started to lead Maggie past.

"Oh, no. Not this time, buster. I'm going with you." Stephanie braced her hands on her hips, blocking their way. "I'm tired of sitting on the sidelines. I want in."

Maggie almost snickered out loud at the look of astonishment on Gunner's face. From his expression, Stephanie's words were the verbal equivalent of a baseball bat upside his noggin.

"But…"

"No, buts. I like Maggie, I have since the first day when I brought her in out of the rain." She winked at Maggie. "If it wasn't for me, she might never have come inside. I'm a part of this team. So, we're all going in there, and strategize and figure out how to solve this problem, as a team, or I'm walking out that door tonight."

Gunner's mouth hung open, and Maggie reached a finger beneath his chin and closed it.

"Chin up, buttercup. We girls stick together." Looping her arm through Stephanie's, she headed for the conference room. Gunner followed behind, mumbling under his breath the whole way.

"You go, girl," Maggie whispered to Stephanie. She could feel the other woman's hand trembling. "You did good. Pick your battles, and don't back down."

Stephanie's back straightened. "I'm probably going to get fired, but I'm sick of being left out. I can do a heck of a lot more than just file and take messages. Oh, and get coffee."

"Girl power." Maggie raised a fist, and Stephanie fist-bumped her, before flinging open the conference room door.

She recognized most of the faces, although there were one or two that she couldn't remember their names. But the room was packed. Carlisle had his ever-present laptop. Andrea had her hand on Carpenter's arm, as if keeping him anchored, because he did not look like a happy camper.

"Any news?" Gunner stepped up behind Maggie, placing his hands on her shoulders, and she felt the heat from his touch spread through her. Knowing he was there, standing up for her—with her—eased some of the tension she hadn't realized she'd been holding, ever since the shooter fired.

"Waiting to hear back from the police department. Good catch on the bullet hitting the carriage."

"Kinda hard to miss." Maggie winced at the sarcasm lacing her words. "Sorry, I'm not used to getting shot at in the middle of my date."

Carpenter chuckled. "Wish I could say the same. Hey," he groused when Andrea slugged him in the arm.

"Ranger Boudreau's going to talk to Remy, see if he can speed things along."

"Yeah, he called, said he was on the way into the station." The grin crossing his face was purely evil. "Apparently, we interrupted things with his fiancée. I don't think she likes me very much right now."

"Stephanie…"

"She's with me." Maggie tugged the other woman to her side, threading her arm with Stephanie's. "She's as much a part of this as anybody."

Carpenter's eyes narrowed as he studied both women, and the urge to squirm hit Maggie full force, but she fought it, knowing he'd think less of her if she backed down. Besides, she wasn't a delicate freaking flower, needing the hero to come riding to her rescue. She was tired of standing on the sidelines, while everybody else rearranged their lives to save her bacon. About time she stepped up.

"I sent Jean-Luc to check out the scene. Other than Nate, who's still out of town, he's our best weapons expert. He's going to see if he can find where the shot originated."

"You thinking EryX has brought in a hired gun?" An older man, seated all the way at the back of the room spoke up. He looked vaguely familiar, though Maggie didn't remember seeing him before. Medium-brown hair threaded through with silver, he lounged against the wall as if this meeting was no big deal, though his posture didn't fool her for one instant. This man was immediately recognizable as a leader, for all his nonchalant posture.

"With the amount of money on the line, that'd be my guess, Gator."

Gator? He must be Jean-Luc and Etienne's father.

"Lemme check around, see if anybody in town fits the profile." He straightened from the wall, and Carpenter lifted his hand in a wait-a-second motion.

"Hang around a few minutes. Let's see if we can get the type and caliber of the bullet. Help us narrow down the usual suspects. Professionals tend to specialize, so we might catch a break."

Gator slouched back against the wall with one sharp nod and an oh-so-casual shrug.

Gunner took her arm and carefully led her to one of the empty chairs. She collapsed into it, the adrenaline rush from the night finally dissipating. It wouldn't be long before she crashed, and crashed hard. She just hoped she didn't make a fool of herself in front of everybody.

"Just a few more minutes, sweetheart, and I'll get you upstairs, okay?" Gunner's whisper in her ear helped center her. Okay, she could handle this.

"Maggie, I want you to think about the incident, everything that happened. Do you remember seeing or hearing anything?"

"I don't think so. Gunner lifted me out of the carriage, and took a step away to text Mr. Boudreau, I mean Etienne, to pick us up. I was less than a foot away from him." She rubbed a hand against her forehead. Why was it everything else about tonight was clear as crystal, yet trying to remember any little detail she might have missed seemed like a herculean task?

"You're doing good. Concentrate on what was around you. Was there any unusual noise?" Carpenter's voice was pitched low and soothing, oozing concern yet contained an underlying persuasion she couldn't ignore. Not that she wanted to—she wanted the shooter caught and strung up by his thumbs. A tiny smirk touched her lips. Okay, if she was being completely honest, it wasn't his thumbs she wanted him strung up by, but her momma brought her up to be a lady.

"I don't think—the horse took a step forward. I remember hearing the sound of its shoe clanging against the cobblestones. I turned toward the sound. and I remember the carriage rolling forward a little bit. I—I think I took a step toward Gunner." She clutched his hand, squeezing tight.

"That single step is probably what saved your life." Carpenter leaned back in his chair, folding his hands across his stomach, a vicious smile on his otherwise handsome face. "Otherwise, we might not be having this conversation."

Gunner lifted Maggie from the chair and sat down, situating her on his lap, with his arms caged around her. It didn't matter the room was filled with his co-workers, she leaned against him, feeling safer now she was in his arms.

"Eryx Pharmaceutical is getting desperate, if they're stupid enough to hire a hit. There's always a trail, if you know how to look." Gator's eyes met Maggie's, and there was a wealth of understanding in their steely blue depths. Without breaking eye contact, he continued. "Fortunately, I know how to hunt, and rarely come back empty-handed. Carlisle, I'd start checking out Oleg Gustaffson, Felix Cabrera, and Yvgeni Dimitriev. See if you can narrow down their current locations."

The silence in the room was deafening, until Carpenter turned to Jean-Luc. "Told you—pay up." He held out his hand, wiggling his fingers.

"I still say you're wrong, but you won this one." Jean-Luc slapped a fifty dollar bill into Carpenter's hand. "Don't worry, I'll get it back."

"Here, honey," Carpenter handed the money to Andrea. "Buy yourself something pretty." Maggie chuckled when the other woman snatched the fifty out of her fiancé's hand and tucked it into her cleavage.

"What's going on?" She whispered in Gunner's ear, unsure of what had just transpired. They were in the midst of a crisis, and yet they were talking bets and passing out money.

"I'll explain later. Suffice it to say, I work with a bunch of lunatics." He breathed the words in her ear.

"Hey, I heard that." Andrea gave a little pout. "We're not all crazy—yet." She winked at Maggie. "Hang around with this crew long enough, they kinda grow on you."

"Gunner, go ahead and take Maggie upstairs and try to get some sleep. Tomorrow's going to be hectic. I'll let you know when I hear back from Remy or Etienne."

"Thanks." Without another word, Gunner stood and carried Maggie out the door. Sleep sounded like a really good idea to her.

This wasn't the ending she'd envisioned to their evening, but she was still with Gunner, and the bad guys couldn't get to her. Not with the building's top security.

"Just a few more minutes, and I'll have you tucked into bed and you can get some sleep." He opened his apartment door to find Ms. Willie standing in the opening to the kitchen, a concerned look on her face.

"Mister Samuel told me what happened. I've got a pot of chamomile tea and some scones set out. Get her all tucked up into bed and make sure she drinks a cuppa. It'll help her sleep like a baby."

"Thank you, Ms. Willie. I don't know what we'd do without you."

"And the good Lord willing, you'll never have to find out. Call me if either of you need *anything*." She stressed the word anything, and he knew precisely what she meant. He was one of the privileged few who knew the older woman had once been an agent for British Intelligence. She'd worked for MI-5 before a tragedy had her leaving it all behind and coming to the States.

She patted his cheek, before closing the door behind her. He made a mental note to send her some thank-you flowers in the morning. All the members of Carpenter's elite team were spoiled rotten due to her, and he didn't want to take it for granted.

"You do look tuckered out, hon." He eased his arm from beneath her, and she lowered her feet to the floor. "I have a favor to ask."

"What?"

A sheepish expression crossed his face. "Would you mind sleeping with me?" He must have seen something on her face, because he hurried to add, "Just sleep. I—need to hold you."

Breathing a sigh of relief, because she'd been wondering how to ask him the same thing, she nodded. "I'd like that."

Taking her hand, he led her back to the master bedroom, tugging back the bedspread. "Go ahead and get changed. I'll get the tea Ms. Willie left and be right back."

Maggie scrambled across the hall, shucking her clothes as she went, and slid on her sleep shirt before rushing back to Gunner's room. Climbing beneath the covers, she pulled them up, tucking them beneath her arms just as he walked through the door.

Setting the tray down on the end table beside the bed, he nudged her hip with his, and she scooted over until he had enough room to perch on the side of the bed. He handed her the dainty glass cup on its saucer, the blueberry scone teetering on the edge.

"Thank you." She took a sip, feeling the warmth spread through her. This was a nicer ending, after the disastrous middle portion, of their date. She'd pictured a completely different scenario when she'd thought about how the night would progress after they'd gotten home.

No, not home. Back to Gunner's place. She couldn't start thinking about this being home. When everything was finished, she'd be heading back to Texas, and he'd be staying here, and continuing his life, his career—without her.

"Finish your tea. I'm going to get ready for bed." He

pressed a kiss to the top of her head, and walked away through a door to the left of his dresser.

Tea finished, she nibbled on the scone, though she wasn't really hungry. It was delicious, and she didn't want to disappoint sweet Ms. Willie, but she could barely hold her eyes open.

Placing the cup and saucer back on the tray, she snuggled down into the depths of Gunner's bed, feeling a little lost in its enormous size. He was a big man, though, and probably needed the extra space. A fleeting moment of jealousy raised its ugly head, but she quickly quashed it. She refused to let her mind think about all the other women he might have entertained here.

Eyes closed, she felt the other side of the bed dip, and Gunner's arms wrap around her, one sliding across her middle, its solid weight an anchor and comfort she could cling to. A sigh escaped, because it felt right to be cradled in his arms.

As she drifted off to sleep, her last thought was not to get too used to this, because eventually she'd have to go home. Alone.

Chapter Twenty

"I checked out the names Gator gave me," Carlisle leaned against the wall of Gunner's kitchen. He'd texted Gunner at the crack of dawn, and Gunner had grudgingly crawled out of the nice warm bed, leaving Maggie sleeping. Yawning big enough to crack his jaw, he inhaled deeply, waiting for the coffee to finish. He wasn't functioning on all cylinders, needing a hearty dose of caffeine, especially after the prior night. He'd lain awake for hours, watching Maggie sleep.

"And?" He looked at the full cup of coffee that had just finished, wanting to chug it down, but he wasn't such a bastard he'd do it. No matter how strong the urge. Instead, he pushed it across the counter to Carlisle and popped another pod into the coffee maker, and stuck a mug into place, inhaling deeply again.

"None of them are in the country. Gustaffson was in Peru as of eight p.m. yesterday. Felix "The Cat" is in Paris. Dimitriev's in Moscow."

"Any word from Remy or Etienne?"

"More bad news. The bullet was so mangled when they dug it out, they couldn't get much of anything. So no ballistics, not even sure of the caliber."

"In other words, we're no closer to finding out who tried to take out Maggie than when we started."

Carlisle took a swig of his coffee, placing the mug back onto the counter. "I didn't say that." The smile on his lips reminded Gunner of a shark. Right before he took a big chomp out of his unsuspecting prey.

"Don't keep me waiting. What've you got?"

"Remember that file I found at Maggie's company? The risks and rewards one?"

"Yeah."

"Well, in all the miles and miles of data, I finally uncovered something very interesting. A name." He picked up his cup, trying to hide his satisfied smirk behind its rim.

"Don't make me beat it out of you—because I will."

"Mason Alexander."

Gunner's mug stopped halfway to his lips. "Are you kidding me? Mason Alexander? Millionaire philanthropist, national goodwill ambassador to South Africa, best friend to the President of the United States Mason Alexander? The man who's predicted to be the next presidential candidate? That Mason Alexander?"

Carlisle's eyes widened slightly, and Gunner knew without turning Maggie stood behind him.

"Morning, darlin'. You heard everything?" Carlisle gave her a wink as she walked into the kitchen and grabbed the mug out of Gunner's hand, taking a sip. Her nose wrinkled at the black coffee.

"Yes. How's he involved?" Handing Gunner's cup back, she placed a french vanilla pod into the coffee maker, and leaned her hip against the counter. She looked all sexy and tousled, and Gunner fought the urge to toss Carlisle out the front door and spend the morning ravishing her. Instead, he'd have to be the grown up and deal with the problem at hand. Then he could make with the ravishment of Ms. Maggie Callahan.

"Mason Alexander has invested very heavily into EryX Pharmaceutical. It's not public knowledge, and it's been funneled through more than two dozen dummy corporations, but it's there if you look hard enough."

"He's a multi-millionaire, it's not surprising he'd be interested in investing in a company that has the potential of making billions of dollars on its latest drug, when it gets FDA approval and is placed on the market." Maggie's fingers tapped against the granite, and Gunner could practically see the gears turning in her brain.

"What happens to all that money if the drug doesn't get to market?" Carlisle posed the question.

"I—don't know. There's tons of money invested in research and development every year. It can take decades for some drugs to get approval."

"Which got me to thinking. What if there isn't really a drug being researched or tested? Could a company phony up a formula, apply for research funds, and never produce a viable product?"

Maggie's eyes widened when she realized where Carlisle was heading with his hypothesis. "Okay, wait a second. There really is a Somnolett. I've seen the patent applications, data, and test studies and protocols for that, along with the marketing plans. None of those came to fruition when the FDA turned down approval."

"But, what happens if there never was a second drug? You said they reformulated Somnolett, and started the process again."

"Right." Maggie smiled when Gunner started pacing in the small space between her and the peninsula where Carlisle stood.

"Follow me here. Let's say the R&D people are offered a good chunk of money, bonuses or whatever, to produce their reimagined formula. The company throws a ton of money into this new formula—only it doesn't exist. They set up a protocol or study, a small enough group they can manage it easily and document it's progress. Instead of giving them this new formula *which doesn't exist*—they are all given placebos."

"Because there is no new drug." Carlisle pipes in, and Gunner can hear the excitement in his voice.

"Exactly. When the study group results start coming in, and the data is collected, none of the patients show any improvement or even a decline, because they're basically taking sugar pills."

"Okay, it's unethical and probably highly illegal, but that doesn't explain why the participants are all dying."

"It's a cover-up." Carlisle's eyes sparkled with excitement. "Think about how each one died. Mostly accidental deaths—no autopsies. And because they were all under a physician's care, chances were good the docs would sign off on the no autopsy order, so no drug screening would be performed."

"Damn, it's all about the money. Millions and millions of dollars being swindled from the stockholders of EryX Pharmaceutical, causing the prices of other drugs to rise sharply to offset the huge losses. It's a vicious cycle—and it all boils down to greed." Gunner looked at Maggie's face, easily reading her stricken look. Biting back the string of curses he wanted to utter, he turned to Carlisle.

"Better wake up the boss. We've got work to do."

When they met up in the conference room, the first thing Gunner noticed was Dean Westin was missing. Matter of fact, he hadn't been there the night before, either. He couldn't help wondering where he'd taken off to, since his brother—*and didn't that take some getting used to*—seemed to want him to hang around.

"Let me get this straight. You think you've figured out what's going on at EryX Pharmaceutical?" The intensity of Carpenter's gaze had Gunner squirming in his chair, and he noticed the other two members of this fine conspiracy weren't exactly still as statues either.

"Came up with a pretty reasonable scenario, boss."

Carpenter tossed a marker toward Gunner, which he caught in midair. "Outline it for me."

Walking up to the big white-board, he wrote the company name at the top and drew a line down and wrote in Mason Alexander's name.

Carpenter only made it halfway to his chair before he sprang up at the sound of Alexander's name.

"Are you freaking kidding me? This all ties back to Mason Alexander?" Maggie watched as the big man doubled over, laughing hard enough he lost his balance, landing on the chair with a firm plop.

"Oh this is too good." He wiped away the tears from laughing so hard. "Guys, I swear, if you can prove Mason Alexander is behind this, I'm giving you the biggest bonuses in company history."

"Um...okay." Gunner turned back to the white-board and outlined the rest of what they'd figured out. There were still a few holes in the theory, but it was sound.

"I can't help wondering why they're still after Maggie." Gunner gave her a wink as he said it, and she blushed. Man, he loved seeing her cheeks light up with pink.

"I might have an answer for that." Dean Westin walked through the conference room door and tossed his cowboy hat onto an empty chair.

"What'd you find out?" Carpenter didn't look surprised to see his half-brother walk in like he owned the place. Gunner's brow wrinkled at the thought that maybe he did own half the place.

"Went back to Houston, did a little nosing around. Bought drinks for a security guard and a lab tech from EryX Pharmaceutical." He looked at Carlisle. "You might recognize them from our little outing the other night."

Carlisle rolled his eyes and waved his happy middle finger at Westin.

"Anyway, I've got a little something here for Maggie." He pulled out his cell phone. "I recorded several voices.

Figured you could listen, see if any of them match up with the two men you heard outside your office."

Maggie sat up straighter in her chair. "I can do that."

Westin laid the phone down on the conference room table, and paused with his finger over a button. "Let me apologize in advance. No disrespect to your friend, Caitlyn, but I needed a topic to get them to open up." He grimaced and swiped his finger across the screen.

"Damn right, I want a piece of that. She's got the best rack in the company. I want to wrap my hands around those..." The voice droned on, talking about all the various ways he'd like to sexually subjugate poor Caitlyn. Gunner watched Maggie close her eyes, her hands balled into fists on the edge of the table.

"That sounds like the pudgy one. He's quite the determined little stalker," Carlisle remarked. "He's one of the two who came into Caitlyn's office while we were there."

"He's definitely one of the two men I heard. Who could forget that nasally whine, though I never saw his face. But I'm sure he was one of the men."

"I hate to say it, but keep listening. There are a couple of other voices I'd like you to check out." Westin continued the recording.

"I don't get your fascination for her. Now if it was that pretty redhead in marketing, I'd love to take her for a spin."

Gunner flung the marker across the room. That jackass was talking about Maggie. His Maggie. His eyes met Westin's, and the other man nodded. Good. They'd make sure this guy never badmouthed another lady again.

"She's definitely hot, but if you want some action, go see Robin in R&D. I've heard she'll screw anything with a penis, and she doesn't mind threesomes either." Coarse laughter spilled from the phone. "Course, you'll have to catch her before she gets behind those locked doors, or you're SOL."

Westin stopped the playback. "Did either of those voices sound familiar?"

Maggie nodded. "Not the last guy, though he's a sexist pig. The one before him."

"Are you sure, Maggie? I need you to be one hundred percent positive." Carpenter leaned forward in his chair, and Gunner could practically feel the excitement radiating from his boss.

"I'm positive. Those two men are the ones I heard outside my office, talking about the company killing those people."

Gunner hadn't noticed Carlisle typing on his laptop. He'd become so inured to the sight, it didn't even register anymore.

"Well, the good news is, we've got an ID on both men. I scanned through the company Human Resources program, and located the photo ID's on both. Larry Donohue is pudgy guy. Low level lab tech, been there for about eight years. Hasn't advanced very far up the ranks. Keeps getting passed over for promotion. He only filed a complaint once, about two years ago."

He grabbed his can of soda, and took a long swig, before hitting a couple more keys. "The other guy, tall and skinny, is Kevin Bacon. Seriously," he paused while everybody in the room laughed, "that really is his name. No relation to the actor. Security guard, been with EryX for six years. Now, Mr. Bacon stayed in the main security pool for three years, before suddenly having a fairly meteoric rise through the ranks to a senior position. He's got clearance for all levels in the building including...Maggie's floor."

"But how would they know anything about what's going on with Somnolett?" Andrea, who'd sat quietly through most of the discussion, posed the question.

"Doesn't matter, we'll figure it out. I'm more interested in what Mason Alexander has to do with all this. Gunner, let's get back to your theory."

Westin snatched up his phone and hat, turning to leave.

"Where the hell do you think you're going?" Carpenter barked the question.

Westin shrugged. "Did my job. Figured I'd head back to Austin."

"Sit. Stay. Good boy. Ouch!" Carpenter rubbed the back of his head, where his fiancée had just smacked him.

"Thanks, babe." Westin grinned at her.

"Can we please focus, people? We need to figure this out so Maggie's out of danger." Gunner picked up another marker and turned back to the infernal white-board.

"As I started to say, Carlisle's digging shows Mason Alexander has funneled money into EryX Pharmaceutical through several dummy corporations. The big question is why?"

"Because he's a..." The rest of Carpenter's answer was muffled by Andrea's hand over his mouth.

"Go on, Gunner." She grinned, leaning over the back of Carpenter's chair.

"Let's look at it like this. EryX Pharmaceutical is at the top of the food chain. They have the most risk with research and development of new drugs, because so few of them actually make it into the marketplace and engender a huge return on investment."

"With you so far, big guy." Westin sat slouched in his chair, with his hands crossed over his abdomen, the same way Gunner had seen Carpenter do a thousand times. It was eerily familiar, because Carpenter's posture at that moment was like a bookend, the only difference Andrea leaning over his shoulder.

"The company has a huge base of stockholders expecting a profit, and if research has fallen behind or isn't producing fast enough, the prices of the other drugs are raised to cover the deficit. But, what if a huge chunk of that money never actually made it into the company's coffers to begin with?"

"Prime example, Somnolett. R&D comes up with a formula for a sleep aid which, if successful, can make the company millions, if not billions, of dollars. But they get shot down by the FDA because there were too many problems, bad side effects, or whatever." Carlisle picked up where Gunner left off.

"The company doesn't want to abandon all the money they've already put into the drug, right? So they change the formula just a little, and apply for FDA approval again, and start tests. Brand new participants. Brand new studies. Brand new cash flow pouring in."

Everyone was following intently, so to keep the flow going, Gunner drew a dollar sign on the white-board.

"Except, they didn't actually produce anything. No new drugs were ever developed. They compiled phony data for the new formulation, changing around figures from the last study. Set up a controlled study group, and gave the participants placebos. Sugar pills. Every single one of them came in thinking they were taking part in a fully funded study. Wait…Maggie, do the people who participate in these studies get paid?"

"Sometimes. Depends on the type of study protocol being done. Usually just a stipend, a couple hundred bucks." Gunner could see her piecing together where he was going.

"If they got paid, there would be a paper trail. I'm not sure, maybe the FDA or somebody started asking for results, and somebody panicked, because they didn't have all the data falsified yet. But for whatever reason, they needed to wipe out all evidence of this particular study group. Which meant eliminating anybody who could be tied back to Somnolett or EryX."

"Again, how does Mason Alexander tie into this?" Carpenter narrowed his gaze at everything Gunner had written on the board. He stood and walked over, taking the marker from Gunner. "I'm starting to see it. Let's say for whatever reason, somebody with clout starts asking questions. Everybody involved with Somnolett from the top down is in a mad scramble to cover their tracks, and make the whole thing disappear. Idiots. You can never hide something this big." He tapped the marker repeatedly beside Alexander's name. "But, you have somebody like Mason Alexander tied in, owning a good chunk of a company like EryX Pharmaceutical. He's planning a presidential run as soon as he can legitimately throw his hat into the ring."

"I thought Mason Alexander was squeaky clean." Westin added, a puzzled expression crossing his face.

"Yeah, that's what everybody thinks. Too bad I know better. And with this," Carpenter tapped the marker against the name again, "the scandal would be big enough to keep him out of the White House."

"You're saying people have died because Mason doesn't want to be associated with EryX Pharmaceutical?" Andrea asked.

"Mason wouldn't deign to get his hands dirty. He'd have no problem hiring somebody else to do the job of eliminating anybody standing in his way." Carpenter paused, looking at each person in the room. "It wouldn't be the first time, either."

The room fell silent at his words, and Gunner absorbed the fact that Maggie's life had been placed in danger because somebody wanted to keep his hands clean. Oh, yeah, the man had to pay.

"We need to trace the money." Maggie stood and walked to the white-board, taking the marker out of Carpenter's hand. "If we follow the money trail, we can expose just about anybody involved with this." She started writing. "First we need to determine if this was a paid study. Since this was a drug that wasn't for treatment of a life-threatening illness like cancer, they could have had people who volunteered for the study in return for compensation."

"Like those commercials you see on TV and hear on the radio? Participants may be compensated and all their medical testing paid for? I hear those all the time." Andrea moved around to sit in the chair Carpenter had vacated.

"Exactly." Maggie wrote another item. "Find out how much money was directed toward research and development of the second formulation of Somnolett. If we're right and no actual funds were spent, that money had to go somewhere."

"We look for large outlays of funds, especially cash. Check bank accounts for people like the two men Maggie identified."

"Give me some time and I'll check their financials. Shouldn't take too long." Carlisle grinned. "Not sure how we're gonna get the figures from EryX Pharmaceutical."

Maggie took a deep breath and faced Carpenter. "Any chance you can give Caitlyn a job—because if she helps us, she's going to get fired. Or tossed in jail."

Carpenter chuckled. "Trust me, she won't spend a day behind bars. And I'll make sure she has another job, if she wants it."

"Okay. Right." Maggie drew in a deep breath, and blew it out. "Looks like we've got a plan. Now let's take these bastards down once and for all."

Chapter Twenty-One

"I am so getting fired." Caitlyn Keyes swiped her key card through the scanner, glancing once more at Dean Westin. She'd been terrified after she'd loaned out her key card the first time, knowing she'd get called into Human Resources and fired—or worse. But when Maggie had called and pleaded with her for help, she couldn't turn her back, not if people were really being killed on the orders of somebody at EryX Pharmaceutical.

So, here she was again, trusting Maggie to pull her ass out of the fire if they got caught.

"Just act natural, darlin'. If anybody asks, I'm your boyfriend, dropping you off because you had car trouble."

"Like they're gonna believe that," she mumbled under her breath. A little mouse like her, who tended to blend into the background wouldn't be dating a studmuffin like Dean Westin.

Yanking the glass door open, she sped through, heading straight for the guard desk. She'd have to sign her guest in—nobody was allowed on the premises without authorization. There'd been another companywide memo just last week about unauthorized visitors. She snickered. *Yeah, I bet they're concerned about strangers accessing the company, including Mr.*

Hottie here and his pal, Mr. Surfer Dude, thanks to me handing over my key card for a little extracurricular B&E.

She latched onto Dean's hand, pulling him toward the bank of elevators for the employee entrance. The faster they got this done, the sooner she'd move on with the next phase of her life. *Whatever that is.* At least Samuel Carpenter assured her she'd have a job. Fingers crossed, phase two would be a little more fun than stage one, because it sure couldn't be any worse.

Several people crowded onto the elevator with them, and she hit the button for the sixth floor. When Dean slid his arm around her shoulders and pulled her against his side, she forced a smile, even though she felt like there was a huge neon sign over her head screaming *look at me, I'm a big fraud.*

"You're doing great, darlin'. Just a little while longer, and it'll all be over," Westin whispered in her ear. The hot breath brushing along her cheek sent a shiver of need spiraling through her.

She blew out, ruffling the bangs across her forehead. It wasn't that she was afraid—much—she trusted Maggie. But the guy standing next to her, with his arm draped casually around her shoulder? There was something about him that set off all kinds of alarm bells. Part of her was screaming *danger, danger, danger!* The other part was standing up singing the hallelujah chorus, and chanting *let's do the horizontal mambo with Mr. Sexy.*

The elevator dinged and she weaved her way through the bodies still crowded around the front of the cramped space, and stepped into the hall, making a beeline for her door.

With a flick of her wrist, the key card unlocked it, and she stepped inside, only to stop dead in her tracks, Westin close on her heels. Her boss and one of the security guards stood like twin pillars beside her desk. A cardboard box sat on her office chair, half-filled with her personal belongings, in a haphazard mess, like somebody had swept their hand along the top of the desk, and scooped everything into one pile.

"What's going on?"

Westin's hands rested on her shoulders, and she couldn't help being grateful he was there. The gleam in her boss's eyes was clear enough. Somehow they'd either discovered her little foray into company espionage, or suspected something. Didn't matter which—she was busted.

Darn it, Mr. Carpenter had assured her his computer guy...what was his name? She kept calling him Mr. Surfer Dude—they'd assured her that he'd covered his tracks, and nobody would discover her key card had been used to access the building after hours.

Looks like I'm fired.

"Is there a problem?" Westin's deep voice reverberated in her ear, his arm still secure around her shoulders. And wasn't she glad he was there?

"Ms. Keyes, I'd like a word with you—in private." Her boss gestured toward his open door.

"I...I"

"Whatever you have to say to her, you can say it in front of me. I'm her fiancé." Caitlyn did her best to school her features, though the jolt of shock rocketing through her had her knees feeling like limp strands of spaghetti. *Fiancé?*

A huge grin spread across her boss's face. "Congratulations! I didn't know you were engaged."

"It was rather sudden," Caitlyn whispered, her gaze ping-ponging between Westin and her boss.

"Why are Caitlyn's things packed? Is there a problem?" Dean's deep voice rumbled, his hand still resting lightly around her shoulder.

"Um, there appears to have been a…misunderstanding. I'm sure we'll get it straightened out, and everything will be fine." Her boss turned to the security guard. "We no longer need you."

The guard frowned. "Are you sure? HR said…"

"Never mind what HR said. I'll handle them." He turned, a sunny smile pasted on his lips. "Caitlyn, if you and your fiancé will come into my office, we can get this minor inconsistency resolved, and get things back to normal."

She turned her head to look at Dean, not sure what to do. They'd planned to quickly get in, get out, leaving a letter of resignation on her desk. Now things were topsy-turvy, and she wasn't sure which way was up.

Westin gave a slight nod, and she turned back to her boss. "Um, okay. Let's straighten up whatever the issue is."

He ushered them into his office, Westin close behind her. Close enough she could feel the comforting warmth radiating from him. And how strange was that feeling? This man that she barely knew made her feel safe, even in the midst of all the chaos.

Once they sat, her boss dove right in. "There's been some sort of mix-up with your key card, Caitlyn. The computer shows you came back to work after hours on Friday evening. You didn't come back into the office, did you?"

She opened her mouth to deny her presence, which technically was the truth. She hadn't been in the office. Westin and his partner, Surfer Dude the computer geek, had been. Before she could answer, Westin reached over and squeezed her hand.

"Caitlyn couldn't have been here then. That's the night we got engaged. We were rather…occupied the entire night."

Caitlyn felt the heat rush into her cheeks at her boss's stare. Wow, who knew Dean Westin could tell such a whopper with a straight face?

"Could anybody have had access to your key card?" Her boss fumbled with his tie, unbuttoning the top button of his dress shirt, looking flustered.

"I don't see how," she answered, doing her best to keep her voice from cracking, something that happened whenever she told a lie. "Nobody could have used my card without my authorization. Besides, as Dean told you, we were busy that night, and my card was in my purse the whole time."

Huffing out a long sigh, her boss watched her, his intense stare making her want to squirm in her chair. But if she gave in to nerves, she'd blow their entire operation out of the water, and they'd never catch the bad guy. She couldn't live with a clear conscience if more people died because she couldn't lie worth a damn.

"I told HR there had to be a reasonable explanation. It had to be a computer glitch. You've never given me any trouble, and your work is exemplary. Thank you for clearing the issue up."

He stood, and Caitlyn raised her hand, stopping him. "Actually, there's a reason why Dean is with me this morning." Glancing toward him, she saw the approval in his gaze, which bolstered her confidence. "I'm sorry to leave you on such short notice, but I'm quitting."

"What?" Surprise marred his ruddy complexion. "I assure you, Caitlyn, there won't be any black marks on your record. This little incident will be forgotten—"

"No, that's not it. I—we're eloping." She offered up the excuse they'd decided on that morning. It was an improbable scenario, but the only one that made sense in light of her needing to leave without arousing any suspicion. Kind of a moot point, really, since they'd already found the computer irregularity.

"Eloping! But..I...you..."

"I understand I'm not giving any notice, but we can't wait, if you know what I mean." She added the little extra lie, figuring she'd embellish a bit to make the story more believable. Westin's body stiffened beside her, though if she hadn't been looking for it, she'd probably have missed it.

"Oh, dear. I mean, congratulations. Mazel tov! I'm happy for you. If you ever want to come back, please don't hesitate to call me."

Caitlyn smiled. "Well, on the bright side, my stuff is already packed." Standing, she leaned forward and held her hand out. "I've enjoyed working here. Thank you for the opportunity."

Without another word, she turned and walked out of the office, Westin at her back. He lifted the box as if it weighed nothing, and she laid the resignation letter and her key card on the desk's empty surface.

"You ready?"

She took one last look around the office, the place where she'd spent the last few years and felt only a twinge of regret. She was leaving the safe and stable life she'd envisioned for the unknown. Starting a new chapter filled with possibilities, and for the first time, felt a thrill of excitement course through her veins.

"New life, here I come."

Chapter Twenty-Two

Maggie rubbed her eyes, then squeezed the bridge of her nose, trying to ease the tension headache building in the background. She'd been staring at numbers for hours, scouring the company's spreadsheets, trying to find any clue their theory was on target. So far they had bupkiss.

"Take a break, hon." Gunner walked up behind her and began massaging her neck, his thumbs digging into the tight muscles. Her groan turned into a moan of pure bliss as he worked out the kinks from sitting hunched over her laptop. With all her studies into forensic accounting, she knew the work was long hours of tediousness, but they didn't have the luxury of time on their side. Not if they wanted to stop Mason Alexander and his cronies from absconding with millions of dollars.

Who'd have thought that one of the most respected men in the country was actually a death dealer, willing to sacrifice innocent human beings all for the sake of greed?

"I can't take a break. The answer's here, I just need to find it." She reached for the mouse, and Gunner's hand covered hers, pulling it back, before tugging her from the chair.

"Sweetheart, you've been at this for almost seven hours

without a break. You need to get up, walk around a bit. Get the blood flowing."

"Seven hours?"

He nodded. "Bet you didn't even stop for lunch, did you?"

Uh oh. He didn't look too happy about that, but she wouldn't lie. It wasn't worth the effort.

"I lost track of time." She arched her back, realizing he was right. While she'd been slogging away, her muscles stiffened to the point she needed to move around, especially if she planned to get right back on the computer after her short break.

"Let's make a deal. I'll order in some dinner, if you'll agree to take a break until it gets here—and eat everything on your plate. Then you can go back to crunching the numbers. Okay?"

She bent over and stretched toward the floor, bouncing a bit to loosen up the muscles. "Can we have pizza?"

He laughed. "You still like Hawaiian style?"

Her answering nod had him grimacing. "Okay, pizza it is. Hawaiian for you and meat lovers for me."

He pulled out his phone and placed the order, and she meandered to the kitchen, pulling down out a bottle of pinot from his wine rack, and poured two glasses.

Turning around, she handed him one, and took a sip of hers. "It's good."

"I took a wine-tasting class a couple of years ago, because apparently I'm a barbarian who didn't drink anything but beer. It was more of a dare from one of the guys on the team, but I found a couple of them I liked."

Walking around him, she crossed over to the window and stared out at the New Orleans view. He'd taken her up to Carpenter's rooftop terrace a couple of days ago, and while she'd appreciated the bridge in the distance, she liked the cityscape visible from his east-facing windows better.

"Food shouldn't take long." He walked up to stand behind her, not too close, but close enough she caught a whiff of the subtle aftershave he'd used. It wasn't the same one he'd used when they'd met. It, like him, had changed over the years, and that subtle difference reinforced the passage of time and distance between them. A reminder each moment time was temporary. Maybe she should grab onto it with both hands, and make memories to store away for those long lonely nights to come—when Gunner walked out of her life for good.

"I'm missing something important. I feel like it's staring me in the face, right in front of me, and I'm not seeing it."

He slid an arm around her middle, pulling her back against his body, and rested his chin atop her head. "Stop worrying so much. You'll figure it out."

Standing in silence, with him a solid warmth at her back, she tried putting aside EryX and everything associated with it, and simply enjoyed the moment. In the arms of the man she'd grown to love all over again. What had begun as an infatuation with a boy on the brink of manhood had morphed and evolved once she'd reconnected with him, and blossomed into what she knew was the love of a lifetime.

His cell beeped, and the arm looped around her middle

loosened. "That'll be dinner. I'll head down and pick it up. Be right back."

She exhaled the breath she'd held as he walked through the door. *What is wrong with me? I'm mooning over the man like I'm the one who's a teenager again. This can't go anywhere.*

But don't you want it too? That little voice in the back of her head whispered. *Take a chance. Live a little. What do you have to lose?*

"Just my heart."

Swallowing down the rest of her wine, she stomped to the kitchen and refilled her glass, topping off Gunner's too, which he'd left on the counter.

The front door opened. "Food's here."

"Great," she answered. "I'm starving."

"Grab a couple napkins, and we'll eat in the living room."

She did, and Gunner opened the lids on the two boxes. The amazing scent of tomatoes, cheese, and sausage hit her first, followed by the yeasty smell of the crust. Her stomach rumbled, reminding her she'd missed lunch.

She grabbed a slice loaded with ham and pineapple, laughing when he shuddered.

"How can you eat pineapple on that? Ruins a perfectly good pizza."

"Don't knock it until you've tried it." She lifted up a chunk of one of the pineapple rings and popped it into her mouth, almost choking on her laughter when he made a gagging sound.

"That's just…"

"Delicious? Yes, it is." She sank her teeth into the crust, pulling off a big piece and stuffing it into her mouth. "Yuf wamf somfth?" She waved the half-eaten piece of pizza in front of his face, nearly choking at his expression of disgust.

"Hell, no. I swear, any red-blooded Italian is cringing at the thought of that monstrosity you're eating."

"Aw, is the big guy scared of a little piece of pineapple?" Her grin turned mischievous. "Come on—I dare ya. Just one bite."

He eyed the new piece she held up, her hand highlighting it in her best Vanna White imitation.

"But it's pineapple—on a pizza. Pineapple belongs in fruit salad or in a smoothie, not on an Italian masterpiece." His petulant tone had her giggling.

"Bawk…bawk…bawk." Another giggle escaped at the disgruntled expression crossing his face, right before he grabbed the slice from her hand.

"One bite, that's it. Deal?"

"It has to be a good bite, not just a tiny nibble. You gotta make sure you get the pineapple and the ham into your mouth and swallow it, or it doesn't count."

"What do I get if I take a bite?"

Hmm, maybe she hadn't thought this through enough, judging from the wicked glint in his eyes. But she'd started this, now she had to finish it.

"What do you want?"

"A kiss." His answer was immediate.

"That seems—fair." Her insides were doing the happy dance. Oh, yes, this was such a good idea. Little tingles skittered down her spine in anticipation.

He eyed the pizza, turning it left and right, even going so far as to look at the bottom of the crust, like it was going to sprout horns or something. Finally, with an aggrieved sigh, he shoved the pointed end in his mouth, taking an enormous bite. And began chewing. And chewing.

"It's good, right?"

His eyes narrowed while he continued chewing the bite, before he finally swallowed. Staring at the piece in his hand, he glared at it, as if it had caused him a personal affront.

"It's okay." Lifting his eyes from the slice to hers, he grinned. "Okay, I confess, it's actually pretty good."

She did the little booty celebration dance on the sofa, wiggling from side to side and holding her hands above her head. "Told ya!"

Her celebration was cut short when Gunner tossed the remainder of the slice back into the box, and yanked Maggie across his lap, straddling his legs, and she squealed, still laughing.

"Hey! I was eating."

"Who's stopping you?" He picked up her half-eaten piece and held it to her lips. "Bite."

Huffing out a breath, she clamped her teeth onto the pizza slice, chewed slowly, and swallowed, her eyes never leaving his.

When his hand moved up to cup her cheek, she leaned into his touch, closing her eyes and letting the sensations wash through her. It was the moments like this that she'd missed when he'd headed off to boot camp. The shared enjoyment of each other's company, laughing and touching—and loving.

"You owe me a kiss." The words were whispered beside her ear. His warm breath sent a coil of need spiraling through her.

Don't do this. Don't fall into the trap of wanting him again. You need to be strong. Fearless and independent.

"A kiss? You want your kiss?" She ran her fingertips along his lower lip, barely touching, yet tantalizing. His tongue peeked out between his lips, moistening them in anticipation.

"Close your eyes."

He eyed her skeptically for a long beat before closing his eyes. She cupped both his cheeks between her palms and tilted his head upward. Leaning closer, she could feel his warm breath against her skin.

"You ready?"

"Oh, yeah."

"Okay then."

With a precise move, she placed a warm, wet, and very loud kiss against his forehead, jumping off his lap and dancing out of his reach, laughing.

"What was that?"

"Well, you asked for a kiss, big guy. You didn't specify where I had to kiss you."

He chuckled. "You win—this time. But I'm onto your sneaky ways now, so watch out."

"You snooze, you lose." She grabbed her half-eaten slice of pizza. "Now I've got to get back to those books and figure out who cooked 'em and how to take 'em down."

"Go get them, hon." He grabbed another slice out of the box, and she snickered, noting it was one of the Hawaiian ones. She'd make a convert of him yet.

Now, to figure out where the money trail led, and catch a killer.

Chapter Twenty-Three

"I got it!" Those were Carlisle's first words when Gunner answered the pounding knock on his front door. "Broke the encryption on the files. Once I did that, figuring out the code for the study participants' physicians and their addresses was a piece of cake."

"You, my friend, are a genius." Gunner stepped aside and Carlisle strolled in like he owned the place. That was the way it worked with pretty much all the guys on the team. Things might change when Nate came back. He had a woman in his life, but the rest of the time the guys pretty much made themselves at home in whoever's apartment they happened to be in at any given moment.

"It's why the boss pays me the big bucks." He grinned when Gunner shot him the middle finger, and continued. "We were right, by the way. Every single person on the study was given a placebo, according to the pharmacy records. The drugs were sent from EryX Pharmaceutical directly to the participating physicians. Even they didn't know whether the patient was taking the actual drug or a placebo. Only the pharmacist at EryX did. This whole thing has been nothing but hocus pocus and trickery. Smoke and mirrors. R&D's records show they never manufactured a single run of the new formula."

Gunner looked over his shoulder, watching for Maggie. She'd been headed for the shower, so they might have a few minutes to talk before she finished.

"Is there anything we can do to ensure Maggie's name stays out of this? Keep her safe?"

Thinking about somebody coming after Maggie once the smoke cleared was like a knife in his gut. When the news of EryX Pharmaceutical's deception broke in the media, he anticipated the vultures of the press to descend on her en masse if they weren't able to keep her part in exposing EryX Pharmaceutical quiet.

"I think the best we can do is minimize the fallout. When these powerful people go to trial, she's going to be subpoenaed. She'll have to testify, and we both know that's going to put a giant bull's-eye right in the center of her forehead."

Gunner glanced down the hall again.

"If I ask you for a favor, can you keep it quiet?"

"Of course." Carlisle's response was immediate.

"You can't even tell Carpenter."

Carlisle paused, studying him for a long time. "I know when to keep my mouth shut."

He exhaled, debating his backup plan. He didn't want to force Carlisle into a position of divided loyalties. The man had been with Carpenter longer than he had. Maybe he'd be better off going through different channels.

"Don't give me that look. Spill it." Carlisle crossed his arms across his chest, a mulish set to his mouth, and Gunner knew he really didn't have a choice. Not if he wanted this done right.

"I need to get new identities—for Maggie and me. Passports, the works."

"Son of a...I knew your stubborn ass would see that as your only option."

"Can you do it or not?"

"I can—but I won't. Gunner, think about what you're asking. Dude, this is something you can't come back from."

Gunner shook his head. "I won't let them hurt Maggie. I can't. She's...everything."

Carlisle studied him, his head cocked to the side. Finally, after what seemed like forever, he nodded.

"I'll do it. But, it's the last resort, got it? We can't afford to lose you. Hell, I can't afford to lose you, you giant ass."

Carlisle shocked the hell out of him by putting his arms around Gunner, hugging him. Truthfully, he'd always considered himself closer to Carlisle than anybody else on the team, even his partner, Nate. Guess Stefan felt the same.

Taking a step back, Carlisle chuckled. "I think we just had one of those chick-flick moments."

"Yeah, well, don't let it happen again, jackass."

"Back at ya, jerk."

Gunner heard footsteps coming down the hall moments before Maggie came into the living room.

"Hi, Stefan. Any news?"

Carlisle grinned, grabbed Maggie around the waist and lifted her off the ground, swinging her around. "I broke the encryption."

Maggie squealed. "That's awesome!"

He lowered her to her feet. "We were right, the second formula was never used. But the good news is, the cleanup can begin, and everybody can breathe safely again—well soon, anyway."

Gunner walked over and slid his arm around Maggie's waist. "It's almost over, honey."

"The boss is headed for New York as we speak. Gonna meet up with Mason Alexander face-to-face. Get a feel for how deep he's into this mess. You ask me, I think he's up to his eyeballs and sinking fast."

"Is it dangerous, Stefan? Carpenter meeting with Mr. Alexander, I mean."

"Nah, the boss can take care of himself. Plus he's got Andrea for backup." He gave Gunner a little salute and turned for the door. "I'm out. You kids have fun."

Gunner heard him laughing as he closed the door behind him. Maggie turned and draped her arms around his neck.

"It's almost over."

"Pretty much. Lots of dealing with the government, tons of paperwork. But, yes, things will get back to normal soon."

Pulling her closer, he rested his chin on the top of her head and wondered how his life would ever be the same. Because come hell or high water, he wasn't losing Maggie— ever again—even if it meant leaving everything behind and running.

Chapter Twenty-Four

Mason Alexander stood in front of the floor-to-ceiling windows of his Manhattan office, gazing out at the world beneath him. The entire expanse before him, with all the busy people skittering around in their menial nine to five jobs—if they only knew the power he wielded over them. They were mere cogs in the machine, the fuel that powered the engine. But the engine and everything in it belonged to him. He didn't need to have an exaggerated idea of self-importance. Mason Alexander knew precisely who he was and the clout he wielded like the finest blade.

His administrative assistant moments earlier had buzzed the intercom, notifying him that Samuel Carpenter waited in the reception area, wanting to speak with him.

What the hell could he want?

The double doors swung inward, and Carpenter strode through. Typical of the arrogant ass, thinking he was so much better than anybody else. And it pissed him off that he hadn't been able to uncover any dirt to bring the smug bastard to heel. But he would. Nobody was that squeaky clean.

"Samuel, what a pleasant surprise. What can I do for you?" He strode forward, hand held out. Always maintain your position of power and authority over others, a lesson he'd learned long ago—at the hands and belt—of the strictest disciplinarian on the planet. His father.

"Alexander." Instead of shaking his hand, Carpenter walked past him and lowered down into one of the two chairs facing Mason's desk. *Jerk.*

"What do you know about EryX Pharmaceutical?" Carpenter leaned back in the chair, one ankle propped atop his knee, and steepled his fingers beneath his chin, the epitome of a relaxed businessman.

Deigning not to answer right away, Mason walked around his desk and eased onto his leather chair, once again striving for that position of authority. He'd be damned if he'd let a piss-ant like Samuel Carpenter get the upper hand.

"EryX? I don't know a lot about them, other than what I've read in the papers, and the usual scuttlebutt on Wall Street. Why the interest?"

Carpenter didn't answer right away, simply staring at him in that annoying way. Like he was gazing deep into his soul, and knew every secret. It made the skin on the back of his neck itch.

"No particular reason."

"Samuel, you didn't fly all the way to Manhattan for what, two minutes of conversation, without a purpose." Carpenter didn't do anything without a reason. He couldn't help wondering what the other man's agenda was—because if Carpenter took an interest in something, it usually meant millions of dollars in profits. Of course, if he started sticking his nose into EryX Pharmaceutical, chances were he'd stir up a hornet's nest of trouble, not only for Mason but others—and he couldn't allow that.

"You know me so well. There are rumors EryX Pharmaceutical is about to have a major breakthrough with one of the drugs they've had in testing. An opportunity too good to pass up. A little birdie told me you might know a bit about it, since several of your subsidiary companies hold shares in EryX."

Carpenter's smile reminded him of a shark, all big teeth, ready to chomp when you least expect it. He was one of the few men he didn't trust, because he didn't own him. Life to Mason was a chess game, and he liked to control all the pieces, ensuring he always won.

"I've got my fingers in lots of pies, Samuel. A subsidiary of mine, you said?"

"Primarily Benedetto Medical."

Though he didn't betray anything by word or deed, Mason felt the wave of excitement radiating from his young nemesis. The same kind of energy he felt whenever one of his investments was about to pay off—big.

"Benedetto? Hmm. I think we might have bought them out in a takeover a couple of years ago. Hold on, let me look."

Pulling out his keyboard tray, he pretended to type, his mind racing through the possibilities. Something was definitely fishy, because he knew first-hand that EryX hadn't made any damned breakthrough with any drugs, especially none in the testing stages.

"Yes, Benedetto Medical is a company we bought last

year, as a matter of fact." He leaned forward conspiratorially. "Between you and me, it was basically a tax write-off, because they were hemorrhaging money. If you've got any money in its stock, I'd consider selling—though you didn't hear that from me. Don't want to be accused of insider trading."

Carpenter chuckled, and Mason had to refrain from rolling his eyes. It was a good thing Carpenter inherited his money from family, because he'd never make a good poker player. Hmm, there was a thought, maybe he should invite him to one of his weekly games—he'd love to take Carpenter for a good chunk of change.

"Really? If it's doing that badly, would you consider selling it?"

"I don't think so." *At least not yet. I need it for a scapegoat when all hell breaks loose at EryX Pharmaceutical.*

"If you change your mind, let me know."

Carpenter stood and started for the door, and paused with his hand on the knob. "By the way, any word on Natalie?"

Mason felt the blood drain from his face. Nobody knew about Natalie, he'd made damned sure of it.

"Who?" Thankfully, his voice didn't crack, though he began to feel frozen deep in his core. If Carpenter suspected something, it was only a matter of time, because with his lousy security company, he'd keep scratching and digging below the surface until he uncovered all his buried secrets.

"Sorry, my mistake. See you around, Alexander." Without another word, he strode through the double doors, leaving them open behind him.

What an ass.

Collapsing into his chair, he couldn't help wondering why Carpenter had come snooping around asking questions about EryX.

Samuel Carpenter warranted watching. One wrong move, and Mason would have to eliminate his rival sooner than he'd anticipated.

On that pleasant thought, he buzzed his assistant and ordered lunch. Time to do a little digging of his own, and see if he could uncover any juicy dirt about the elusive Samuel Carpenter.

"He's in this up to the whites of his eyes." Stretching his legs out in the spacious limo, Samuel smiled softly when Andrea snuggled against his side. He hated letting her out of his sight for even a minute, but confronting Mason Alexander needed to be done alone. Besides, Alexander had a weakness for beautiful young women, and he didn't want that hound dog sniffing around his gal.

"Did he say anything useful?"

"Wasn't so much what he said. It was the look on his face when I mentioned EryX."

"Did he take the bait?"

Before they'd left New Orleans, they'd decided it might be a good idea to dangle a carrot in front of Mason Alexander's nose, with the offer to buy Benedetto Medical. Alexander had been honest when he said the company was on the verge of bankruptcy. Plus it had been smart to buy it as a tax write-off. The company had been in the red for the last several years. For the last two, it had been funneling a ton of money into EryX Pharmaceutical, specifically into research and development.

He'd left Maggie and Gunner back in New Orleans, scouring the financial reports, because it was very odd that a company on the verge of losing everything, had the where-withal to shovel buckets of money into another company.

"Benedetto Medical was mentioned. He's oh-so-sorry but he isn't selling right now. Though he did mention if I owned any stock in it, I'd be well-advised to dump it ASAP."

"Wish you'd been wearing a wire for that. We could've sicced the SEC on his ass."

Samuel chuckled. He loved Andrea's vicious side when she went into protective mode. And she'd decided Maggie needed protecting, which meant finding and taking out any threat. She'd been well-trained by the CIA, and had quickly become one of his finest assets.

"Don't worry, love. I put a bit of a scare into him."

Andrea pulled away and stared, a puzzled look on her face. "What kind of scare? Did you threaten him?"

"Nothing overt, so you don't have to worry. There's one particular skeleton rattling around in Mason Alexander's closet, which if it ever came to light, would not only curtail any chance for the White House, but also land him in prison for the rest of his life."

The sting from Andrea's punch to his arm hurt, all the more because it was unexpected.

"Hey!"

"You've got the kind of dirt that can take him out of the picture for good? Why is he still walking around?"

"Because, my love, I want them all. Not just Alexander, but all the people involved with the Somnolett cover-up. Mason may be the top dog, but there are others involved. If we don't take them down, who's to say they won't turn around and do the exact same thing again. More people could die."

She sighed before leaning back against his side. "I hate this. It seems like for every lousy cockroach we squash, a dozen more come crawling out of the woodwork."

He brushed a soft kiss against the top of her head. "Don't worry. Just consider me a big ole can of bug spray. The kind that kills them dead."

He could feel her whole body shaking beside him, her fist against her mouth to keep from laughing out loud. He loved that she got him—his sense of humor, his quirks. Everything. And loved him anyway.

"I think I deserve a good lunch, after dealing with that particular cockroach. Anyplace in particular you'd like?"

She quirked her finger, motioning him closer and leaned in to whisper in his ear, "How about room service?"

Chapter Twenty-Five

G unner watched Maggie hunker over the laptop, studying the numbers. She'd been at it for days. Long, unending days without much of a reprieve. They didn't make a lick of sense to him, but for her it was like looking at an intricate dance, each step leading to the next, to form the perfect choreography. At least that was how she explained it. As far as he could tell, it was all a bunch of gibberish.

"I think we need a break."

Her head popped up from behind the monitor, and she peered at him. "Huh?"

"That's it. Save your file, and put on your shoes. We're going for a walk."

"Gunner, I need to—"

"You need to get away from this," he swept his hand toward his table, where dozens of printed pages were spread across its gleaming surface, along with a box of highlight markers and a portable printer.

"I don't have time for a walk. I'm close, I can feel it."

"And you'll still be close when you get back, probably with a clear head from getting a little fresh air." Walking over, he put his hands on her shoulders, squeezing lightly. "You've been at this long enough, you need a break. We won't be gone long. A short walk to get the blood flowing and ease your stiff muscles."

With a heavy sigh, she saved her work and stood, looking under the table for the shoes she'd kicked off when she'd tucked her legs beneath her on the chair.

"Okay, but only for a little while. It's like I'm right there—the answer is close—I can feel it."

"Half an hour won't make much difference then. And you'll feel better getting out of my apartment."

They rode the elevator down to the lobby. Stephanie was behind the reception desk, on the phone with a client. Gunner waved as he ushered Maggie out the door.

Sliding his arm around her waist, they headed down Canal Street, looking at the buildings undergoing construction and refurbishing. It was going through its own mini-rejuvenation, bringing the older buildings back to their former glory.

"Thank you."

"No problem. I was going stir crazy, and I live there. Didn't want you to start feeling trapped."

"Gunner, you've never made me feel trapped. I've never been more free, more myself, than when I'm with you."

"Good. I like hearing that."

They walked another couple of blocks, before ducking into a bakery nestled between two taller buildings. The glass-fronted displays were filled with an assortment of sweet and savory pastries, breads and croissants. Gunner decided on a strawberry shortcake cupcake and a glass of lemonade. He watched Maggie debating between a chocolate turtle brownie and a slice of white chocolate raspberry cheesecake, so he ordered both along with a glass of sweet tea.

There were a couple of little bistro tables scattered by the big glass-paned windows emblazoned with the bakery's name, and a couple more outside on the sidewalk, beneath the awning.

"Hate to say it but we need to stay inside."

Shrugging, Maggie headed toward a table with her drink, and Gunner followed with the rest of their order, placing it on the table she'd chosen by the window.

The day was gorgeous with a brilliant blue sky and big puffy white clouds. It was warm, but not unbearably hot.

"This is nice. Feels like you're in a small town, even though you're in the middle of the city."

"It's one of the things I love about living here. There is such a variety of life here. No matter what you're looking for, New Orleans has it."

They ate their snack in relative silence, before Gunner noticed Maggie growing even quieter.

"What's wrong?"

She lowered her gaze to the table, and whispered, "Do you see those two men across the street? To the right a couple of doors down?"

Pretending to take a big sip of his lemonade, he studied the people across the street, noting immediately the ones she referred to.

"Yes."

"They've been watching us, ever since we sat down."

A frisson of awareness skittered along Gunner's spine.

"You sure?"

She nodded. "Positive. I think they've been following us ever since we left C.S.S."

"You're good. I didn't spot them until a couple of blocks ago."

"You knew they were there?"

He smiled and brought her hand to his lips, kissing the knuckles. "I knew. They work for C.S.S. That's Ranger and Sebastian Boudreau, Etienne's brothers."

Her shoulder's slumped. "I don't know if I should wave at them or punch you for not telling me."

"Sugar, I'm not letting anything happen to you."

Before he could say another word, she closed the small space between them and kissed him.

It wasn't a kiss that leads to hours in bed. There were no fireworks going off overhead. No, this was a simple, sweet kiss filled with tenderness and something else. Something more than he dared dream. This kiss was more than two people who'd once been lovers, and were testing their chemistry.

No. This kiss was filled with promise. An awakening of all those things he'd yearned for but never found without anybody but Maggie.

He finally pulled back, staring into her beautiful eyes, and could tell she was as confused by the simple kiss as he.

"Gunner, I…"

"Down!" The yell came from across the street. Acting on instinct, Gunner's body covered Maggie's, as he pushed her to the floor, shielding her. The *pop, pop, pop* sounded followed by the sound of breaking glass. Somebody was shooting at them in broad daylight, with dozens of people on the streets.

A white sedan sped away, with Ranger racing on foot behind it, phone in hand. Good man, he was trying to catch a photo of the plate. Carlisle could run it, see if they could get a hit.

"You okay?" Sebastian Boudreau leaned over, offering Gunner a hand. He eased off Maggie, pushing the hair off her face.

"You okay, honey?" Scanning her body, he didn't see any blood, no patches of red to show she'd been shot.

"I'm fine." Her eyes widened, and a trembling hand reached for him. "You're not though. You're bleeding."

"It's just a scratch."

"Gunner, you've been shot."

He shook his head. "Nope, a chunk of glass skinned across my arm. I'm fine. Promise."

Sebastian slid his gun into a shoulder holster beneath his windbreaker. Good thinking. It would be just like the cops to take one look at the ex-SEAL, spot the gun, and haul his ass in for questioning.

Ranger jogged up, phone still in his hand. "You recognize either one of these jerks?"

Maggie shook her head, but Gunner nodded. "Hell, yeah. Those are the two yahoos that grabbed me at the airport."

"They're either getting brave or desperate, taking pot-shots in public."

Sebastian glanced between Gunner and Maggie. "Makes me wonder who they were aiming for, the big guy or Ms. Callahan."

"Don't know, don't care. Let's get Maggie back to my place, before they decide to take a second chance."

Gunner gave the owner a card with his information, to pay for repairing the window. Then, the three men surrounded Maggie, with Ranger in front, Gunner at Maggie's side at street level, and Sebastian bringing up the rear.

The walk back wasn't the leisurely stroll they'd left with earlier. In less time than it had taken to get to the bakery, they were back behind the security of C.S.S., and back in his apartment.

Gunner thanked the other two team members, not only for their vigilance, but their quick response. Having two former Navy SEALs on the team definitely came in handy, even if they were squids.

"You need anything? I've got a bottle of whiskey…"

"I'm fine. Where's your first aid kit?"

He lifted a brow. "Under the bathroom sink."

Without another word, she walked away, returning a minute later with the white box.

"Sit. Let's get you cleaned up."

Crap. He'd forgotten all about the blood on his arm. Obviously Maggie hadn't. Honestly, he wasn't worried about a little scratch. He'd had a whole lot worse when he'd been a marine, serving his country.

"I can't believe somebody shot at us, right out on the street. Have they lost their minds?" Maggie's mumbles were barely audible, and Gunner knew she wasn't talking to him.

He winced when she wiped the scrape clean with an alcohol swab, before dabbing on some antibacterial ointment, and applying a Band-Aid.

"There." She snapped the first aid kit closed with an audible click. He reached over and caught her hand.

"Honey, it's okay. I'm not hurt, it's barely a scratch."

"If Ranger and Sebastian hadn't been there, it would have been more than a scratch. Don't you get it? This isn't going to stop."

Pulling her into his arms, he held her close, felt the shudders rocking through her. His hand slid up and down her spine in a slow caress. There wasn't anything sexual about it, it was meant to comfort and reassure her.

"Maggie, we will catch them. You've got the best minds in the business working this case. You'll figure out what EryX is hiding in the books, and we'll shut them down."

"I don't want you to die, Gunner. I couldn't bear it if I lost you again." Her words were mumbled against his chest, and soaked into him like rain onto parched earth.

"Mags, honey, you're not going to lose me. I won't lose you either. I'm not sure what divine force brought us back together, but not even the combined forces of Hell will drag me away from you ever again."

Tears swam in her gorgeous eyes, and her fingertips rose to touch his lips.

"I love you, Gunner. Maybe it's too soon, and you're not ready to hear it, but I won't deny or hide my feelings anymore. We could have died today, and you wouldn't have known how I feel."

The fist squeezing his heart eased and loosened with each word, and his whole being filled with warmth. He wasn't alone. The love he felt swept over him like a tsunami, pulling his heart along in its wake.

"Maggie Callahan, I love you. I fell in love with you when I was a boy, and the man that I am now loves you. Don't ever leave me."

"Never."

Their lips met, each kiss, each caress of lips and tongue was a vow, a promise, unspoken yet heard. His hands speared through her hair, angling her head and controlling the depth of the kiss, making love to her mouth.

She finally drew back, breathing deeply. "Wow. Who knew?"

"Me." He whispered against her nape. "I've always known, but I was afraid. Afraid to risk it all and be rejected."

He pulled her close, pressing her body against his tight enough he didn't know where he ended and she began. He buried his face in the curve of her throat, breathing in her scent, a subtle blend of gardenia and Maggie. Always beneath the surface, there was Maggie.

"I love you so much, Mags. Make love with me?"

Without hesitation, without another word, she stood, took his hand and led him down the hall.

Stopping in front of his bedroom door, she looked over her shoulder and smiled.

"Yes."

Chapter Twenty-Six

M aggie studied the laptop screen, before pulling a couple of the printed spreadsheet pages toward her, checking the highlighted sections. Darn it, why couldn't she figure out where the money had gone?

There were huge infusions of cash, lots of it, from multiple corporations connected with Mason Alexander, offshoots and subsidiaries of the company, pouring money into their research and development.

A good chunk of that money was earmarked for Somnolett. That, in and of itself, was unusual. Most of the time funds were dispersed into a general account, to be used on whichever project took precedent and needed an infusion of cash.

Something felt off about these books, because they were too clean, too pristine.

Maybe that was it. A good bookkeeper would make sure the numbers balanced, but wouldn't necessarily dig any deeper than that. Unfortunately, in today's economy, most people were overworked and underpaid, so they didn't have the time or the desire to dig deeper.

Yet there was this little niggling at the back of her brain, telling her she was looking right at the problem, except it wouldn't take shape. As much as she liked solving puzzles, unlike a jigsaw puzzle, she didn't have a pretty scenic picture to look at.

"How's it going?" Gunner walked to the table, and placed a quick kiss against her neck, before ambling to the kitchen, wearing only a pair of boxers. His hand scratched lazily against his stomach, and her eyes followed every movement.

"You want more coffee?"

"Ugh, no thanks. I feel like I've already OD'd on the stuff."

He popped a pod into the coffee maker, before grabbing a glass and filing it from the water dispenser in the fridge's door.

"Here." He plunked the glass down beside her laptop. "You gotta stay hydrated."

"Yes, sir." She gave him a mocking salute instead of waving her middle finger at him, which had been her first instinct.

"It's right in front of me. I know it, I can feel it. But the darn answer is eluding me."

"Wanna talk about it? Toss a few ideas around? Sometimes brainstorming it out loud helps to show the bigger picture."

Her hand dragged through her hair, twisting it into a knot at the base of her neck before letting it go. "Can't hurt."

"What's your gut telling you? You've been studying the numbers—if the answer's there, you've seen it."

"It's like everything is precise and orderly. Too perfect.

The exact amounts add up every time, down to the penny."

"I don't deal with numbers much. Isn't that how bookkeeping works? The numbers are supposed to balance."

"Yes, but not like this. You have the exact same amounts coming in and going out. Not at the same times, mind you, but when you add them all up, it's…"

She broke off, staring at one of the spreadsheets. "Gunner, that's it! Why didn't I see it?"

"What? I still don't get it."

"It has nothing to do with the drug, with Somnolett. It's all about the money."

"We knew the money was being funneled out into other people's pockets. That's why they've been killing off the people in the study, remember?"

"That's just it. The deaths are a smokescreen. To draw attention away from what's really going on."

Maggie stood up and threw her arms around Gunner's neck. "Can you get Carpenter? I only want to explain this once."

"Let me make a call." He walked back to the bedroom, presumably to get his phone. She couldn't believe it finally made sense. At least from the money end. The killings, as horrible as it sounded, were secondary to the real story.

"He'll be down in five minutes." Gunner walked back into the room, his phone in his hand.

Maggie grinned. "You might want to put on some pants before he gets here."

He rolled his eyes, before heading back down the hall, reappearing wearing pants, and pulling a T-shirt over his head.

Carpenter walked in, not bothering to knock. "What'd you find?"

"They're laundering money." Maggie announced, knowing they'd get it. "It's being moved around multiple places, but the figures are too pristine to be anything else."

"That makes perfect sense." The smile on Carpenter's face had Maggie grinning. She loved it when the puzzle pieces fell into place, but it was even better when somebody else understood what she'd found.

"Multiple companies are shifting funds into EryX's R&D division. That money is then earmarked specifically for Somnolett, which transfers it to another specific account. The money is then held in that account, supposedly to be used for the drug trials, the protocols, supplies, compounds, salaries, and everything else having to do with Somnolett."

"You've got a list of all the companies?"

"I'll get it for you. But I can tell you most of the money came in from companies that Carlisle has listed as belonging to Mason Alexander."

Carpenter's eyes lit. "We've got him."

"Is it going to be enough to arrest Alexander?" Gunner stood behind Maggie, placing his hands atop her shoulders. "I'm not letting Maggie stick her neck out if it's not. He's got too much money and way too much influence."

"We're not going to make any rash decisions here, Gunner." Carpenter nodded toward Maggie. "I'd never put your woman at risk. We make sure that every I is dotted and every T is crossed before we take this to the feds."

"I'll get you everything I can from the money aspect." Maggie's hand hovered over the printouts of the spreadsheets. "It's all here, and I'll get you enough documentation nobody can miss it."

With a nod, Carpenter headed toward the door, motioning Gunner to follow him. Maggie's teeth toyed with her bottom lip, wondering what Carpenter said to put that look of fury across Gunner's face.

Without another word, Carpenter left, and Gunner locked the door behind him. Without waiting for him to come to her, she stepped close, felt the heat radiating from his body.

"It's going to be okay, babe. Now that we're on the right track, it's only a matter of time before we'll take down Mason Alexander and everybody else involved with EryX Pharmaceutical."

"Can we get them all? Somebody always seems to fall through the cracks."

Her hand reached up to cup his cheek, rubbing against the slight scruff. Running her nails across it, it made a scratching sound, and she grinned.

"From everything I've read in my classes, and cases I've followed in the news, once you pull the legs out from beneath the key players, the rest of them start falling like dominos. We'll get them."

Without another word, she wrapped her arms around him, pressing as close as she could, and felt the slight tremor that ran through him.

"I don't care what it takes, hon, I need to keep you safe.

Screw Mason Alexander and the rest of them, let 'em rot. All I care about is you."

She leaned back enough to see the heat in his eyes. Knew he meant every word, and felt a warmth unfurl in her chest and spread throughout her body. Though he had said the words earlier, his actions now spoke loud and clear the one thing she wanted to hear.

He loved her.

Which was a good thing, because she loved him more than life itself. Had truly never stopped loving him. Though she'd been barely older than a teenager herself, she'd fallen fast and hard, and neither time nor distance had killed her feelings. They'd simply lain dormant, waiting to spring forth again.

"Nothing's going to happen to me, Gunner. I've got too much to live for, especially now." Taking his face between her hands, she tilted it until he was looking at her, their gazes locked.

"I said it before, and I'm saying it again. I love you, Wilson Everett."

Since her body was pressed against his, she felt the shudder course through him, watched his eyes widen at her words.

"Maggie, oh Maggie." He rested his forehead against hers. "I love you too."

"I'm so glad."

"How could I not love you? You're more than I ever dreamed possible. I can't believe I found you again, and that you're mine."

She laughed. "Well, technically, I found you again, but I know what you mean. We were always meant to be together. The first time wasn't the right time, but...it's funny. We're both different people and yet we're the same. You're still the one person I trust more than any other. The single soul in the whole universe who gets the real me—and loves me anyway."

The smile that lit his face was worth everything, and Maggie swore she'd do everything in her power to see that smile for the rest of her life.

"I need to make love to you, my Maggie."

Eyes closed, she let his words pour over her, like raindrops across a parched garden. There wasn't anything she wanted more than to be in his arms, but they had things to do and jerks to toss in jail.

"I want that too, my love, but we've got a job to do. People are still dying, and we've got to stop EryX Pharmaceutical."

"But..."

She chuckled at the pouty look on his face, though she knew he only did it for her benefit.

"Catch the bad guys first, then we'll spend the next week in bed, big guy." She couldn't resist pressing a kiss to his lips. Pouring everything she felt into that kiss. Every moment of hurt, despair, along with the joy and hope.

When Gunner started to deepen the kiss, she broke it, stepping back. "Huh-uh." She wagged a finger under his nose. "Go do whatever it is you need to do for Carpenter. I'm gonna hit the books again, and get him that list."

"Just so you know, I'll be back to collect on that promise."

"What promise?"

"The one in your kiss." He grabbed her before she could dart away, pressing a fierce kiss against her lips. "Lock the door behind me, and don't answer it for anybody. Got it?"

"I'd say yes, daddy, but I don't want a spanking." Watching the twinkle in his eyes, she knew she'd be paying for that taunt later.

"Brat." His finger twined around a lock of her hair before he let it slide loose, and headed for the door and walked out. Within seconds, there was a rap on the door, followed by a growled, "lock it."

Grinning, she turned the deadbolt.

"Good girl."

Chuckling, she headed back to her laptop. She had some bad guys to catch.

Chapter Twenty-Seven

"I think I've identified everybody in the Somnolett." Carlisle handed the list to Carpenter. "As of two hours ago, all of them are still alive."

"Let's see if we can't keep them that way." Carpenter's eyes scanned the list, and Gunner stood, leaning in the doorway, watching the exchange between the two men. This was one of the things he loved about working on the elite team for C.S.S. They'd gotten into such a rhythm working together, they could almost read each other's minds. He laughed silently. Yeah, it was like those old married couples, where they'd finish each other's sentences.

"You gonna put guards on all the remaining participants?"

Carpenter looked at him, nodding. "Looking at this list, we should be able to get them covered pretty quick. We have two in California, one in Minneapolis, one in Evansville, two in New York City, one in Fort Lauderdale, and another two in Miami. Three more in Texas."

"Not too bad. Austin can cover the Texas people. Send somebody from the Jacksonville office for the Florida cases." Gunner moved to the conference table, and plunked down into an empty chair.

"Sacramento can handle the California cases." Carlisle added. "The Midwest you're gonna have to fly people in."

"I'll call Dean, he can handle those."

Gunner quirked a brow at his boss. Now that he mentioned it, Westin had been scarce recently.

"He skipped out and went back to Texas. He's a sneaky bastard." He chuckled. "I think it was all Andrea's talk about bridesmaid dresses and hotel venues. I think it spooked him."

Gunner doubted that anything spooked Dean Westin, but kept his mouth shut. Now that he knew Maggie loved him, he'd give the guy a break, especially since it seemed Carpenter really liked the guy. He'd reserve judgment—for now.

"I've gotta say, Gunner, your Maggie has done a great job of figuring out the money laundering angle. We were so focused on the people dying, we couldn't see the forest for the trees."

A sense of pride filled him. Maggie had figured it out, and was even now upstairs working to gather the evidence needed to bring down Mason Alexander.

"She's brilliant." Carpenter leaned back in his chair, steepling his hands beneath his chin, and gave Gunner his big ole crocodile grin. "Anybody who can get the goods on Mason Alexander is great in my book."

"What do you have against the man, boss?" Carlisle leaned back in his chair, for once not focused solely on his computer screen. "I know the guy's a sleaze-bag, but this seems personal."

Carpenter was silent for so long, Gunner began to wonder if he was going to answer. When he did, his words chilled him to the bone.

"He killed someone."

"What? Why isn't he in jail?"

Carpenter slid his chair back enough he could prop his feet on the end of the table. "Several years ago, when I was a still wet-behind-the-ears DEA agent, I ran across a case. Nothing out of the ordinary, college kids partying. Although they were more affluent than your average college kid."

Gunner knew those were the kind of cases Carpenter liked to work on, because of his sister. When Lily had died of a drug overdose, having been lured to drugs by her roommate and his brother, both of whom were from a powerful, rich family, he'd committed himself to seeking out the more affluent drug peddlers. It didn't bring Lily back, but it helped to ease the hurt, and exposed the ugly truth about drug manufacturers and users not just being the poor and underprivileged."

"One of the young women I came across at that time was named Natalie St. Cloud. Pretty, young, and naïve. Headed for a good life with a college education. You know the kind of girl who'd work, have two or three kids by the time she was thirty, and be happily married."

"I take it Ms. St. Cloud didn't get her happily ever after?" There was an undercurrent in Carlisle's voice Gunner had never heard before, and it worried him.

Carlisle hadn't been the same ever since working a case a few months previous, where a young woman was held hostage. Though he and Ranger had been able to help in rescuing the woman, she'd paid an awful price. Carlisle was having a hard time letting go. He might have to take him out for a drink, see if there was anything he could do.

"In her junior year, Natalie became involved with an older man. Three guesses who. He was married at the time. The S.O.B. couldn't resist a pretty young thing like Natalie, who'd started working for him part time, to supplement the money for her classes and books."

The bitterness in Carpenter's voice ate at Gunner. He'd spent more than one night keeping his boss company, while finishing off a bottle of Jack Daniels, and hearing horror stories from the front lines. Made what he'd been through in the marines seem like a walk in the freaking park.

"Let me guess—she got knocked up?" Carlisle made a scoffing sound when Carpenter nodded. "It's like a bad romance novel plot twist."

"Yeah, well here's a plot twist for you. We found Natalie's body at a crack house. Supposedly she'd overdosed. Only we couldn't find anybody who believed it. Her family, her friends, her coworkers—nobody ever saw her take anything stronger than an aspirin, and even that was under protest. This girl was so clean, she squeaked."

"You think Alexander had something to do with it?"

"Hell, yeah. When I confronted him, he gloated. Taunted me, saying I'd never find the proof." Carpenter ran a hand through his blond hair, mussing it even more. "And he was right. I came damned close, but nothing that would hold up in a court of law. The one witness who could place

Alexander at the scene gave me a verbal statement, and then conveniently disappeared. His body was found weeks later."

"In other words, Mason Alexander is more dangerous than we imagined, and he won't be stopped. Not with his eyes set on sixteen hundred Pennsylvania Avenue." Gunner slumped in his chair.

"Mason's in for a surprise." The vicious gleam in Carpenter's eyes had Gunner straightening back up in his seat. He knew that look. The boss man had a plan.

"Whatever it is, I'm in." When Carpenter started to shake his head, Gunner held up his hand. "Maggie's life is on the line here. You will let me in—all the way in—or I'll go off on my own. You want me going rogue, fine, because keeping Maggie safe from this piece of filth is more important than my job."

"Put a sock in it, cowboy."

Carlisle snickered when Carpenter aimed finger guns toward Gunner.

"I didn't say you were out. But I'll need all the information Maggie's gathering to add to my own stash."

Stash?

"Let's just say the DEA and the FBI don't have all the evidence I collected. Since they weren't going to build a case against Mason, I figured I'd keep some of what I collected as a safeguard. Because sometimes, even with the best security, evidence has a way of disappearing."

Too true. Gunner saw it happen more than he'd like to admit. People with money tended to have more clout, and could pay bigger bribes.

"I'm in." Carlisle held up his hand, as if volunteering.

"What is this, first grade? Put your hand down, Geek Boy."

Gunner laughed at the nickname the team had given their computer expert years earlier. Dang, he loved these guys like brothers.

"Okay," Carpenter leaned forward, rubbing his hands together with Machiavellian glee. "Here's the plan."

Chapter Twenty-Eight

Maggie stood and stretched, pressing her hands against the small of her back. She'd been sitting hunched over the laptop for hours, but she was finally done.

Following the money trail, she'd been able to document every single transaction, where it originated, how long it was held in each account, and when and where it was electronically transferred. How this had gone on for so long was anybody's guess, but obviously enough people had been paid hush money to keep their mouths shut.

It didn't matter. There was more than enough evidence to take to the authorities, with most of the top players at EryX Pharmaceutical guilty of money laundering. And the man they'd been working for—Mason Alexander—was up to his eyeballs, since it was his money they'd been purportedly cleaning.

"It's over." She pinched herself, just to make sure she wasn't dreaming. Sticking a thumb drive into the port on her laptop, she copied all the information she'd gathered. She'd give it to Carlisle, so he could print it out. Plus she wanted to make sure there was a backup of her work—just in case.

The ringing of her cell phone had her smiling. It was the ringtone she'd put in for Gunner—Chances Are. It was an

KATHY IVAN

oldie, a classic, but they'd danced to it once over and over, and every time she'd heard it since, it reminded her of him.

"Hey, where are you?"

He chuckled. "French Quarter. I had to hand deliver some information to another client. That closes out everything I was working on, and now I can concentrate all my energy on you."

And didn't that send a little tingle racing through her? Gunner focused solely on her pleasure was a delightful thought.

"I finished. Getting ready to take the information and turn it over to Carlisle. It's his baby now, but there's enough to put a lot of people in prison for a long time, including Mason Alexander."

"Sweetheart, that's awesome!" She heard the pride in his voice, and it warmed her inside. Though she didn't need his approval, knowing she'd done something that helped the team coordinate a complete plan of attack gave her a feeling of accomplishment. It felt good to utilize the skills she'd been studying for so long, and making a major contribution to bringing down bad guys who were hurting others? That feeling was worth its weight in gold.

"We need to celebrate. Since it's early, I'll pick up some champagne and OJ, and some croissants from this little bakery I know, and we'll celebrate with mimosas. In bed."

Just like that she was hot and needy, and wanting him with an unquenchable fire. "I like that idea. I'll be waiting."

"Be back soon."

After hanging up, she headed to the door. The faster she

got this info to Carlisle, the quicker it was out of her hands and she could concentrate on the man who was fast becoming the center of her universe. And she didn't mind— not one bit.

Gunner strolled down through the French Quarter, heading for this little bistro he knew that made the flakiest croissants he'd ever eaten. Jean-Luc had taken him there the first time, and he'd been going back ever since. He couldn't wait to share them with Maggie. After he picked up the croissants, he had one more stop to get the champagne, and he'd head back.

He strode past the little tables grouped together outside the front door of Michel's Patisserie. The scents of freshly baked breads and pastries hit him the second he opened the door, and his stomach rumbled in anticipation.

"Mr. Gunner, a pleasure to see you again." Michel, the owner and principal baker, stood behind the counter, sliding a tray of chocolate croissants into the display case. "It's been a long time, my friend."

"It has. Work's kept me busy."

"What will it be today? No, wait here." Michel disappeared into the back, and Gunner knew he was in for a treat. He'd once done a favor for Michel, dealing with a bully who was threatening Michel's teenage daughter. Ever since, Michel made sure he got something special whenever he came to the bakery.

When he came out of the back, he had a white box in his

hand, with the bakery's logo imprinted on the top. "Here, you must try this."

"What is it?" Gunner started to lift the lid, and Michel swatted at his hand.

"No, no. Do not open until you are home. It is a surprise—but you will like it, I promise."

Gunner grinned. When Michel said something was good, he was guaranteed to like it. The hard part would be sneaking it into the building without setting off Ms. Willie's radar.

Reaching for his wallet, he stopped at the frown on Michel's face. Why was he surprised? The man hadn't let him pay for anything in ages.

"Thank you." Gunner leaned closer to the baker and whispered, "It's for my girl. I'm sure she'll love it."

The other man's face lit up with a huge smile. "Mr. Gunner, you have found that special someone? Mais oui, this is excellent news, my friend. Excellent news, indeed."

He thanked Michel and walked out, ready to make his final stop before heading back to the apartment. Humming a little, he nodded to the older woman walking past him in the opposite direction, a yappy dog tugging on its leash. A hand slapped against the back of his neck, and he started to turn, but his knees buckled, nearly dropping him to the ground.

An unfamiliar black sedan pulled up beside him, as the two men half dragged, half carried him toward it. The pastry box slipped from his hands, tumbling to the ground, its lid falling open. The last thing he saw were his favorite almond filled cookies scattered along the sidewalk.

Struggling against the two men was useless, and they tossed him into the trunk. The lid slammed shut with a bang, and his eyes rolled back in his head as darkness fell.

Chapter Twenty-Nine

Gunner looked around, trying to gauge where he'd ended up. The last time he'd opened his eyes, he'd been in a dark, black place. With the vibrations and thumps, he'd been pretty sure he was in the trunk of a car.

I have got to stop getting snatched off the street. Sheesh, how many times can one guy end up a hostage? This is getting really old.

Whoever opened the trunk had gotten a boot to the face, but it hadn't been enough, because he'd felt electricity shock through his body, and he'd twitched, rolling away from the pain.

He did remember puking his guts up all over the shoes of whoever was standing outside the trunk.

Score one for me.

At least this time he was prone on a couch instead of tied to a metal chair. A quick check showed no cuffs or bonds of any kind. With utmost care, he sat up, looking around.

"Glad to see you awake, Mr. Everett."

Mason Alexander sat off to his right, in a pub chair, a casual smirk on his face. *Perfect.*

"Figured the second time's the charm, Alexander?"

He chuckled, a hand smoothing down the front of his

suit jacket. "Worked that out, did you?"

"Yep, that's me, king of MENSA."

Alexander's smile quickly turned to a frown. "I do not appreciate a smart-ass, Mr. Everett. Speak to me with respect."

Gunner shook his head, trying for a pitiful expression. "Respect is earned, Mason, and you ain't earned mine." Leaning back against the cushions, he propped his feet on the coffee table. *Take that, jackass.*

"I need to speak with Ms. Callahan. I have a few…questions."

"Funny, we've got a few questions for you too."

The whole time he talked, he only partially focused on Mason Alexander. The rest of his brain worked trying to figure out where the hell he was, and how he could escape.

"Mr. Everett, Ms. Callahan will be perfectly safe. I simply need to know how much information she pilfered from EryX Pharmaceutical."

"More than enough to send your sorry ass to prison for the rest of your life. And if you think I'm gonna let you talk to her, you've got a screw loose."

Alexander watched him, his steel blue gaze icy with disdain. "You seem to think you have a choice in the matter, Mr. Everett…or do you prefer Wilson?"

He grimaced at the use of his given name, hoping Alexander didn't notice. The last thing he needed was to give the man more ammunition.

"Carpenter won't let you get within five hundred feet of Maggie."

"Carpenter?" Alexander chortled, laughing hard enough it brought tears to his eyes. He watched the older man wipe them away, still chuckling softly. Gunner cursed under his breath. This guy was definitely a few bricks shy if he underestimated Samuel Carpenter.

"If you're counting on Samuel Carpenter for anything except a large paycheck, you are sorely mistaken. The man is incompetent, as proven time and again when he worked for the federal government."

Gunner seethed, biting his tongue hard enough he could taste blood. "If anybody's underestimating someone it's you, if you don't believe Samuel Carpenter will take you down. If there's dirt to be found, nobody is better at uncovering the truth." He paused, letting his words sink in. "What's the matter, Mason? You hiding something from Carpenter?"

Again with the smoothing down of his hand over his jacket. Hmm, that seemed to be a habit when he got flustered. Gunner filed that information away in his brain, ready to use it later.

"Mr. Everett, my record is clean. There's nothing in my past for anyone to uncover—because I haven't done anything illegal."

"Really? How about something immoral? Unethical?"

A flush of red spread across Alexander's face. *Looks like I struck a nerve. Let's dig a little deeper.*

"We've all got a few regrets. I know I do. Want to swap war stories, old man?"

Mason Alexander jumped to his feet, his fists balled at his sides, the gentlemanly façade fading. "You don't know anything about me, boy. And if you're smart, you'd better keep it that way."

"Tsk, tsk. Who says I don't know anything about the great Mason Alexander. The man who would be king—oh wait, America doesn't have a king. Right, Mr. President-wanna-be?"

The other man took a step toward Gunner, a murderous glint in his eyes. "You don't have a clue what you're talking about."

Gunner quirked a brow, goading him further. "Don't I? I've been friends with Samuel for a long time. Years. Who do you think he talks to? There are no secrets. The bodies never stay buried—not forever anyway."

Alexander studied him intently, and Gunner sat motionless on the sofa, refusing to be the first to blink. He hadn't revealed anything to the man, only teases and taunts, but apparently the barbs struck home. *Good. Let him sweat.*

Mason's hand slid across his jacket front again. Oh, yeah, definitely nervous. "We've gotten a bit off topic, Mr. Everett. Let's get back to Ms. Callahan, shall we?"

Reaching into his pocket, he pulled out a phone. Gunner recognized it instantly. It was his phone. The smile that played across the other man's lips made Gunner seethe. He wanted to leap across the space and wrap his hands around the other man's throat. Squeeze, until he was no longer a threat to Maggie or anybody else.

"Won't do you a damned bit of good without the password." Thankfully, he'd learned early on in the service to always keep things password protected or better yet encrypted. Something Carlisle had drilled even deeper once they'd begun working closely together. Geek Boy had taught him a few tricks along the way, including locking his phone.

"Really? It took my computer expert less than twenty minutes to break your password." Mason's finger slid across the screen, and Gunner bit back another curse. "It looks like you've been a very bad boy. Although I do like this one of Ms. Callahan."

Maggie was going to kill him. Unable to resist the temptation of her sleeping beside him, he'd snapped several pics, with her hair spilling across the pillows, a tiny smile tugging at the corners of her lips.

"She's very pretty. Maybe I'll keep her when this is over."

"You better mean the phone, or I'm going to rip your spleen out through your nose." Gunner almost didn't recognize his own voice, or the deep gravely threat beneath his words. Every thought, every instinct, screamed to protect the woman he loved.

Mason's head tilted back as he laughed, long and hard, and Gunner fought the urge to leap from the sofa and wrap his hands around the other man's throat. "Not yet," he whispered, "not yet."

"Mr. Everett, you are immensely entertaining. However, I'm afraid our time together must end." Lifting his hand, he motioned to somebody beyond Gunner's view, and the two goons who'd snatched him at the airport stepped forward.

"Lock him up. And this time, make sure you use something stronger than duct tape." His eyes met Gunner's. "Good help is so hard to find these days. You wouldn't be interested in working for me, would you?"

Gunner bared his teeth. "Not if we were the last two people on the planet."

"That's what I thought. You seem like the do-gooder, Boy Scout type. Oh, well…"

The two men grabbed him simultaneously, and though he struggled, they held tight, slapping a pair of cuffs on his wrists behind his back.

Haven't we done this dance before?

Faking a calmness he didn't feel, he let them lead him from the room, grimacing when he heard the *tap, tap, tap* of a finger hitting the keys on his phone.

Please, Maggie, don't listen. It's not me. Take the message to Carpenter. He'll know what to do.

Mason Alexander's smug laughter was the last thing he heard as he was led away.

Chapter Thirty

Maggie heard the text alert on her phone, and glanced at the screen. Her heart leapt in her chest when she saw it was Gunner. Swiping her finger across the screen, she read the message.

We have Mr. Everett. If you want to see him live through the day, you'll come alone. DO NOT mention this text to anybody or he dies.

Maggie's hands shook so hard, she dropped her phone onto the table top. The message came from Gunner's phone, which meant somebody had taken him.

She didn't recognize the address. Shoot, she didn't know anything in or around New Orleans except the few places Gunner had taken her. Dropping onto her seat, she pulled up the map program and typed in the address, though she had to start over twice, because her hands were shaking so hard she kept mistyping it.

How was she going to get there? Maybe she could take Gunner's truck? Frantic, she tore open the drawer where she'd seen him toss his keys before, praying they would still be there. Her hands pushed aside papers and old receipts, take-out menus, and a couple of decks of cards before she found them.

Okay, one problem solved. Now came the really hard part. Sneaking out without anybody seeing her. Her first thought was the fire escape that ran down the side of the building. Gunner told her it was monitored on security camera twenty-four seven, so that was a bust. If she went out the front, Stephanie would see her. Unless—maybe she could somehow distract Stephanie away from the front desk for a few minutes.

In no time at all, she had the directions downloaded to her phone, the keys in her hand, and was headed out the door. Taking the stairs seemed her best bet, and she raced down each flight, stopping right before she reached the bottom step.

Stealthily, she eased around the corner, glancing toward the front reception desk, looking for Stephanie. She still hadn't figured out how she was going to get the woman away from her desk, so she'd have a straight shot to the front door, but she'd come up with something.

Except the desk sat empty. As a matter of fact, she hadn't heard or seen any of the guys for a while. Ms. Willie had been absent a bit for the last few days, turning a bright pink whenever anybody quizzed her about her absence.

Stephanie, on the other hand, always remained front and center at her desk. She complained to anybody who would listen that there way too much paperwork, and not enough action for her taste. The girl wanted to be out in the field so bad she could taste it.

Yet, here her desk sat eerily empty, but Maggie wasn't

about to look a gift horse in the mouth. She raced for the front door, and stumbled out onto the street before anybody could stop her.

Racing around the corner, she bounded down the alley, reaching the parking lot within minutes. A quick press on the key fob, and she was behind the wheel of Gunner's truck. There wasn't any choice but to move the seat, because when she sat back, she didn't come close to reaching the pedals.

Taking a deep breath and praying Gunner was alright, she started the truck and pulled out of the alley and onto Canal Street, and away from Carpenter Security.

Chapter Thirty-One

Night had fallen by the time she reached the address on her phone's GPS. She parked in front of an opulent home, the circular drive flanked on either end by large urns with pelicans perched atop atop each with wings spread wide. Which seemed oddly fitting, since it was the state bird.

Looking at the house and its surrounding acreage, her heart plummeted into her stomach. She had a really bad feeling she knew who the property belonged to—Mason Alexander.

Might as well get it over with. Nobody's getting rescued with me sitting on my ass in the truck.

Taking a deep breath, she walked to the front door and knocked. It was opened immediately by a tall man, built like a tank. One of those steroid-abusing, body-builder, Mr. Universe wanna-be types. He gave her the once over before scanning the drive and front of the house.

"You followed?" The high-pitched voice coming from him in no way matched his exterior. She bit her lip to keep from chuckling aloud. It reminded her of a squeaky toy that a dog played with, not what you'd expect from some muscle-bound goon holding her boyfriend hostage.

"No."

Grabbing her arm none too gently, he pulled her into the house, closing the door behind her with a loud thunk. Maggie looked around, taking in the solid hardwood floors, the wainscoting, and high ceilings. The light buttery-yellow paint warmed up the entryway. Under normal circumstances, she'd have said it looked like a nice home. Today? It reminded her of a prison.

"Where's Gunner?"

Mr. Universe didn't answer, simply urged her along by tugging on her arm. Yanking it out of his grasp, she frowned. "You don't have to manhandle me. I came. Now where's Gunner?"

"He's indisposed at the moment, Ms. Callahan." Maggie spun toward the voice, not surprised to see Mason Alexander standing inside what had to be the home's library slash office. Two of the walls were floor-to-ceiling bookshelves, crammed with hardcover books which looked like they'd never been touched. What a waste.

Shaking her head, she took a closer look at the books' spines, noting obscure titles that probably nobody but an egghead would even consider good reading material. Where were the classics? The paperbacks with creased spines and missing dust jackets? The paperbacks with dog-earred pages?

"I want to see Gunner," she demanded, proud her voice came out firm and steady. Inside she was shaking like an aspen in the wind, surprised her knees hadn't buckled already.

"I believe we need to chat first. Please," he motioned to one of two chairs sitting in front of a large oak desk. "Join me."

Maggie kept her eyes glued to Alexander while she skirted around him, and walked the rest of the way into the library. The carpet beneath her feet was thick and luxurious, done in a warm rust shade. Didn't matter how fine the furnishings and fixtures were, the place gave her the willies.

"What do you want?"

"Everything, Ms. Callahan. I want all the information you took from EryX Pharmaceutical. Every page. Every flash drive. Every napkin you jotted notes onto. Anything that pertains to Somnolett."

"I..."

"Don't lie, my dear. Your cyber fingerprints are all over everything in the main system. Yours and Caitlyn Keyes. Apparently she's been a very bad girl too."

Maggie swallowed past the lump in her throat. Darn it, they'd been so careful. She knew Carlisle hadn't left behind any cyber-footprints. It must have been the blip with her keycard Caitlyn discussed with her boss, when she went back to EryX with Dean Westin the second time.

"She doesn't know anything."

Alexander shook his head. "A lot of people get pulled into events they have no business sticking their noses into. They become what's known as collateral damage."

Maggie crossed her legs, fidgeting with the edge of her blouse. Stalling only prolonged the inevitable. She only hoped Gunner would forgive her, but she couldn't see him killed. Not because of her.

"Truthfully, Mr. Alexander, it took me a while to figure

things out. You were clever, I'll give you that. Unless an expert forensic accountant went into EryX Pharmaceutical's records looking for specific discrepancies, the books appear squeaky clean. All the totals balance, right down to the penny."

"Yet you weren't fooled." A pained expression crossed his face. "May I ask, what tipped you off?"

He didn't know? Was he willfully blind or just desensitized to people dying? "It was the deaths."

"Deaths? I don't remember there being any deaths in the information I received."

She studied him intently, trying to read his expression. Could he be lying? He looked legitimately puzzled, almost shocked, at her words. Maybe she could feed him a little information, play along. Pretend she was cooperating, and she might get a little insight into what the hell was going on, because she was beginning to think she'd taken a wrong turn and landed in La-La Land.

"You already know I work—worked—for EryX Pharmaceutical in sales and marketing." She waited for his nod. "My boss and I came into the office on Labor Day, wanting to get caught up on some of the paperwork that had fallen behind, and get a jump start on the next quarter. There weren't a lot of people there, and my boss left before me."

"Conscientious worker. I like that."

She almost rolled her eyes. Like she cared if he approved of her work ethics? The man was responsible for enough crimes to land him on the FBI's most wanted list, or would if they suspected anything.

She continued as if he hadn't spoken. "My boss didn't mind if I studied at my desk when things were slow. It was quiet, so I spent a little while catching up on some classwork. When I got ready to leave, there were two men outside my office door. I admit it, I was nosy, so I listened."

His lips curled upward at the corners. "I can understand that. You can learn a lot of interesting things when you listen in on others' conversations. I'm assuming you heard something that intrigued you."

She shook her head. "No, it sickened me. They were talking about the people who'd died. All of them part of the Somnolett protocol study. Too many people, it should have been an immediate red flag to pull the drug from use. But nothing came across my desk stating the study had been terminated."

"Hmm. That's very interesting. I wasn't aware of any fatalities related to Somnolett."

"They weren't. Somnolett didn't kill anybody, because Somnolett doesn't exist, does it, Mr. Alexander?"

Maggie's stare met his directly, without flinching under his anger, and she could see the exact moment when he figured out she knew more than he'd realized. She probably should have kept her mouth shut, but he sat there with a smug look on his face, nonchalant about people being killed and pretending to know nothing about it.

"You really have done your homework, Ms. Callahan. You're correct, the second formulation of Somnolett doesn't exist. A proxy formula was written but never produced. The opportunity for profit was too good to pass up."

"No matter how much blood you got on your hands?"

Standing, he turned his back to her, and glanced out the huge window behind his chair. Outside, the sky was beginning to change colors, with the sunset painting it in vivid hues like the brushstrokes of a master artist. "That's where your theory goes off the tracks. No one died because of Somnolett. A ton of money has been made from the R&D scheme, but all the people in the study were given placebos."

Was it possible he didn't know? They'd never considered the possibility somebody else might be calling the shots, since Mason Alexander had the most to gain.

"Mr. Alexander, several people died after participating in the study. Each appeared accidental or suicide, but Somnolett connects each one of them back to EryX Pharmaceutical. The two men I overheard talked about the people dying, admitted the deaths weren't accidents. That's when I stuck my nose into things, as you so elegantly put it."

He spun around and took a step toward her and she flinched, her spine flush against the chair's back. "I don't believe you."

"Who would you believe? Gunner will tell you the same things I have—or maybe you'd like to talk to Samuel Carpenter?"

If she hadn't been watching him so closely, she probably wouldn't have noticed the wince of pain cross his face at the mention of Carpenter's name. Pacing behind the elegant desk, he crossed back and forth in front of the window, running a hand through his salt and pepper hair.

"Carpenter knows about this? The man is out to crucify me. I might as well put a bullet in my brain."

"Samuel believes me. But—and it's a big but—if you didn't have anything to do with the people being killed, there might be a way out of this."

Maggie had to do some quick thinking, because Alexander still had Gunner heaven only knew where, and she'd do whatever it took to save him, including sacrificing herself.

"I didn't order anybody killed. This was strictly about money."

"Don't you mean money laundering?"

He shot her a glare. "Call it whatever you want, it's about huge profits. Keeping my companies in the black. But I didn't condone anybody dying."

"The only way out of this is to cooperate. Make a deal."

He barked out a laugh and it wasn't a pretty sound. She could hear the tinge of desperation in it.

"If Samuel Carpenter is building a case against me, nothing I say will change his mind. The man hates me."

"Convince me and Gunner. We'll take care of making sure Samuel Carpenter goes along with any bargain we strike with you. But I'm not going to negotiate on your behalf until Gunner's sitting right here next to me."

She held her breath when she finished talking. This was a make or break situation. If he decided not to listen to her, she was dead and probably Gunner, too. Crossing her fingers, she waited silently.

Looking past her, he nodded toward the bodyguard who

stood just inside the doorway. "Bring Mr. Everett here."

Maggie let out her breath in a silent exhale. Now all she had to do was convince Mason Alexander that they didn't believe he was a stone-cold killer.

Chapter Thirty-Two

"Tell me you've got him."

"Boss, how many times do I have to tell you, I'm good, but I'm not a miracle worker." Carlisle looked up from his laptop, and pushed his glasses back up his nose.

"I had you clone everyone's phone for a reason, Geek Boy. That's why it's written into the employee contracts."

"And I've got everyone's phone, including Maggie's when she wasn't looking—by the way, you get to explain that little fact to her. But, I can only go as fast as…got ya." Carlisle started scrolling with his mouse. "Looks like Gunner's phone texted Maggie forty minutes ago. Wasn't Gunner though. Whoever it was gave her an address with instructions to come there."

"And the GPS?"

"Shows Gunner's phone is at the address texted to Maggie."

"Perfect." Carpenter turned to the other men in his living room. "Jean-Luc, Ranger, and—"

"Me." Dean Westin walked into the living room, one towel around his hips and another drying his hair. Carpenter scowled at him, before grousing, "Be ready to roll in five minutes or you get left behind."

Westin disappeared down the hall without another word.

"Dayam, boss you gotta hear this." Carlisle's voice was filled with more excitement than Carpenter had heard from him in months, ever since the whole incident with Sarah Sloane's missing sister.

He stood and walked around the sofa to peer over Carlisle's shoulder. There was a graph across the top of the screen with what looked like voice analytics.

"I think I'm in love with Maggie Callahan." With the push of a button, voices began playing out of the speakers.

"I can understand that. You can learn a lot of interesting things when you listen in on others' conversations. I'm assuming you heard something that intrigued you."

"No, it sickened me. They were talking about the people who'd died. All of them part of the Somnolett protocol study. So many people, it should have been an immediate red flag to pull the drug from use. But nothing had come across my desk stating the study had been terminated."

"Hmm. That's very interesting. I wasn't aware of any fatalities related to Somnolett."

"They weren't. Somnolett didn't kill anybody, because Somnolett doesn't exist, does it, Mr. Alexander?"

"Maggie must have switched on the recording mechanism on her cell phone, and she's recording their entire conversation. This proves Mason Alexander is the one who sent her the text from Gunner's phone." Carlisle rubbed his hands together and grinned. "Can we go get him now?"

"Everybody gear up. Mason Alexander will have mercenaries for bodyguards, and they won't hesitate to shoot.

Kevlar and body armor for everybody. Jean-Luc, you comfortable being the point man?"

Carpenter knew Jean-Luc was the best shot among the men assembled, though he rarely called upon him to play sniper. That usually fell to Gunner or Nate—both of whom weren't available. As much as he hated putting the other man in the tenuous position of taking another life, he knew Jean-Luc would do the job, even with the ensuing nightmares that accompanied it.

"I've got it." He noticed the look that crossed Jean-Luc's face, which disappeared almost as fast as it appeared. Made a mental note—Jean-Luc must take some mandatory time off as soon as this op was finished. The man was stretched taut as razor wire.

"Keep the connection open and bring that laptop. I want to hear what Alexander has to say about EryX Pharmaceutical." Carlisle picked up the laptop and headed for the front door. Carpenter scowled. "And put on a damned vest."

Not bothering to see if his order was followed, he stormed out the front door of his apartment. Andrea was going to be pissed she missed all the excitement. Thank goodness she'd gone out with Ms. Willie, helping out on some secret project the other woman was working on.

"Let's go get our man, and take down Mason Alexander."

In the parking lot, they piled into two black SUVs, Etienne Boudreau driving one and Ranger driving the other. He trusted the Boudreau brothers. They knew their way around New Orleans better than anybody else on the team, having been born and raised here.

Not bothering to turn around, he knew Carlisle would hear him in the back seat. "Keep monitoring the line. Let me know if Alexander figures out what Maggie's up to. I'm going to call Remy and inform the authorities of what's going down."

There was a grim satisfaction in Carpenter's gut that he'd finally be able to make Mason Alexander pay the price for his past crimes.

Chapter Thirty-Three

G unner tugged at the handcuffs encircling his wrists. Apparently the two yahoos who'd kidnapped him the first time learned from their mistakes. This time he'd been secured to an iron pipe running down the length of the wall. Outside. In the elements.

Not that it wasn't a nice posh backyard. Swimming pool, fire-pit, patio, and elegantly manicured grass as far as the eye could see, sloping downhill to a dock on the lake. A rich man's vacation home, complete with a luxury speedboat to play with.

Yet here he sat on the damp grass, handcuffed to the side of the house, unarmed. He might panic if they were closer to the wild bayous, but he doubted anything nasty would crawl out of the lake.

Footsteps approached from around the corner, and he resisted the urge to struggle against the cuffs, instead leaning back against the wall, acting like he didn't have a care in the world.

"Boss wants to see you."

"Aw, shucks, I was just starting to enjoy the ambience."

"Keep your trap shut. I ain't taking no more of your lip."

Gunner rolled his eyes. This moron had no idea how

much talking he could do, especially if he put his mind to it. But that could wait, because apparently Alexander wanted to see him.

Goon number two uncuffed his wrists, while the first one kept his Sig trained on him. He could probably take them both out without much effort. After all, he'd done it before under worse conditions, but he had to admit he was curious to see what Mason Alexander wanted.

"Come on, smart-ass."

Goon number two reattached the cuff to Gunner's left wrist, but at least this time they were cuffed in front of him. They led him around the side of the house and through the kitchen entrance.

He stumbled when one of them shoved him, and he spun around with a growled warning, but froze when he heard her voice.

"Maggie?"

Ignoring the two behind him, he raced toward the sound of Maggie's voice, coming from somewhere in the house. A hand wrapped around the back of his shirt, yanking him to a halt.

"Let me go."

"Calm down. Mr. Alexander wants to see you."

Gunner inhaled a deep breath, forcing himself to still the urge to bash in the heads of these two idiots and get to Maggie, but he'd play things their way—for now.

"Take me to him then."

With another jerk on his collar, he was released and he managed to walk precisely and carefully, toward the two voices he could now hear distinctly.

What the hell is Maggie doing here?

Alexander spotted him first, and his expression never changed from the cordial tone he used with Maggie. "Mr. Everett, please, join us."

He took a step into the room, then another, one foot in front of the other until he stood beside Maggie's chair. Raising his cuffed hands, he gently touched her cheek.

"What are you doing here?"

Her eyes widened when she'd spotted the handcuffs.

"Those aren't necessary." She touched the cuffs, though she spoke directly to Alexander.

"Let me be the judge of that, Ms. Callahan. Mr. Everett, please, sit."

Gunner felt like he'd walked in on the second act of a three-act play, and didn't have a clue what had already happened, or was about to. And he didn't like it one bit. Maggie shouldn't be here. He'd left her tucked up safe in his apartment, where she should still be, not sitting in front of the bad guy, making nice.

"What'd I miss?"

Maggie smiled and implored him with her eyes to play along. "Mr. Alexander and I have been discussing the situation with EryX Pharmaceutical."

"I'll just bet you have," he muttered under his breath.

"Mr. Alexander assures me he had nothing to do with the deaths involving Somnolett. In fact, he didn't know anybody had been killed until I told him."

Gunner studied the other man's face, trying to read the

veracity of that statement. He did look a little shaken. When he'd first confronted Gunner an hour ago, he'd been in command, arrogant in that way only the ultra-rich could. Now he'd lost that edge of confidence. Maybe sweet Maggie had found a chink in his armor.

"I may be a lot of things, but I am not a killer."

Gunner wanted to throw his words back in his face, bring up what Carpenter had told him about Natalie St. Cloud. Mason Alexander might sound sincere, but he was a snake in the grass, and he didn't trust him. The second he did, he'd find himself snake-bit with no antidote.

"What part are you playing in the whole EryX fiasco then? We've uncovered enough underhanded dealings, money laundering, and other criminal activity to put you and all your cohorts away for a very long time. Somehow, I don't think you'll look good in prison orange."

Gunner watched the color leech from Alexander's face. There was a pinched white look around his lips, and his breathing increased until he was nearly panting. *Crap, that's all we need, for him to keel over from a heart attack or a stroke.*

"I've already explained to Ms. Callahan, I don't know anything about people being killed. I was strictly in it for the huge profitability offered."

"Gunner, I believe him. We've got him dead to rights for the money laundering. His companies have been funneling money in from South America and Russia, through his subsidiary companies. Once the money went into Mason's business accounts, they in turn funneled it into EryX Pharmaceutical. Then it was basically channeled into the

R&D division, and then back out again to Alexander's companies paid as dividends and stock options which could be sold. That way it was squeaky clean, and nobody was the wiser."

"South America and Russia?" He eyed Alexander, noting again the pinched look around his eyes. "Please tell me you aren't involved with the cartel? Because we won't even get a chance to throw you in jail. Your wife will be visiting you at the cemetery."

"That's why I want you to call Carpenter. I want to make a deal, and he's got connections—way more than I've got." Alexander collapsed into the chair behind the desk, and rested his hands on top. "I can testify. Name names. You wouldn't believe how high this goes."

Gunner gave him a pitying glance. "You threatened my woman. I don't think I can forgive that."

"Mr. Everett, I don't kill people. I merely wanted to find out what she knew, and convince her to keep her mouth shut. I would have made it worth her while financially. Everything is spinning out of control. It wasn't supposed to be like this."

"How exactly was it supposed to be, Mason?"

Gunner wanted to chortle at the look of shock on Alexander's face when he spotted Carpenter leaning against the study's doorjamb. Goon number one lay on the floor unconscious at his feet.

"Samuel. I guess I shouldn't be surprised."

"You always did underestimate me." At Gunner's brief nod, he continued. "I think it would be best if we moved this

Chapter Thirty-Four

"Everybody down!"

Maggie dove for the floor, and Gunner landed on top of her, his body shielding hers. Her heart was beating so fast, it could jump from her chest, yet her only thought was Gunner. He was still cuffed and unable to defend himself.

"You okay, sweetheart?"

"I'm fine," she whispered.

He started to climb off her, and she clutched at his biceps. "Where do you think you're going?"

"I'm going to check on Alexander. Carpenter and the others are looking for the shooter or shooters. Let me see how he's doing."

Maggie didn't want to let him go, but knew he was right. He half-walked, half-crawled to where Alexander was sprawled across the desk, and she watched the *drip, drip, drip* of red trickling off the front. Blood.

"You got a phone?" At her nod, he prompted, "Call nine-one-one. Tell the police what's going on and that we need an ambulance."

Hands shaking, Maggie pulled out her phone, noting the recorder was still active. Shutting it off, she dialed for help.

"Nine-one-one, what's your emergency?"

KATHY IVAN

"We have a shooting at ninety-seven twenty-one Harborview Court. We need an ambulance and the police right away." She tried to keep her voice calm, though she wanted to curl up in a ball and hide away from everything.

"Officers are being dispatched. You said one person has been shot? Can you tell if they're breathing?"

Maggie looked at Gunner. He nodded. "Yes, but it's labored. GSW to the left side of the chest."

Maggie relayed the information, and passed back the instructions she gave to Gunner, though he'd already done everything before she could talk. It was clear he'd dealt with bullet wounds before. Probably his marine training.

"Please stay on the line until the officers arrive. Can you give me your name?"

Maggie told her, giving her as much pertinent information as she could, while she watched Gunner struggling to keep Alexander alive.

"Dammit, he's stopped breathing." As she watched, he started chest compressions, and mouth-to-mouth. The cuffs made a clanking sound with each movement.

Maggie told the dispatcher what was happening, and fear seized her gut as she watched, helpless to do anything but talk.

"Ma'am, the officers should be arriving any second. Is there still active gunfire?"

Maggie listened intently. "I don't hear anything."

As soon as the words left her mouth, she heard the familiar whining screech of police and EMT sirens.

"They're here," she told the operator.

"Okay, let them in to do their job." With that Maggie hung up, as two EMTs rushed into the room, with their gear in hand. Gunner immediately stepped back to let them do their jobs.

"Are you okay?" Her hands ran across his chest and up over his shoulders, she couldn't help it. He'd made himself a target in front of the window where Alexander had been shot, trying to help the other man.

"Shh, baby, I'm fine. Don't know how he's doing though." They watched the paramedics work, alternating chest compressions and mouth-to-mouth.

"I've got a pulse." The paramedics' movements were almost a blur as they hooked up an IV, and placed an oxygen mask over Alexander's nose and mouth.

Maggie sagged against Gunner. As horrible as Mason Alexander was, she didn't want him to die. It might seem heartless, but there were too many unanswered questions. Most especially, if he didn't order the people killed—who did?

Carpenter and the rest of the team stood in the foyer, staying well out of the way, while the police took the two bad guys who'd come in with Gunner into custody. Mason Alexander was wheeled out on a stretcher, and loaded into the back of the EMT rescue truck, which took off with a wail of sirens, headed toward the hospital.

Leaving them alone with a bunch of cops with a bunch of questions. Like who'd been shooting at them, and why?

Chapter Thirty-Five

"Looks like Mason's gonna make it."

Gunner held Maggie against his side, as Carpenter updated the team. Everyone gathered in Carpenter's living room, the entire team including Andrea and Ms. Willie, though they'd missed all the excitement. *And man, issn't Andrea pissed about that?*

"He made it through surgery, though it was touch and go there for a bit. The doctors said he wouldn't have made it if you hadn't done CPR." He nodded to Gunner, who shrugged. No need to tell anybody that he'd considered letting the bastard bleed out.

"Wasn't like I had a choice. Couldn't let the S.O.B. die without telling us who's actually pulling the strings at EryX."

"We got a lot of answers, thanks to Maggie and her quick thinking." Carlisle winked at her, and Gunner shot him the evil eye. "Smart move, activating the recorder on your phone."

Maggie blushed. "I hoped I'd get him to talk, even if just a little. I never anticipated things turning out the way they did."

"Next time, you come to me. Even when the bad guy says not to." Carpenter chided, shaking his finger. "Especially when the bad guy says not to tell me. That should have been your first clue. Don't you watch TV or movies?"

"Sheesh. Sorry."

Laughter erupted around her, breaking the tension.

"Seriously, guys, how'd you know where to find us?" Maggie leaned forward, dislodging the arm he'd wrapped around her shoulder, and Gunner draped it across the back of the couch, though he'd much rather it still be around his gal. He couldn't believe she'd willingly walked into danger— for him.

"Every member of Carpenter Security agrees to have their cellphones cloned. It's part of their employee agreement. We never take advantage of the fact—but in a case like this, it showed us the text sent to you from Gunner's phone, and the GPS pinpointed where his phone pinged the cell tower. Which, coincidentally, just happened to be the same location as the address Alexander sent you."

She looked from Carlisle to Carpenter and back again, eyes narrowed. "Did you do that to my phone too? Is that how you knew about mer recording Mason?"

Gunner almost snickered when Carlisle wouldn't meet Maggie's gaze. Not that he blamed him…much. She could be a virago when crossed. Duping her phone without her consent?

"Look, I only did it to protect you. We've had too many incidences where being able to track a cellphone could have been the difference between life and death."

"Don't blame Carlisle. He was doing his job."

She leaned back with a huffed out sigh. "I get it. Next

time though, just ask."

"Promise." Carlisle gave her another wink, and Gunner wrapped his arm around her, his glare warning the other man off. Not that he expected Carlisle to make a move. The guy was still engrossed with Sarah's sister, though he couldn't help wondering how the guy thought he could make the relationship work. He was here in New Orleans, and she was over a thousand miles away in San Diego. Still, he hoped they'd find a way. After the hell Savannah had gone through, she deserved a good guy. And Stefan Carlisle was the best.

"When can you question Alexander?" Gunner figured getting them back on topic might be a good idea.

"The cops have locked down his room so tight, a gnat couldn't get in. He's going to be facing so many charges, outside of money laundering and racketeering, he's going away for a long time." Carpenter sipped his coffee, grimacing before putting it back onto the coffee table.

"We need to get to him, find out who else is behind EryX Pharmaceutical. I honestly don't think he knew about the participants dying. Seemed genuinely shocked." Gunner remembered the look on Alexander's face the second the bullet struck.

"He mentioned South America and Russia. I'd wager he's been funneling money in from the cartel, cleaning it through EryX, getting his portion, and transferring the cleaned funds back to the mafia-controlled legitimate enterprises." Maggie leaned forward, and Gunner tugged her back, tucking her against his side. He wasn't letting her go, not for a second. She still didn't realize how much danger she'd been in, and he planned to keep her glued to his side for the duration.

"Which leaves me wondering who at EryX is pulling the strings. Because this wasn't something cooked up by low level bookkeepers." He smiled at Maggie. "No offense."

She laughed. "None taken, since I wasn't working there as a bookkeeper. But I agree, it had to be somebody with enough clout to either manage or bully people into making those books add up."

Gunner watched her tap her index finger against her lips. "Might be more than one person."

"She turned to look at him. "What do you mean?"

"Somebody pretty high up the food chain, because Mason Alexander doesn't deal with menial employees. That would be beneath him. So we need to look at who actually runs the place—has the most clout."

All eyes turned to Maggie. "Ian Buchanan is the Chairman and CEO. Has been for the last ten years, ever since his father retired."

"Buchanan Senior had a stroke and the son stepped in." Carlisle added to Maggie's statement. "The company was hemorrhaging money at that time, it looks like."

"I remember something about that. My grandfather talked about how Buchanan had run the company into the ground." Carpenter leaned forward, jostling Andrea, who was perched on the arm of his chair. "He said he wouldn't touch Eryx Pharmaceutical with a ten foot pole. Too big a risk."

Gunner considered what they'd said, different scenarios

running through his mind. It wasn't unheard of for a son to take a leadership role in a company his father had run for decades. Old pappy had probably been grooming him to take over ever since he was knee high.

"What changed?" Everybody looked at him like he'd grown two heads or something. Then he realized they didn't have a clue what he'd been thinking. "You said the company was hemorrhaging money. Then Buchanan Senior steps down due to a stroke. Or was that just the rumor that was spread, so the son could transition into the top position without too many questions asked?"

Carpenter studied him with that intense stare he used when his mind was playing options. Sometimes Gunner swore the man had a computer for a brain, inputting the facts and spitting out the best solution for any given situation.

"It could have been done. Wouldn't be a big shocker. A change of leadership can infuse new blood and new capital into a venture, even with an established company like EryX Pharmaceutical."

"Looks like about four months after the son took over there was a major breakthrough in the R&D department with a diabetic drug." Carlisle spun around the laptop. "A drug that could be taken along with insulin to regulate diabetic sugar spikes. It was considered a miracle for diabetics who struggled to get their sugars under control."

"And poured a ton of money into a nearly bankrupt company." Dean Westin leaned forward, his movements mirroring Carpenter's, and Gunner's gaze shifted from one man to the other. Now that he knew the truth, it was obvious they were brothers.

"Carlisle, get me everything you can dig up on Ian Buchanan. Right down to what color socks he's wearing."

"You got it, boss. I'm heading to my place. Got a couple other searches running, I need to check. Unless you need me…"

"No, go."

"Honey, a little tact." Andrea smiled at Carlisle. "What he means is, thank you for your hard work, Stefan."

Carpenter rolled his eyes, and yanked Andrea onto his lap. She let out a little squeak.

"What she said."

Everyone laughed, and Carlisle left. Gunner opened his mouth, but before he could say anything his phone rang. Looking at the caller ID, he saw Remy Lamoreaux's picture and number. Remy had become a good friend since he'd moved to New Orleans, and was a detective with the New Orleans Police Department.

"Hey, Remy. What's up?"

"I'm at Tulane Medical. Mason Alexander just coded. The docs got him resuscitated, but they don't think he'll make it."

Gunner looked at Carpenter and shook his head. "The surgeons said he was gonna pull through. What the hell happened?"

"Nobody's sure, but they think he had a stroke after the surgery. If you've got questions for him, I'd suggest you get your backside here ASAP."

"We're on our way."

He ended the call, and squeezed Maggie against his side. "Mason Alexander just coded. They don't expect him to make it."

Without hesitation, Carpenter lifted Andrea off his lap and stood. "Let's roll."

Chapter Thirty-Six

The ICU waiting room was crowded with people, most of them from C.S.S. Maggie held Gunner's hand, needing to feel the connection between them. So much had happened in the last twenty-four hours, it was all one big blur.

There were two police guards stationed outside Mason Alexander's hospital room, as well as his own personal bodyguard inside. His wife was in transit, flying across the country to get to his side. She'd been at a charity benefit in San Francisco when the news broke about Alexander being shot. They hadn't been able to keep it out of the press. He was too well-known to hide that little tidbit from the gossip mongers.

Carpenter and Remy had been allowed into the room, though only because Remy was a cop and pulled rank. Otherwise, everybody else sat, awaiting word on his condition and whether he could answer any questions.

It seemed like they'd been there for hours, though it was probably less than one. She hated hospitals. Sterile and unfeeling, they always felt cold and unwelcoming, no matter how hard the staff tried to be cheerful and friendly. And she was freezing. They kept the temperatures lower because of all the equipment, but that didn't change the fact she had goosebumps skittering across her arms.

"Come here." Gunner's voice was a whisper in her ear. His arms wrapped around her, and she felt the warmth of his body heat begin seeping into her. The man was like a giant furnace, and right now she welcomed his embrace.

The nurses' station in front of the Intensive Care rooms was a jungle of monitors and flashing lights. She didn't understand any of it. The men and women she assumed were nurses moved quietly and efficiently about their duties.

The door to Mason Alexander's room swung inward and Remy and Carpenter walked out. From their expressions, things had just gone from bad to worse.

"Alexander?" Gunner was the first to ask. Carpenter shook his head, and Maggie felt a squeezing in her chest. She didn't like the man, and he'd been partially responsible for the entire fiasco at EryX, but she hadn't wanted to see him dead.

"He's hanging by a thread, but it looks bad. I don't want to talk here," Carpenter added. "Too unsecured. Head back to the office, and we'll debrief."

"I've got to get to the station and file the report." Remy looked tired. Gunner knew they were grossly understaffed at the police department. Remy had been pulling a lot of extra shifts, and it was obviously wearing on him. Probably on his fiancée too. He was engaged to a pretty little firecracker named Jinx Marucci, who kept him on his toes.

"Thanks for the head's up, Remy." Carpenter gave him a brief slap on the shoulder, and headed toward the elevator.

Gunner and Maggie followed, and he could hear the others who'd been in the waiting room with them talking quietly with Remy. They'd meet up with them back at the office, to hear what—if anything—Alexander had said.

The car ride back was fairly quiet, and he pulled the truck into the parking area behind the building and cut the engine. "Gunner, this all seems like a dream. Surreal and yet all-too-real. Mason Alexander is dead because of the mess at Eryx Pharmaceutical. And I'm to blame."

Gunner's head swung toward her. "This is not your fault. You aren't the one who pulled the trigger."

"But if I'd kept my mouth shut, he'd still be alive."

"And how many others from the study protocol would be dead? The whole situation wouldn't have stopped until every person with knowledge of Somnolett was eliminated. You stopped more people from being killed to cover up a conspiracy."

He pulled her across the bench seat, until she was flush against him, with his arms encircling her. "Sweetheart, Mason Alexander made his choices when he began laundering money through Eryx Pharmaceutical. When you think about it, and the precise and organized way the whole operation was done, it probably wasn't the first time. He's the one who got into bed with the cartel, with his eyes wide open."

She sighed. "I know that in my head. But part of me wishes this had never happened. That I'd wake up and it would be Labor Day, and I could call and tell them I wasn't coming to work. Then this would all be just a nightmare."

His body stiffened and she realized what she'd said.

"I don't mean the part about seeing you again. That I wouldn't change, even if I could. You, Gunner—you're what's kept me going. You make me feel safe. Feel cherished." What she really wanted to say was that he made her feel loved.

"I'm glad you feel that way, honey. If I could, I'd erase every moment of danger, keep you safe no matter what. But I can't regret you coming back into my life. I feel like I finally started living again when I saw you, standing in the bathroom doorway, dripping wet. You were the most beautiful sight I've ever seen, and I felt like I'd finally found the one thing I'd spent my life searching for without realizing it."

"Gunner..."

His finger tilted her chin up, and she met his green-eyed intense stare. "Maggie Callahan, I've been searching my whole life for you. I let you get away once, which is a mistake I've regretted more than words can express." With a touch as gentle as a feather stroking against her skin, he brushed the hair off the side of her face. "I know I've told you before, but I have to say it again. Shout it from the rooftops. I love you, my Maggie. Now isn't the right time, or the right place, but I can't hold it in another second longer. Seeing you going toe-to-toe with Mason Alexander, realizing the peril you were in, sweetheart, it scared me stupid."

Maggie huffed out a laugh. "Scared me too. Oh, Gunner, I love you too. I never stopped loving you. I've always regretted letting you walk away, but it was the right thing.

Fate has brought us together again, and I never want to leave. No matter what happens, I want us to be together—always."

Gunner gently cupped Maggie's face between his hands, and brushed a soft kiss against her lips. She could taste the coffee he'd drank at the hospital, and the essence of him.

Her lips opened beneath his, and she kissed him back, loving the feel of his mouth on hers. A loud rap against the driver's window had her jerking out of Gunner's arms, and she spied a grinning Dean Westin on the other side. Gunner rolled the window down barely an inch.

"Dude, you've got a perfectly good room upstairs."

Gunner banged his head against the steering wheel, while Maggie giggled. Right now really wasn't the best time or place to have this discussion, though she wouldn't change one second of it. Knowing Gunner loved her was—priceless.

"We're coming, jackass. Tell Carpenter we'll be right in."

"Sure you will. I'll tell him ten minutes. Don't be late." Westin chuckled and walked away, heading for the back entrance.

He swung around to face her, the tenderness in his expression stealing her breath. "I'm not sorry, honey. Well, I'm actually sorry that Westin caught us making out like a couple of teenagers, but not about telling you I love you. Now, let's find out if Carpenter got anything from Alexander." The look in his eyes caused heat to flare in her cheeks. "Then I'm taking you upstairs, locking the rest of the world out, and making love to you for the rest of the night."

"Sounds like a plan to me, cowboy. Let's go."

Chapter Thirty-Seven

With everyone crowded into Carpenter's living room, seating was limited, and Gunner didn't mind having Maggie perched on his knee. Nope, not one bit. The atmosphere was somber, even for this normally rowdy bunch.

"The physicians confirmed Mason Alexander did suffer a stroke." Carpenter stood by his fireplace, his shoulder propped against the bricks.

"Was he conscious at all when you went in?" Etienne Boudreau occupied Carpenter's usual chair, leaning forward, with his forearms resting on his thighs.

"He was conscious, but he can't speak. But he was coherent enough to understand my questions, and nod yes or no answers."

"Did he know who shot him?" Gunner asked the question that had been bugging him ever since the police had whisked Alexander away. He had so many unanswered questions, and now it looked like he might never get the answers he wanted.

"He knows, but there's no way to get the answers. If he recovers, which the docs say would be a miracle, it could take years before he's able to communicate in any recognizable fashion." Carpenter blew out a ragged breath. "Poor bastard."

Maggie tentatively raised her hand, and Gunner bit back his smile. She'd learn soon enough, with this group you jumped in with both feet, because if you hesitated, they'd roll right over the top of you.

"Somebody had to have ordered the hit on Alexander. Which means we've got another player in the game, right? I didn't find anybody receiving funds from EryX who worked outside the company—except Mason Alexander. How do you figure out who this other person is?"

"Good question," Carpenter said. "Nothing Mason did would surprise me, but I listened to the recording you made, Maggie, and I believe him when he claimed to not know anything about the murders."

"So do I. When I brought them up, he looked stunned. It was only for a moment, and he tried to hide it, but I saw the shock on his face."

"My gut instinct tells me the Russian mob is involved. They're not above utilizing prominent people to do their dirty work, like laundering vast sums of money. I've had dealings with them in the past, and I know a guy who owes me a favor. I plan on calling in that marker, and have him do a little snooping."

Gunner silently chuckled at that assessment. Why was he not surprised Carpenter had connections with the Russian mafia? The man knew everybody. Plus there had been rumblings in New Orleans from the Russian contingency the last several months.

When Vladimir Dubshenko had been ousted from his position of power over the New Orleans Russian mob, it had left a vacuum with powerful men jockeying for control of the city. There were one or two frontrunners, a couple of nasty pieces of work who'd been taking potshots at each other, and he wondered if one of them had finally come out on top.

"You know a guy in the Russian mafia?" Andrea strode over to stare up at Carpenter. "I swear, you know the most interesting people."

"Let's just say I did something for Anatole Sokolov, and he feels he owes me a blood debt."

"Anatole Sokolov?" Jean-Luc choked out the name, before burying his face in his hands, his shoulders shaking with laughter. "One of the biggest leaders in Bratva, and he owes you a blood debt."

Carpenter stood with his shoulder against the fireplace, and an arm wrapped around his fiancee's waist, but Gunner could see a distinctive twinkle in his gaze. The man loved tossing out little bombshells that threw his team for a loop.

"Can we get back on track here? Mason Alexander. Now that he's out of the picture, and you've turned all the evidence over to the feds, the danger to Maggie is over, right?"

"Arrest warrants have been issued for nearly a dozen people, either associated with Benedetto Medical or EryX Pharmaceutical." Carlisle answered Gunner's question. "Maggie, you'll be glad to hear that Ian Buchanan has been cleared. Apparently, he's spent the last several months in and out of the country, dealing with a family crisis, and had turned over the running of the company to the CFO—who was neck deep in this whole scheme."

"So, it's really over?" Maggie's voice held a breathless quality, and Gunner pulled her closer, offering her his silent comfort and support.

"You're safe, Maggie. What you've done, coming forward once you found out something was wrong, that was remarkably brave." Carpenter straightened from his nonchalant lean against the fireplace and walked over to squat in front of Maggie, taking her hands in his. "You saved a lot of lives, at the risk of your own. Most people will probably never hear about what you did, but you should always remember that your actions—your bravery—made a difference to a lot of people's lives."

Gunner tried to swallow past the sudden lump in his throat. Damn, his boss could be quite eloquent when he wanted to. He watched Maggie's eyes fill with tears, saw the faint smile touch Carpenter's lips before he stood.

"Okay, folks, the party's over. Everybody go home and get a good night's sleep, because tomorrow is going to be a long day."

Gunner helped Maggie stand, and he started for the door, following in the wake of the mass exodus, but there was a question nagging him, and he wanted to ask it before he left.

"Boss," he said quietly, capturing Carpenter's attention. "I noticed Gator and Ms. Willie haven't been around much the last couple of days. Is everything okay?"

"You know, now that you mention it, I haven't seen

much of either of them. It's not like Ms. Willie to disappear without a word."

Maggie tugged on his sleeve, and he leaned down. Standing on tiptoe, she cupped her hand around his ear and whispered, "Look at Andrea's face. She knows something."

Sure enough, Andrea's cheeks were pink and she wouldn't meet his gaze.

"Andrea?"

She glanced over his shoulder, refusing to meet his eyes, and mumbled, "I need to pick up these cups," and started grabbing the scattered dishes. Carpenter stopped her with a brief touch on her hand.

"Sugar, what's going on?"

Gunner almost snickered at the guilty look on her face. For a trained C.I.A. operative, Andrea couldn't lie worth a darn.

"Ms. Willie's fine. She needed a few days off to work on…something…personal. With Gator." She added that last bit so fast, it was nearly unintelligible.

"She's gone off with Gator Boudreau?" A myriad of emotions swept across Carpenter's face, before finally devolving into outrage. "I'm gonna kill him."

"Wait!" Andrea grabbed his wrist, holding on as he stomped toward the front door. "It's not like that, I swear. She's just helping him. Something to do with one of his neighbor's needing a little TLC." Andrea scowled at him. "Don't you trust her?"

"Of course I trust her. She's like a mother to me."

Gunner could almost predict the next words coming out

of Andrea's mouth.

"Then respect her wishes and cut her a little slack. The woman has never asked you for a minute off the entire time I've known both of you. For the first time, she's doing something that doesn't have Samuel Carpenter at its epicenter. Deal with it."

"And on that note, I think we'll be going." Gunner grabbed Maggie's hand and tugged her toward the front door, and out to the elevator, pressing the button before dissolving into laughter.

"Did you see his face?" Maggie stood hunched over, her hands resting on her knees. Gunner had his back to the wall, using it for support, because he was still laughing.

"I think he'd have been less surprised if Andrea had stuck him with a cattle prod, than to think Ms. Willie might actually have a life outside of Samuel Carpenter and C.S.S."

Gunner straightened and pulled Maggie into his arms. "Speaking of having a life outside C.S.S., I think we should finish what we started a little while ago."

Maggie melted into his embrace, and whispered, "How fast can we get downstairs?"

Epilogue

Jean-Luc stepped out of the shower, and wrapped a towel around his hips. Grabbing a second one, he rubbed it briskly over his head and chest, soaking up all the moisture, then tossed it into the hamper.

He was tired, although if asked, he'd swear everything was fine. The past few cases had been nasty business, with him spending a lot of time out of the office and hitting the streets.

The good thing was, they'd been resolved with the good guys winning, and the bad guys in jail awaiting prosecution. This last case, the one Maggie Callahan had brought to their doorstep had been especially nasty. It had taken the combined efforts of every member of the Carpenter Security's elite team to stop a series of murders, money laundering and fraud.

But they'd done it. Gunner and Maggie were on track to get their happily ever after, as Andrea liked to call it.

Cupid had struck hard with C.S.S.'s teammates lately. Three couples in the last few months. Samuel and Andrea had been the first, followed by Nate and Sheri. And now it looked like Gunner and Maggie would be the next happy couple.

I hope that arrow-wielding mischief-maker in a diaper keeps his heart-tipped darts to himself. I don't need a woman in my life. Not now, maybe not ever.

He dressed quickly, grabbing a beer on the way through the kitchen. Staying at Gator's house for a couple of days while his dad was off working on some secret project seemed like a great idea. Samuel hadn't raised a fuss when he'd asked for a couple of days off. Nope, he'd taken one look at him and told Stephanie Jean-Luc was out of rotation for seventy-two hours.

Walking out the back door, he tilted his head back and let the sun's rays warm his face. The temperature in the afternoons was still warm, though the evenings had taken on the coolness of fall.

He eased down onto the first step on the edge of the porch, and took a long swallow of his beer. Maybe he'd grab the boat in the morning, take a trip out to visit Ranger and Sarah at the cabin. Although maybe he'd better call first. They were still in that extended honeymoon phase, and he didn't need to walk in on something he never wanted to see again. Once had been more than enough, thank you very much.

Elbows resting on his knees, the beer bottle dangled from his hand as he watched the driveway. The front of the house faced the water, so anybody coming by car ended up following the drive to the back of the house.

An older Toyota Corolla approached at a cautious speed. He didn't recognize the car. Maybe it was one of his father's friends, though they usually came by boat.

It pulled to a stop and sat with the engine idling for a couple of long minutes before it finally shut off. When the driver's door opened, he spotted a pair of feminine feet with dainty sandals emerge. When she stood, he got a good look at the woman—and didn't recognize her.

Long blonde hair fell in a straight curtain over her shoulders. It was long enough to fall to the middle of her back, he guessed. Sunglasses covered her eyes, but she still raised a hand to block out the glare as she looked in his direction.

Closing the door, he noted the prim button front white shirt paired with a denim skirt that hit just above her knees.

He decided to let her make the first move. If she was looking for Gator, he'd point her in the right direction. If not, he'd send her on her way, because he didn't have time for anything but another beer and some quiet time.

"Are you Mister Boudreau?" Her voice was a husky contralto, and his body responded, though he feigned indifference.

"One of them."

With a quick motion, she pulled the sunglasses off, and he found himself staring into brown eyes the color of his favorite caramels.

"I'm looking for Jean-Luc Boudreau."

With a weary sigh, he stood. "I'm Jean-Luc. What can I do for you?"

Shaking her head, she took a step forward, bringing her close enough he realized she was a little bit of a thing. Couldn't be more than five foot two or three.

"It's not what you can do for me, Mr. Boudreau. You

need to come with me."

"Lady, I'm not going anywhere with you, so you can climb back into your car and head back the way you came."

"I'm not going anywhere without you, Boudreau, so suck it up and get in the damned car."

Jean-Luc almost laughed out loud at the look of irritation on the blonde's face. She wasn't classically beautiful, but right now she was spitting fire and cute as a box of kittens, and just about as spunky.

"No offense, ma'am, but unless you give me a very good reason, which you haven't so far, I'm going to park my backside on this step and finish my beer."

"A good reason? You want a good reason? How about the fact my best friend is in the hospital dying? She's barely holding on, and begged me to find you."

Jean-Luc heard her anguish beneath the anger, sensed the pain she tried desperately to hide. "Who's looking for me?"

Eyes flashing fire, she strode forward until mere inches separated them. This close, he could see the smattering of freckles across her pert nose.

"Your wife."

NEWSLETTER SIGN UP

Don't want to miss out on any new books, contests, and free stuff? Sign up to get my newsletter. I promise not to spam you, and only send out notifications/e-mails whenever there's a new release or contest/giveaway.

http://eepurl.com/baqdRX

REVIEWS ARE IMPORTANT!

People are always asking how they can help spread the word about my books. One of the best ways to do that is by word of mouth. Telling your friends about the books and recommending them. If you find a book or series or author that you love – talk about it. The next best thing is to write a review. Writing a review for a book does have to be long or detailed. It can be as simple as saying "I loved the book."

I hope you enjoyed reading Hidden Agenda. If you liked the story, I hope you'll consider leaving a review for the book at the vendor where you purchased it and at Goodreads. Reviews are the best way to spread the word to others looking for good books. It truly helps.

Deadly Justice © Kathy Ivan
(New Orleans Connection Series #6)

A quest for justice…

After a devastating betrayal, ex-DEA agent Samuel *"The Ghost"* Carpenter devotes his life to searching for the person who cost him not only his job but nearly his life. When he discovers a link between the man he's hunting and a beautiful executive assistant, he realizes the path to his target is seduction—a task he's all too eager to undertake, since he can't seem to resist the alluring beauty.

…turns into a dangerous seduction.

Andrea Kirkland can't fathom the sudden interest rich and powerful Samuel Carpenter's showing, but she's not stupid. He's got a deeply-hidden agenda and she's a means to an end. Except, she has secrets of her own, and despite their instantaneous chemistry, she's not above using Carpenter to further her own vendetta.

On a whirlwind journey from Dallas to New Orleans, passion explodes between them. But when a murderer strikes, Carpenter must choose between his mission of vengeance or face losing the woman he loves to a vindictive madman hellbent on revenge.

Get it Now!

BOOKS BY KATHY IVAN

www.kathyivan.com/books.html

NEW ORLEANS CONNECTION SERIES
Desperate Choices
Connor's Gamble
Relentless Pursuit
Ultimate Betrayal
Keeping Secrets
Sex, Lies and Apple Pies
Deadly Justice
Saving Sarah
(part of Susan Stoker's Special Forces Kindle World)
Deadly Obsession
Hidden Agenda
Saving Savannah
(part of Susan Stoker's Special Forceps kindle World)

LOVIN' LAS VEGAS SERIES
It Happened In Vegas
Crazy Vegas Love
Marriage, Vegas Style
A Virgin In Vegas
Vegas, Baby!
Yours For The Holidays
Match Made In Vegas
Wicked Wagers (box set books 1-4)

OTHER BOOKS BY KATHY IVAN
Second Chances (Destiny's Desire Book #1)
Losing Cassie (Destiny's Desire Book #2)
The Remingtons: Could This Be Love
(Part of Melissa Foster's Kindle World)

MEET KATHY IVAN

USA TODAY Bestselling author Kathy Ivan spent most of her life with her nose between the pages of a book. It didn't matter if the book was a paranormal romance, romantic suspense, action and adventure thrillers, sweet & spicy, or a sexy novella. Kathy turned her obsession with reading into the next logical step, writing. Her books transport you to the sultry splendor of the French Quarter in New Orleans in her award-winning romantic suspense, or to Las Vegas in her contemporary romantic comedies. Kathy tells stories people can't get enough of; reuniting old loves, betrayal of trust, finding kidnapped children, psychics and even a ghost or two. But one thing they all have in common – love (and some pretty steamy sex scenes too). You can find more on Kathy at

WEBSITE:
www.kathyivan.com

FACEBOOK:
facebook.com/kathyivanauthor

TWITTER:
twitter.com/@kathyivan

EDITORIAL REVIEWS

"Kathy Ivan's books give you everything you're looking for and so much more".

—Geri Foster,
USA Today and NYT Bestselling Author of the
Falcon Securities Series

"This is the first I have read from Kathy Ivan and it won't be the last."

—Night Owl Reviews

"I highly recommend Desperate Choices. Readers can't go wrong here!"

—Melissa, Joyfully Reviewed

"I loved how the author wove a very intricate storyline with plenty of intriguing details that led to the final reveal…"

—Night Owl Reviews

Desperate Choices—Winner 2012 International Digital Award—Suspense

Desperate Choices—Best of Romance 2011 –Joyfully Reviewed

Printed in Great Britain
by Amazon